To the Stars
by
Jess Levins

Also by Jess Levins

HOSPITAL ANGEL
To The Stars

Watch for more at https://www.JessLevins.com.

For my daughter

Jill A. Levins

COPYRIGHT

TO THE STARS

Copyright @ 2022 Jess Levins

Cover Design by Tallulah Lucy

Library of Congress Cataloging-in-Publication Data

ISBN 979-8-9867-7323-3-0 Paperback

ISBN 979-8-9867-7322-3 eBook

CHAPTER 1 EXPULSION

Thomas Wilson hated this time of day. The school allowed an entire period for lunch, but you could only remain in the cafeteria for a half period. The students spent the balance of the period outside, where they socialized or worked on their studies. Thomas had been waiting for the day when two boys who were close friends would separately exit the cafeteria. As soon as the first boy stepped out, Thomas attacked him from the side and the boy landed on his back with Thomas on top. Thomas sat on him and continued to hit him.

"I give up," the boy said. "Please stop."

Thomas was breathing hard but could not rest. He allowed the boy to get off the ground and run away. Thomas rushed to his hiding place by the door. A second bigger boy walked out of the cafeteria, and Thomas again attacked without warning. This time the boy landed facedown. Thomas sat on the boy's back and continued to hit him in the back of the head until the boy started crying. This surprised Thomas and he stopped hitting him.

Thomas leaned down next to the boy's ear. "Leave me alone," Thomas whispered so only the boy could hear. The other students had quietly watched the fights.

Thomas got up and walked over to an empty bench. He sat on the bench, and after a few minutes, his breathing slowed down. He quietly waited until the start of his next class.

THE NEXT DAY THOMAS found himself in a room outside the Principal's office, waiting for his mother to arrive. Principal Tindal asked him how a ten-year-old could cause her so much trouble. She had served as a principal for four years. Previously, she had been a teacher for fifteen years. Today she reminisced about her days as a teacher. Most days, she enjoyed being a principal, but not today. She was forty-one years old and slightly overweight. Her brown hair had a few streaks of gray. Premature bags were showing beneath her eyes from the added stress of running the school and dealing with an overbearing School Board. She took her job seriously, and her authoritarian demeanor allowed her to stay in control of most situations. Today she wore casual, conservative business clothes as expected for a school principal. Her attire consisted of a button-down navy blouse, matching pants, and black shoes with soft soles for comfortable walking.

Earlier in the day, the School Board and Superintendent had criticized her during a joint conference call. They had just held an emergency meeting. The Superintendent let her know the Board was disappointed with her management of the recent fighting incident involving three students. They described the incident as told by the parents of two of the students. They told her to expel the third student who had started the fight. She started to object until reminded by the Superintendent that her employment could be terminated by a majority vote of the School Board.

Principal Tindal called the third student, Thomas Wilson, to her office. She had been distraught from her conversation with the School Board and lost her composure with the student. When he denied the accusations, she screamed at him and called him a little demon before getting her emotions under control. Afterward, Principal Tindal felt disappointed with herself since she had never behaved in that fashion toward a student. At that point, Thomas lowered his head and stopped trying to explain. She directed him to the waiting room while she contacted his parents.

ALINA WILSON RECEIVED a message saying she needed to come to the school immediately to discuss her son's behavior. The school did not provide any additional information. She felt relieved Thomas had not been injured. It might be an urgent matter, but it was not an emergency. She had been dressed casually at home when she received the call. As a corporate executive's spouse, Alina knew the importance of being properly attired. She took the time to change into a custom-fitted, semiformal black dress with matching shoes and a complementary designer purse. Alina felt blessed. She had smooth, unblemished skin, except for the beginning of slight wrinkles at the edge of her eyes. She eliminated the wrinkles by touching the edge of each eye with an atomizer.

When Alina arrived at her son's school, the receptionist escorted her to the Principal's office. Thomas stood up, but the Principal told him to remain in the outer room. The walls were poorly insulated, and Thomas heard the entire conversation. He listened as the Principal explained to his mother how he had physically attacked his classmates in two separate instances on the previous day. The parents of these classmates filed complaints with the School Board.

The private school depended on donations to supplement the tuition fees, and the parents of these children were huge donors. Also, one parent served on several of the School Board's committees.

Thomas heard his mother volunteer to increase their donations to the school, but Principal Tindal said it would not affect her decision. The Principal looked at Alina with sad eyes.

"Thomas has been permanently expelled from our school." Thomas heard his mother gasp.

"You cannot be serious. I could understand a suspension, but expulsion does not make any sense. Surely, you can give Thomas another chance."

"I am sorry. The School Board has already decided, and it is no longer within my control. Thomas is academically an excellent student, and you should consider enrolling him into public school."

They exited the Principal's office, and Thomas stood up.

"I am sorry for what I said to you earlier," the Principal said to Thomas.

Principal Tindal turned back to Mrs. Wilson. "Goodbye."

The Principal returned to her office and closed the door. Thomas picked up his backpack and left the school with his mother.

They drove home in silence with the vehicle on auto. Thomas turned to his mother and broke the silence. "Mom, it was not my fault."

Alina glanced at her son and wondered how often she had seen the same innocent face and heard the same comment. Thomas always seemed to get into trouble. Her two older children were well-mannered and never gave her any grief.

Alina then remembered what Principal Tindal said to Thomas before they left. "Thomas, why did the Principal apologize to you?"

"She screamed at me and called me a demon," Thomas replied in a subdued voice.

Alina changed from being depressed to being furious. No one had the right to call her son a demon. Alina started to return to the school and tell Principal Tindal how wrong it was for a principal to call her son a demon. She considered filing a complaint against the Principal and the school. After further consideration, she decided it would be a waste of time. They arrived home, but Alina's anger had not subsided.

"Go to your room and wait for your father to come home," Alina said as she shook her head.

Alina called Ben Wilson, her husband, and told him what had happened. She asked him to come home. Alina seldom made such a request. She needed him, and he hoped she would always ask for his help when making crucial family decisions.

When Ben arrived home, he saw his well-dressed wife. "You look nice," Ben said. He followed up with a hug and a kiss.

Ben forgot why he came home early, as he felt amorous, but Alina spoiled the moment when she pulled back. "You need to go see your son."

Ben groaned in disappointment. Alina laughed and then got serious as she again explained how Thomas had been expelled. She told him the Principal had suggested they enroll Thomas into the local public school.

After twenty-two years, Alina still loved her husband and knew he still loved her. He always had a way of making her feel special. They married right out of college. They struggled in the beginning when Ben's father died, and Ben became the owner of the failing family business. They worked together each day. They lived in the free housing available to all citizens to save money. During the first three years, the company barely broke even. However, the business made a profit in the fourth year and did well thereafter. Those initial struggles made them appreciate their current executive lifestyle with a large home and acreage for their horses.

Ben walked down the hall and entered his son's room. He saw Thomas lying on his back in the center of the bed and sat on the bed beside him.

Ben raised his eyebrows. "Your mother said you got expelled from school for fighting. Tell me what happened."

Thomas gladly told his side as he sat up. "Almost every day, two boys at school beat me up. Yesterday, the boys came to the outside break area separately, so I fought one boy as soon as he came outside. Then, when the other boy came out, I fought him. I won both fights.

Today, Principal Tindal called me to the office but did not want to hear my side. Then she called mom."

"How long has this been going on?"

Thomas hung his head. "The whole school year. I do not want to go back to school. Can I go to work with you?"

"Son, go play, and we will discuss the school issue later."

Ben went to his home office and called his attorney. He explained what had happened.

"I want the videos for the outside break area at my son's school for the entire term."

"It should not be a problem," the attorney replied. "No assumption of privacy exists for an outside area viewable by the public. Also, a precedent has been established in several prior cases."

Ben went into the kitchen and gave Alina another hug. "I will take Thomas with me tomorrow. I want you to hold off enrolling him in the public school."

THOMAS WALKED INTO the entertainment center, grabbed a snack, and sat down. His brother Stephen, who was four years older, had just finished his homework.

Stephen looked up and saw Thomas. "Why the sad face?"

"I got expelled from school. Mom came to school and picked me up. The teacher called me a demon. Mom called Dad, and he came home early."

Stephen chuckled. "Wow, you have outdone yourself this time, squirt. This is even worse than when you painted your room."

Thomas remembered how upset his mother had been when he painted his room and got paint on everything, including himself. He remembered waiting in his room, all covered in paint, until his father came home. Thomas explained to his father how he wanted his room to look like a spaceship. He had done a pretty thorough job painting the room black, along with the bed, dressers, floor, clothing, and everything else. The stars he tried to paint were a bigger mess. He remembered the next day when he came home and went into his bedroom. While at school, his father hired a tech specialist who turned his room into a realistic spaceship with a view of the stars. He could use his voice to change to various points in the Galactic, including approaches to space stations. To this day, his room was still his favorite place in their home, and at night, he enjoyed moving through the Galactic before falling asleep.

Stephen snapped Thomas out of his daydreaming. "So, your teacher called you a demon," Stephen snickered. "It kind of fits. My brother, the demon. You are a demon and are going to send everyone to hell." Stephen had a broad grin that stretched the width of his entire face.

Stephen saw Thomas' sad face. "Hey, I know it seems bad, but it will get better."

"Are you sure?" Thomas asked.

"Yes, I am sure."

Just then, their sister Joan walked in. She was two years older than Thomas. "I just heard. Thomas, I am so sorry. How do you keep getting into so much trouble?"

"I do not know. It is not my fault," Thomas said in a sad voice.

Joan gave Thomas a sympathetic look. She loved him, but he constantly got into trouble, particularly with their mother.

"Hey Joan, the Principal renamed Thomas. His new name is Demon."

Joan frowned in disbelief. "Thomas, the Principal called you a demon?"

Thomas lowered his head again. "Yes."

Joan went over to her younger brother and sat down next to him. She put her arm around his shoulders. "Thomas, you are not a demon, and the Principal should never have said that."

Thomas sighed. "But what if I am a demon?"

"You are not a demon!" Joan responded with a forceful voice. Joan decided to cheer up her younger brother. "Let's have some fun and play three-way Fantasies."

Joan nodded to Stephen when Thomas was not looking. They put on the immersion headgear and waited for the game to assign the avatars. They heard Thomas groan and realized his avatar was a demon. They could not help giggling, and finally, Thomas joined them.

Each player had fifty wasp space fighters. Thomas had never won a game against either of his siblings. In a three-way game, he always got eliminated first. Thomas remembered winning his two fights at school by separating his opponents and fighting one at a time. He thought about their previous games and realized his sister always concentrated on defense while his brother attacked. His brother and sister were nearly equal in the number of wins, as shown on the cumulation scores. In past games, Thomas played without a strategy and wound up between Joan and Stephen while they attacked his ships. Each wasp carried ten missiles, but it only took five hits to eliminate a wasp. Instead of attacking, Thomas retreated and looped all his wasps around the edge of the boundaries to place Joan's ships in the middle, but he did not engage.

Joan moved her wasps behind asteroids as she engaged Stephen's fighters. She would fire missiles from a fighter and then move it back behind an asteroid. Her ships were only exposed briefly while locking onto Stephen's ships and firing a missile.

Stephen attacked the front lines with thirty wasps but had ten fighters circle around and attack Joan's portside flank. He had the remaining ten wasps attack Joan's formation from the starboard side. Joan destroyed more of Stephen's fighters in his frontal attack, but Stephen's wasps were eliminating Joan's ships in the flanking maneuvers. Stephen lost twelve wasps in the frontal attack, but his flanking maneuvers had eliminated eighteen of Joan's fighters. The battle continued while Thomas remained out of the fight.

Thomas had an idea. He took all fifty of his wasps and flew them below the battle to the portside of Joan's formation. He held his fire until he lined up five of his wasps against each of Stephen's enemy ships. Then his fighters fired their missiles simultaneously, taking out all ten of Stephen's ships. The surprise attack left Stephen with twenty-eight ships. Now, Joan had the advantage with thirty-two fighters.

Thomas withdrew all of his wasps and moved below Joan's starboard side. Stephen was not about to be caught unaware a second time and turned his ten fighters to engage the new enemy. Thomas had all fifty of his wasp fighters firing missiles against Stephen's smaller group. All ten of Stephen's wasps were destroyed without Thomas losing any of his ships. Joan and Stephen lost additional ships in their battle against each other. Thomas glanced at the scoreboard. Stephen only had nine fighters, while Joan had twenty-seven ships.

Joan moved from her defensive position and attacked Stephen's remaining ships. Thomas waited until they were fully engaged. He then moved up behind Joan's fleet and opened fire. After the rear engagement, the battle was never in doubt. Anytime a ship took two hits, Thomas would move it back and let a ship with full shields move in front. Also, he rebalanced his missiles among his fighters to provide every ship with the maximum firepower.

At the end, Thomas observed the scoreboard results. Over ninety percent of his missiles hit their target, and he had not lost a single ship. Thomas could not be happier. This was the first time he won the game of Fantasies against his two older siblings. Thomas knew he would never lose again and smiled.

After the game, Stephen turned to his younger brother. "Being a demon may be good for you. After all, you just won your first game of

Fantasies." They did not know the win by their little brother would change the Galactic.

They all received a signal through their wristbands, calling them for dinner. After Thomas left the game room, Stephen turned toward his sister.

"I agreed we should let Thomas win, but he annihilated us."

They both shook their head as they followed Thomas to the dining room. They laughed together when they heard Thomas excitedly explain to their parents how he had won the game. The conversation during dinner was subdued. They avoided discussing the school expulsion.

After dinner, Ben said, "Thomas, your mother and I decided you can go to work with me tomorrow, while we figure out what to do about your schooling." Thomas thought this might be his best day ever as he went to his room.

Thomas lay on his bed, and the more he thought about it, the more excited he became about going to work with his father. He relaxed and watched the stars in his simulated spaceship. It would shut down automatically as soon as he fell asleep.

As Ben and Joan lay in bed, Alina expressed her concern. "I am worried about Thomas' future."

"Do not worry about Thomas. He is full of energy and is enthusiastic about everything. He has an extra spark I do not see in other kids his age. I am proud of our other two children. They will do well, but Thomas is special. Thomas is going to accomplish great things."

Ben's comment surprised Alina. "I will be happy if he just completes his education," she said.

Ben had a good feeling about Thomas, but he agreed with his wife. As parents, Thomas had been more challenging than their other children. Ben built spaceships. The best ships were more difficult to build, and he felt the same might be true of his youngest son.

THE NEXT DAY, EVERYONE had a quick breakfast. Thomas climbed into the passenger side of his father's vehicle, and they headed to work. Once they arrived, Ben gave Thomas a tour of the facility since it had been several years since his last visit. Thomas liked the design area the best. A tech said he would be happy to entertain Thomas for a while.

When Ben sat down at his desk, he saw a communication from his attorney. He opened the file and saw videos of the break area for each day of school. He became angrier as he watched. The two bullies attacked Thomas together and it was never a fair fight.

Ben called his attorney. "I want you to set up a meeting with the School Board and the parents of the boys who have been attacking my son." After discussing a few more details, the attorney agreed to arrange a meeting.

That night, after Thomas had gone to bed, Ben asked Alina to join him in his home office and started showing her the videos. The fights were always two against one. In some fights, one boy would hold Thomas while the other boy punched him in the stomach. Other times, they would kick Thomas as he lay balled up on the ground. After watching just a few of the videos, Alina started crying, and Ben stopped the viewing. Alina finally stopped crying and dried her eyes.

"I cannot believe I did not know. I am a horrible mother. Thomas never complained. Occasionally, he would come home with scrapes and bruises. When I mentioned it, he would say it happened while they were outside. I just thought they were playing too hard."

Then, Ben showed Alina the fights, where Thomas beat up the two bullies by fighting one at a time.

"Well, they finally got what they deserved," Alina said.

TWO NIGHTS LATER, THEY met with the School Board and the four parents of the two children who had been attacking Thomas. Ben's attorney and the school's attorney attended. The other parents were upset. They insulted Ben and Alina before taking their seats.

Ben's attorney started showing the videos. After viewing a dozen episodes with the date of each incident, he stopped the viewing. He then explained he had hundreds of similar engagements between the three children. He then showed the final fights and explained these were the only fair fights. The room remained quiet after the viewing.

Then, the school's attorney said any filings of criminal or civil charges against the two youths were none of his concern. Then he asked if Ben and Alina would hold off filing a civil complaint against the school until he had a chance to prepare a settlement offer. He further explained the school did not tolerate bullying and they would expel the two students who had been attacking Thomas. The attorney for the school had a whispered conversation with the directors of the School Board. The attorney then addressed Ben and Alina.

"Thomas can return to school with a clean record."

The parents of the two youths who had been bullying Thomas were distraught. They pleaded with Ben and Alina not to file criminal charges against their sons. Ben's attorney asked for a minute to talk to his clients.

Ben, Alina, and their attorney walked outside to discuss the matter. Alina wanted to have charges filed, but the attorney told her the two young men were minors and would at most receive a reprimand. She should consider these parents had not filed criminal charges against her son when they thought Thomas had started the fights. Eventually, Ben and Alina felt the parents were honestly dismayed at what they saw in the videos. Hopefully, each of the couples would address their son's behavior. They returned to the conference room.

Ben's attorney addressed everyone. "I am representing three clients harmed by the school. My clients will wait for the school's settlement offer, but we expect a quick response. The school is responsible for providing a safe environment for the children. Proper supervision was lacking, and no one reviewed the videos before expelling my client. The school allowed Thomas to be physically assaulted and battered every day. Each such incident represents a potentially separate charge against the school. Besides the physical harm, Thomas has suffered emotionally, and no longer wants to attend any school."

The attorney paused and then continued. "My second client, Alina Wilson, has several claims against the school. She suffered embarrassment and humiliation when the Principal expelled her son. Also, Alina suffered emotionally when she witnessed the beatings her son endured. My third client, Ben Wilson, also endured distress. He and his wife must deal with trying to heal their son's emotional scars. We will file a complaint with the court if we do not have a settlement within two weeks."

Ben's attorney turned to the parents. Each set of parents were concerned about what may happen to their son. "My clients will forego filing criminal and civil charges, but you need to change your children's behavior. Next time, they may not be so lucky."

All four of the parents thanked Ben and Alina for not pressing charges. Then each set of parents blamed the other parents' child for being a bad influence on their son.

As they were leaving, Ben's attorney said he would contact them as soon as he received a response from the school.

Alina enjoyed the ride home since Thomas could return to school. She felt confused when Ben explained they needed to consider all their options before making a final decision.

Ben and Alina were both upset with what Thomas had endured. Neither of them had ever been in a fight or bullied. Their time at school was pleasant, and the occasional boredom represented their worst experience. Thinking about the videos, Ben remembered Thomas had not cried during any of the fights he had lost. Also, Thomas looked troubled when he had beaten each of the other boys. He appeared to be performing a necessary but unpleasant task. Ben was glad Thomas had fought back and won but liked that Thomas had not enjoyed harming the other boys.

DURING BREAKFAST THE following morning, Ben explained to their other children what had happened at the school meeting. Alina smiled and told Thomas he could return to school.

"Please, I do not want to return to school. I want to keep going to work with dad." Alina saw the look of desperation in Thomas' eyes.

Alina sighed. "We will talk about it later. For now, you can go to work with your father."

"Thomas, did you ever tell your teacher about the fights with the two boys?" Ben asked.

"Yes, at the beginning of school, all three of us went to the office. The two boys said I started the fights. They returned to their class while I sat in detention. Mom received a note and told me to behave in school."

It took a moment for Alina to recall the note. "The note only said you were disciplined for failing to follow school rules." Alina felt even worse since she had not asked Thomas what rules he had broken.

Ben saw the look on Alina's face. "I share the blame. I remember you telling me Thomas had gotten detention. I just thought it was a minor event." Ben and Alina regretted not taking a greater interest in the note and in Thomas' schooling.

Ben broke the silence and stood up. "Time to go to work." Thomas smiled as he headed out the door with his father. Ben could not help smiling too.

For the next three days, Thomas continued to go to work with his father. The employees enjoyed spending time with Thomas. So far, they had not tired of his endless questions. They expressed surprise at Thomas' knowledge of spaceships.

The General Maintenance Manager, Ralph Miller, enjoyed answering the questions and kept giving Thomas parts to fix. Ben and Ralph were lifelong friends. Ralph held the rank of First Officer on a commercial ship when Ben married Ralph's sister. Ralph served as Ben's best man at the wedding. During the reception, Ben convinced Ralph to work for him. He took over ship repairs and ship maintenance operations. This allowed Ben to concentrate solely on new ship construction.

While building and overhauling spaceships, Ben became familiar with the training modules installed on every vessel. In most cases, these modules were newer and better than the units used by the planetary schools. Also, a motivated person could proceed at an accelerated pace. The modules contained the standard academic courses plus specialized training certifications for every position on a ship, including maintenance, engineering, navigation, tactical, and administrative positions. Ben wondered why spacer children seemed more intelligent than planet-based children of the same age. Now he realized they simply had a more structured approach to learning and better training modules. Ben decided to home-school his son and ordered the best training module available. He had the module installed in an empty office. Ben notified his attorney he would accept a settlement from the school for the cost of the training module plus legal fees.

Ben's attorney called him the next day. He had asked for two training modules plus legal fees. The attorney explained why he asked for two modules. One training module would be at the shipyard and the other at Ben's home. Then, Thomas could study at work or at home and speed up his learning progression. The attorney for the school responded the following day. They accepted the offer since a court trial would be costly and harm the school's reputation. Also, the school knew a court verdict could be considerably more expensive than the proposed settlement.

Ben observed the intelligence and abilities of all his children. Thomas was the more physically fit and had an insatiable curiosity which unfortunately got him into trouble with his mother. Ben further recognized Thomas as the most driven of his children and how he always pushed the boundaries. Ben felt the best course of action would be to keep Thomas challenged and busy.

Ben observed how most individuals had little drive or motivation. Unfortunately, the few individuals with ambition lacked the qualifications or opportunities to achieve their goals. Ben decided his son would receive the best technical education and management training.

Ben's father instilled in him the importance of information. As a result, Ben had accumulated information on ships, planets, space stations, and stargates. Over the years, he had continuously collected public information. Also, he gathered private data from the various vessels repaired by his shipyard. His suppliers supplemented this information. Ben had observed how knowledge made the difference between success and failure in nearly every enterprise, whether in private, public, or political endeavors.

Over a trillion humans lived on over a thousand Core Planets. There had not been a new settlement in close to a hundred years. Few members of the Core Planets possessed the drive, motivation, or enthusiasm to move to newly terraformed planets. The Core provided a minimum standard of living to every citizen. Because of this standard, the Core citizens were unwilling to face the challenges of settling on a new world. This standard included basic housing, adequate food, healthcare, and public transportation.

Relocation to an Outer Planet or Rim World provided opportunities and individual freedoms. Unfortunately, the dangerous living conditions resulted in a significantly lower life expectancy than any of the Core Planets. The worlds inhabited in the Rim were not referred to as planets, since the terraforming did not fall within the Imperium's range for classification as earthlike. Everyone knew the living conditions on the Rim Worlds were extremely harsh. While better than the Rim, the conditions on most Outer Planets were worse than the Core Planets. However, a few Outer Planets had a high standard of living.

The navy protected the Core Planets. There were a few brilliant and ambitious individuals within the military with minds not destroyed by the demands to follow orders without thinking. Ben met Admiral Nelson years earlier, and no finer mind existed in the Galactic.

Thomas showed an unusual ability to think and question everything. He recently asked why individuals did not have tech implants to allow for quicker communication with an AI. Ben tried to explain it would cause dependence on technology to such an extent the brain would atrophy, and an AI would then have direct control over a person's thinking ability. When the explanation failed to sway Thomas, he explained how only the brightest and wealthiest individuals who already had an advantage would receive such implants. Again, the answer failed to satisfy Thomas.

Ben took a deep breath. "The intergalactic law states that anyone caught with an AI implant will be executed without a trial. Also, any citizen reporting an incidence of an AI implant is paid a reward large enough to live on one of the pleasure worlds. Plus, anyone participating in such modification will spend the rest of their life on a prison planet in the Rim."

Finally, Ben felt relieved when Thomas accepted his last explanation. Ben explained the law but did not understand the absolute restrictions. Years earlier, he listened to a group of old spacers telling late-night stories. He found one story particularly interesting. It told how millions of people with implants had suddenly died at the same time for no apparent reason. Ben remembered listening to the incredibly old spacer. He thought the story sounded believable. Ben asked the spacer if anyone had discovered why they had died. With a glazed look, the old spacer said he asked numerous individuals the same question. One day, a government bureaucrat told him to stop asking questions. He clearly understood his life would be forfeited if he continued trying to find out what had happened.

Ben agreed to let Thomas split his time between study and real-life on-the-job training. Thomas spent sufficient time in each department so he would understand every aspect of ship construction. Thomas kept up with the basic studies and matched his ancillary courses to coincide with the departments in which he worked. He had exemplary math skills, which allowed him to excel in technical fields. Thomas had a firm understanding of engineering and computer systems. Also, he obtained a shuttle pilot's license. He made friends throughout the shipyard. The workers liked his excitable personality and willingness to work on any job, regardless of the difficulty. He always showed up to help when a crew got behind schedule. Thomas routinely assisted on ships needing emergency repairs but handled routine maintenance when no emergency required his skills. Also, Thomas loved to fly and always volunteered to fly a shuttle when the shipyard needed a pickup or delivery.

THOMAS RECEIVED AN all-frequency distress call while piloting a loaded construction shuttle to the shipyard. The transmission said their impulse engines were damaged. The ship continued to transmit its coordinates. Thomas knew the vessel was far from a Stargate, but it was within a short jump of the shipyard. They could not engage their jump engines unless they achieved the minimum required velocity using their impulse engines. Thomas had picked up distress signals in the past but left any emergency rescue to more experienced ships. In contrast, this distress call originated from a Rim World ship. Therefore, no commercial vessel would answer the emergency transmission. Eventually, the military would investigate, but the delay might result in the death of all the survivors. Also, the construction shuttle would be perfect for a rescue mission since it was designed for building new ships and repairing old vessels. Thomas answered the call.

"This is Thomas Wilson, aboard the Shuttle Y14E with Wilson Enterprises. What is the nature of your emergency?"

"This is Captain Higgins with the Luxora. We were attacked by marauders and made a risky hard jump. Our life support is on backup. The impulse engines are offline, and the hull has multiple holes. The bulkheads automatically sealed off the damaged parts of the ship. Our engineer and maintenance tech died during the attack, and we cannot affect repairs. Please help us."

Thomas called the shipyard and sent his Uncle Ralph a message informing him of the emergency. He jumped before receiving a response. He brought the shuttle out of hyperspace, and it only took a moment to locate the Luxora. It took a little over four hours for Thomas to reach the ship using the shuttle's impulse engines.

Thomas took several trips around the ship. Only a portion of the ship had power. His first task required getting life support back online.

Wilson Enterprises had schematics on every ship in the Galactic. Thomas displayed the information on the ship and located the four power units that provided life support. Power units were usually kept fully charged since energy flowed directly into the units from impulse and jump engines, depending on which were in use. A unit in a damaged section of the ship could not be repaired, one unit registered as fully depleted, and one unit showed fully charged, but the cabling had been damaged. The one functional power unit provided backup power to part of the ship. Thomas inspected the depleted unit and determined it could not hold a charge due to several cracks in the housing.

Thomas contacted Captain Higgins. "This is Pilot Thomas Wilson with Wilson Enterprises. I will try to get the power unit with the damaged cable back online."

It took Thomas several hours to replace the cable and reengage the unit. Thomas backed the shuttle away from the ship and watched as power flowed into the undamaged sections. The external sensors of the Luxora were back online.

"Your shuttle is quite large," Captain Higgins said. "I have never seen such a shuttle."

"It is a heavy-duty construction shuttle," Thomas said with pride. "It is used for building new ships and repairing old ships. This shuttle can do just about anything. I am going to cut away panels of your hull from the section with the most damage and use the material to patch two of the smaller holes. There is another hull breach in the engine room, but it will be easier to repair from inside the ship once I assess the damage to the engines."

"You introduced yourself as Thomas Wilson," Captain Higgins said. "Are you related to the owner of Wilson Enterprises?"

"Yes, my parents own the business. I am their youngest son. I will proceed with the repairs to your hull."

Patching the smaller holes took little time since he used the shuttle's AI to cut an exact patch for each hole. The shuttle's arms held the hull patches in place while the welding extensions sealed the seams. The Captain and his crew watched and were extremely impressed.

Thomas contacted the Captain. "I patched the two hull breaches we discussed. I will see about repairing your impulse engines."

The engine room was still in the vacuum of space. Thomas located a hole made by a precision weapon. The attacker meant to disable the impulse engines without destroying the ship. Whoever had attacked the ship, avoided hitting the jump engines, but their efforts to prevent such damage had allowed the vessel to escape. Thomas decided to patch the small hole after completing the engine repairs. He did not want anyone entering the engine room until he finished the repairs and returned to the safety of his shuttle.

Thomas positioned the shuttle against an access panel for the engine room and activated the seal. He filled a repair pack with tools and entered through the hatch. Thomas decided not to come through the hull breach since there were several sharp edges, and he did not want to risk damaging his suit. Thomas found two bodies. Both were wearing spacesuits. One suit had a tear the person had tried unsuccessfully to patch, and the other suit had run out of air. Neither spacesuit had been maintained, and he did not see any spare oxygen bottles. Thomas did his best to ignore the bodies as he proceeded with the repairs. The ship would remain without gravity unless he could repair the impulse engines. Both engines were damaged, but in different places. Thomas checked the parts cabinets and shook his head in disappointment. He used his AI to analyze the damage. The AI results confirmed his expectations. He could repair one engine using the spare parts plus parts from the more damaged engine.

Thomas explained to the captain what he planned to do. He worked until he could no longer hold a wrench and returned to his shuttle for food and sleep. After he rested, he took a shower and used the food processor to prepare a meal. Thomas saw several messages from his uncle and his father. He sent a return message saying the repairs were nearly complete. Also, he sent them his coordinates as requested since the damaged ship had stopped sending a distress signal. Thomas did not communicate directly since he suspected they would order him to return home immediately.

The engines were modular, which reduced the repair time. Thomas replaced the damaged modular in one engine with an undamaged module from the other engine. After finishing the repairs, Thomas examined the electronics and upgraded the controllers using universal chips. Thomas got the electronic system back online. Next, he used the ship's computer to activate the cameras within the ship since he was curious about the ship's crew. The Luxora had a motley crew. Several crew members were barely human. They would all stand out in a crowd.

Thomas activated his communicator. "Captain, I am activating the engine to check out the repairs. Please stand by."

Thomas kept the repaired engine offline. He did not want to release access to the bridge until he felt the engine had sufficient power to reach the minimum velocity to engage the jump engines. Thomas set all engine parameters to the midrange settings. He started the engine and brought it to idle. He then adjusted each setting up or down until he reached the optimal positions.

Next, Thomas retrieved a leak repair kit from his shuttle. The repair kit worked well for the engine room hull penetration. Thomas decided not to take any chances. He returned to his shuttle, remotely pressurized the engine room, and released control to the bridge.

"Captain Higgins, you now have control of the ship's engines. I have entered the coordinates for our shipyard. Once there, your ship can be properly repaired."

"Pilot Wilson, you have our eternal gratitude. Please join us on our bridge so I can thank you properly." Captain Higgins and the bridge crew waited for the response.

"Thanks for the offer, but it is time for me to return to the shipyard. I will be happy to meet with you when you arrive." Captain Higgins hid his disappointment, but he had a backup plan.

"Before you leave, we would ask one more favor. A hatch in a remote corridor of the ship is stuck in a closed position and a female crew member is trapped there. She could use your help to return to the main part of the ship."

Thomas asked and received the location of the trapped crew woman. Captain Higgins was unaware the ship's cameras could be remotely monitored. It only took a moment for Thomas to access the correct camera. He saw an attractive but older female who appeared to be in her mid to late twenties. He moved his shuttle to the closest airlock and latched onto the ship. Thomas took a moment to take some precautions before opening the shuttle's rear door. He left the pilot's seat and approached the airlock to the ship. He opened both the inner and outer doors. However, Thomas remained in the shuttle.

"You can come aboard," Thomas shouted. "I can take you to another part of the ship."

"I have a sprained ankle and could use your help getting to the shuttle," the female said.

"You will have to make it on your own since I am not leaving the shuttle."

"Very well, I am coming."

Thomas returned to the pilot's chair with his back to the rear door. He carefully watched the corridor of the ship and saw a hatch open. Four men rushed through the corridor toward his shuttle. He signaled the AI to close the rear door with an emergency override and applied lateral thrush to separate the shuttle from the ship. Then, he applied forward thrust to put some distance between him and the ship. He watched through the monitor as two men were sucked out of the airlock before they could get the inner hatch closed.

Thomas brought the shuttle a short distance from the ship before stopping. He planned to turn around when he felt a blaster against the back of his head.

"Well played," the woman said. "You almost succeeded, but you have just become the newest member of our crew. The two crew members who died were not well-liked, but the Captain will see to your punishment. He is the only person on the ship who is allowed to kill a member of his crew. You can turn around but do it slowly." Thomas rotated his chair around and was wearing a severe expression.

"The men killed themselves," Thomas said.

The woman could not hide her surprise. "Why, you are just a kid. How old are you?"

"I am fifteen, but I will be sixteen in a few months," Thomas said with a frown.

"Captain, I have secured the shuttle, but you will not believe this. The pilot is just a kid. He is only fifteen years old."

"Well, we still have a new member of our crew who can keep the ship running. Also, we have a priceless shuttle and a valuable hostage, which may result in a large ransom. I will meet you in the shuttle bay."

"You heard the Captain," she said.

"You do not understand. An advanced AI controls the shuttle. When you pointed the blaster at me, the AI implemented the Defense Protocol."

Defense Protocol was the verbal program initiation phrase he had set up before letting her aboard. The shuttle's engines shut down. Also, the AI sent a signal to the new controllers Thomas had installed in the engine room. The signal shut down all power aboard the Luxora.

"What did you do?" The woman shouted. "Turn the power back on."

She received a communication from Captain Higgins, and all the color drained from her face.

"I no longer have control of the shuttle. The AI is now in control. As you said, I am just a kid. I do not have the authority to override the AI. Also, the AI does not care if you kill me or not. It is just following its programming. If you give me the gun and get off the shuttle, it will probably turn your ship's power back on."

She walked to the back of the shuttle so she could talk to Captain Higgins without being overheard. Then Thomas felt the disruptions from multiple ships dropping out of jump.

"A destroyer and three frigates have arrived," the AI stated.

A voice came over the shuttle's speakers. "This is Captain Horwitz to the Luxora. Prepare to be boarded. Any resistance and you will be destroyed."

The woman walked over to Thomas and handed him the blaster.

"Captain Horwitz, this is Thomas Wilson. The power throughout the Luxora is turned off. Would you like me to turn it back on?"

Captain Horwitz laughed. "That would be advantageous, but first, join me on the bridge. Your parents are on board, and they are pretty upset with you. You can land in our shuttle bay."

Thomas knew navy formalities. "Yes, sir," he replied.

Thomas looked at the woman. "You can sit in the co-pilot seat."

"The navy is going to place everyone on the Luxora under arrest," she said as she took the seat. "I was wondering if you would let me hide on the shuttle?"

"Please," she said. Thomas had planned to say no before she said please.

"Very well. If you get hungry, you can use the food processor. The AI will not let you fly the shuttle, so do not touch anything else."

Thomas landed the shuttle as directed. As soon as he exited the shuttle, an officer asked Thomas to follow him to the bridge. When he entered the bridge, his mother rushed over and hugged him. Then she scolded him and asked if he had lost what little sense God had given him. His father just shook his head.

"Mom, you are embarrassing me," Thomas said. The Captain and the rest of the bridge officers were unsuccessful in hiding their grins.

The Captain rescued Thomas. "What can you tell me about the pirate ship?"

"I answered their distress beacon. When I arrived, they were in serious trouble. The hull had been breached in four places. I could only patch three holes since I did not have sufficient hull material on board the shuttle. I restored life support by getting two of the four power units back online. Both impulse engines were damaged and offline, but I repaired the less damaged engine. The engine is only operating at eighty percent and will need a complete rebuild to get any better. I performed an upgrade to their neural network and internal tech. You do not have to worry about them shooting at you because I turned off their armament. I also have access to their internal cameras. Would you like me to put their bridge on screen?"

"Please proceed," the Captain said with amusement.

Thomas walked over to the Communications Officer. "May I use your station?" The Officer looked toward Captain Horwitz, and the Captain nodded his head.

Thomas sat down and brought up the bridge of the pirate's ship, but it was dark. Thomas stood up and used his wristband to restore power to the ship. They could hear Captain Higgins as he screamed profanities, including all the ways he intended to kill Thomas. Captain Horwitz addressed the pirate ship but received no response.

"Sorry, sir," Thomas said. "Let me turn back on their external monitors." Thomas used his wristband again. "Sir, he can see and hear you now."

The pirate Captain looked up and stopped talking. "This is Captain Horwitz; I have a destroyer and three frigates. You have a choice. Surrender or be destroyed. Personally, I hate pirates and would rather blow your ship apart."

Captain Higgins knew he had no choice. "We surrender, do not shoot, we surrender. There must be some mistake. We are a civilian ship conducting honest trade."

Captain Horwitz nodded to his First Officer, who immediately arranged for a boarding party to take control of the Luxora.

Thomas had one more surprise. "Sir, before taking their Nav System offline, I plotted the jump coordinates to take them to our shipyard for repairs. I can enter new jump coordinates remotely if you tell me where you plan to take the ship."

The Navigator spoke up. "How were you able to take control of their ship and keep control?"

"I used a double AI interface with a special program I devised," Thomas said and grinned. "The first interface hit their neural network straight on and overloaded their systems while the second part of the program took control. Then I changed all the security codes to allow me to control their ship. I designed the program to make repairing ships in our shipyard easier. Sir, can I accompany the boarding party?"

"Are you out of your mind?" Alina shouted. "You cannot go on the pirate ship. Were you not listening? The pirate captain wants to kill you!"

Captain Horwitz laughed again and shook his head. "Thank you for your offer. Still, I have to honor your mother's concerns. I would like you and your parents to remain as our guests for a couple of days until we get this sorted out."

The Captain assigned a yeoman to assist them during their extended visit. Captain Horwitz asked his Intelligence Officer to do a background check on Thomas Wilson.

The following morning, Thomas accompanied by his parents met with the Captain and several of his officers in a conference room. Thomas provided them with additional details of everything that had taken place except for the stowaway on his shuttle. Everyone enjoyed his story except for his mother, who interrupted several times to tell Thomas how his recklessness could have gotten him killed.

Later, they had dinner as guests at the Captain's table. Thomas and the Captain were alone for a moment before sitting down for the meal.

"Thomas, if you ever want to join the navy or attend the academy, let me know. With my recommendation, you could receive advanced standing at the academy and be out in one year with a commission. I suggest you avoid discussing it with your mother until after you are enrolled."

Thomas spent both nights sharing a room with three junior officers while his parents were provided with a private stateroom. Everyone on the ship heard about how Thomas took control of the pirate ship. The Chief Engineer joined them for breakfast. He congratulated Thomas on his repairs to the pirate ship and gave him a tour of his department. Thomas thoroughly enjoyed himself, and the Chief Engineer loved answering his questions. They had a final meeting with Captain Horwitz and his First Officer.

"What is to become of the pirates?" Thomas asked.

Captain Horwitz was livid. "We have to let them go."

"How can you let them go?" Alina asked. "They are pirates, and they threatened to kill my son."

"Yes, we all know they are pirates," Captain Horwitz said. "Unfortunately, we searched their ship but could find no evidence that would allow us to arrest them. We either have to catch them in the act of piracy or find contraband on their ship or a witness willing to testify against them. What upsets me is knowing they will attack future ships."

"Sir, I still have access to their ship's network," Thomas said. "I could add a defense-only protocol allowing the ship to defend itself if attacked. Subject to the programming, if the Luxora attempted to fire first, their guns would become inoperative, and their shields would drop."

Captain Horwitz looked straight at Thomas. "How difficult would it be for them to remove the protocol?"

"No one on their ship has the ability to override the program. It would require someone good with tech. Also, I could put in a trap to shut down everything except life support if someone tried to change the protocol."

"How long would it take you to prepare the protocol you just described?" Captain Horwitz asked.

"It is already completed. Ensign Alverez and I worked on various protocols last night before deciding on the one I just described. I shared a cabin with him and two other ensigns. They also helped with suggestions on how best to sabotage the pirate ship. I would need to use your ship's AI since it has the necessary range." The Captain made a call, and within a few minutes, the three ensigns arrived.

"I understand you three did not sleep much last night."

"No sir, we were working on a personal project, and it took most of the night," Ensign Alverez answered on behalf of the group.

"Thomas Wilson has informed me of a defense protocol which may prevent our pirate friends from attacking future ships. I cannot authorize making modifications to a civilian ship. However, if a civilian used our AI and accidentally sent a protocol to another ship, it would be a civilian matter. Perhaps the three of you could give Thomas a tour of our tech department."

"Yes, sir." They all grinned. "We would be happy to give Thomas a tour of our ship, and we will specifically warn him not to touch certain displays."

"Dismissed." Thomas and the ensigns could be heard as they excitedly ran down the aisle toward the tech center. Thomas accidentally touched a sensor on a holographic monitor, which sent an override program to the Luxora. They had added one more subroutine, which would notify them whenever the Luxora attempted to fire their guns. Thomas received a message on his wristband letting him know his parents were in the shuttle bay, ready to depart. Thomas said his goodbyes and left to join his parents. Over the years, the story of Thomas and the pirates would be told over drinks. It would grow with the retelling.

THOMAS TOOK THE PILOT'S seat, and his father sat next to him as the co-pilot. Once they entered jump, Thomas and Ben joined Alina in the storage area. They folded down a table and three chairs. Once they were all sitting around the table, Thomas folded out an additional chair.

"You can come out now," Thomas said. The young woman came out of the bathroom.

"I never got your name," Thomas said.

"I am Lukia Madisum."

"Mom, dad, this is Lukia Madisum. Lukia, these are my parents, Ben and Alina Wilson."

"Who is this woman, and what is she doing on our shuttle?" Alina asked.

Thomas had already rehearsed a story. "She was a prisoner on the pirate ship, and I rescued her. I agreed to give her a ride to our planet." His father raised his eyebrows.

"You poor thing," Alina said. "I cannot imagine how horrible that must have been. Do you mind talking about it, or is it too painful?"

"No, the pain has dulled with time. I am from the planet Horae. Raiders regularly attack our planet. I was sixteen when they attacked our village. They took what they wanted, and they took me. Both my parents were shot trying to stop them. I do not know if either of them survived. I also had a fourteen-year-old brother and an eleven-year-old sister. It happened nine years ago, so they will be adults if they are alive."

Thomas thought Lukia had played her part beautifully and did not realize she was being entirely truthful. His mother took an immediate liking to Lukia. While Lukia and Alina were talking, Ben nodded his head toward the front of the shuttle. They went to the pilot's area. Ben asked for the true story, and Thomas gave him an honest answer. Thomas was surprised Ben did not seem bothered by having a pirate onboard their shuttle.

Ben managed to speak to Lukia in private during the trip. "Thomas told me you assisted the pirates by pointing a blaster at him. In the Core, food is free and minimum accommodations are also free, along with free healthcare. I will help you register once we arrive at our home planet of Fidem. We are in the shipbuilding business. If you would like a job, come, and see me. I will give you a second chance, but there will not be a third."

They arrived home without further incidents. Several months later, Lukia applied for a job at Wilson Enterprises and became an employee. It was not long until a manager promoted her to supervisor. Lukia was a self-taught pilot, but she studied and passed the courses to become a licensed shuttle pilot.

CHAPTER 2 ARENA HOCKEY

B en knew Thomas was doing exceptionally well with his general and specialized education. Thomas continued to advance rapidly through the modules. He completed college courses and obtained certifications in a wide variety of ship functions. However, Ben was concerned Thomas would lack the social skills to interact successfully with the wide variety of people he would meet in the future. Ben discussed his concerns with Ralph, his brother-in-law, and Ralph recommended Ben get Thomas involved in a team activity.

A religious order called Fidem settled the planet over nine hundred years earlier, and Fidem became the name of the planet. The original planet's charter outlawed all professional sports, and no one could receive remuneration for participating in any sports. In addition, no university offered sports scholarships. Sports and exercise were still encouraged by the various governing bodies. Still, these same governing bodies required athletes to earn their livelihood from regular jobs. They failed to comprehend how athletes needed to practice extremely hard to become competitive at a specific sport.

Over the years, the religious order lost its absolute power, and church membership became voluntary. Around a hundred years earlier, the government amended the planet's charter to allow for professional sports. Regrettably, for sports, they set the salary at minimum wage for all players. Athletes were to live in poverty or have regular jobs. Also, players could only be paid starting four weeks before the beginning of the season, and all wages ended upon completion of the last game of the season.

Further, to prevent abuse, the total income for an athlete from all sources could not exceed the medium pay for all planetary citizens. Therefore, athletes primarily played for the joy of the game. The outstanding players typically left Fidem and immigrated to a planet without restrictions on player remuneration.

Even with the low player salaries, most teams were not very profitable. After paying team salaries for the players and coaches, the funds collected from gate receipts barely covered the costs for player equipment, use of the facilities, and other expenses. The income from sponsors helped, but sponsors received minimum benefits from the advertising.

Ben started researching the sporting industry or the lack thereof. Several months later, he received information from a business associate saying Jeffery Tredal, the local arena hockey team owner, had severe financial problems. Further, the team lost its only remaining sponsor and was losing money.

Ben informed Alina that he and Thomas would attend the next arena hockey game. None of the other family members had any interest in joining them. Ben contacted the owner, and two tickets were waiting at the gate. Thomas and Ben watched the game from the owner's box.

There were few spectators because the team had only won one game over the past two seasons. The hockey teams played in a zero-gravity arena. The game was awful, with the home team losing nine to nothing. The visiting team rested all their starters during the third period.

Ben and Thomas remained in the booth with the owner after the game ended. Ben told Thomas to stay quiet after the game and observe the discussion. Thomas saw Jeffery was distraught and nervous. Ben told Jeffery he might be interested in purchasing the team. After further discussions, Jeffrey presented Ben with an asking price. Ben shook his head.

"The team is losing money and has no sponsors. I doubt anyone else is interested in buying the team. The price you are asking is too much. I will wait and purchase the team once you file for bankruptcy."

Ben stood up to leave, but Jeffery asked him to sit back down. Jeffery then presented a much lower asking price but stated his major creditors would have to approve the sale. They both agreed to let their respective attorneys draw up a purchase agreement.

Ben and Thomas left the arena. On the drive home, Ben asked Thomas what he had learned.

"Knowing the company was losing money and had no sponsors changed everything."

"You are correct. Knowledge increases your odds of having a better outcome. You need useful information whether you are buying, selling, or trading. You need to know what is important to the other person. People make decisions, not corporations."

"Dad, why is the sale subject to his creditors?"

"The major creditors could take legal action to block the sale unless they receive some of the proceeds. Normally, this would not be an issue. However, if Mr. Tredal files for bankruptcy, these creditors would likely receive none of the money owed to them. Mr. Tredal will probably provide payments to various creditors to get their support. The creditors will agree to this, even though they will receive less than what is owed. Even secured creditors would not want a bankruptcy filing because they would receive significantly less in bankruptcy than in a regular sale. Also, in bankruptcy, the judge could undo the sale on behalf of the creditors. A judge would not undo the sale if the primary creditors signed off on the purchase. This has been the accepted legal approach for thousands of years. You must consider what other parties might do, even if they are not directly involved with the negotiations. This is a good transaction for everyone. Jeffery will no longer lose money funding the team and will have cash for his other businesses. Hopefully, the sale will allow him to survive without filing for bankruptcy."

At sixteen, Thomas only understood part of his father's explanation, but he would remember their conversation.

They executed an agreement to transfer ownership of the team subject to a list of creditors giving their approval. Several weeks later, Ben became the new owner of the team.

BEN AND THOMAS ATTENDED the last game of the season. As expected, the team lost. After the game, they visited the locker room. The players were mostly talking about what they would do during the off-season.

The Coach approached Ben. "I guess you are the new owner."

"You are correct. We could not meet with you or introduce ourselves to the players before we completed the purchase."

"Thank you," the Coach said. "As part of the sale, we received all our back pay. I hope Jeffrey told you I am retiring. Hiring a new coach will be your first job. Let me introduce you to the players."

The Coach told the players he was retiring. The announcement did not surprise the players, but they wished him well. Then, the Coach introduced Ben as the new owner. Ben gave a short speech since he knew the players were ready to leave. The team captain asked the only question. He wanted to know if they still had jobs. Ben assured all the players their contracts would be honored. The players became animated and clapped when told they would be paid on time in the future.

The players did not make much money, and few people were interested in watching a game when they could submerge themselves in a simulation.

"The team needs a new name," Ben said to Thomas on the drive home. "I will let you select the name."

"Demons, the new name is Demons," Thomas said without hesitating.

Ben laughed. "Demons it is."

SEVERAL WEEKS LATER, Ben's office assistant announced: "Coach Pendleton is here for his appointment." Coach Pendleton entered Ben's office, and after the introductions, he took a seat.

"You asked me to come here to discuss the opening you have for a coach. You are the owner of an arena hockey team that finished in last place every season for the last five years."

"Yes, you are correct," Ben said. "I am a businessperson, so let us save some time. You won a world championship, and before getting fired for finishing in fourth place two years ago, you finished in the top three every year. I know your employment contract has a non-compete clause preventing you from signing with any Eastern Division team for another three years. Also, your former employer spread several rumors preventing Western Division teams from wanting to hire you."

The Coach grimaced. "I do not know how you got my prior contract information. It was supposed to be confidential, but you are well informed."

"Coach, I have investigated the rumors. I have concluded these rumors are completely false. Our team finished in last place again this year, so we have the first draft picks in each round. I will give you complete autonomy in decisions concerning the team, with two exceptions. First, you must stay within the budget set for the team. Second, my son is to be one of the twenty players on the team. He will dress out for each game and play at least one full period in each preseason game. Also, he will play in the third period of any regular-season game if the team is four or more points behind. No team has ever overcome a four-point deficit in the final period. Otherwise, you will only play my son when it helps the team."

"What position did your son play, and how old is he?"

"My son is 16 years old and has never played on a team."

The Coach was concerned. "No one under the age of eighteen has ever played professional hockey. He could get hurt by the adult men who play this game. Also, we would be giving him a position on the team which a professional player could fill."

Ben made his final point. "Coach, the bottom four or five players on any team seldom play a single minute during the regular season. Having my son sit on the bench will not hurt the team. The rules do not specify the age of a player. Are you telling me you cannot be competitive with nineteen adult players and a minor?"

"I get complete control on all other team matters as long as I stay within the budget?"

"Yes," Ben answered.

"This control includes trading players or draft picks and signing free agents."

"Yes," Ben replied again.

Coach Pendleton thought for a moment. "The last question, how much are you offering me?" Ben transmitted a copy of the employment contract to the Coach.

"Look it over," Ben said. "I need to have your answer within ten cycles." They said their goodbyes, and Coach Pendleton left the office.

Four days later, Ben received an acknowledgment from the Coach accepting the offer. Ben posted an announcement of the new Coach and the team's new name.

Next, he met with the arena owner and purchased it at a fraction of what it would cost to build a similar structure. He knew if the team started winning, the owner would want a higher price based on gate receipts. Also, with a little marketing, the arena could host other events.

Ben used his business reputation to get sponsors from independent, privately owned companies. These businesses were not subject to the oversite associated with publicly traded companies. Each company expected to receive enough advertising benefits to offset the small amount it contributed as a sponsor. While it is costly to own a team, Ben still expected to make a profit or at least break-even financially.

DURING THE OFF-SEASON, Thomas used his codes to enter the arena each day after completing his shipyard work and study lessons. He had full use of the arena for training.

Thomas had spent over a thousand hours in the shipyard working without gravity on various ships. His young, slimmer frame gave him an advantage over the other dock workers when working in tight junctions or narrow crawl spaces. The crews would laugh at his enthusiasm, when he jumped at the chance, to work in areas they were happy to avoid. Also, they were impressed when they inspected his finished work and found it exceptional in all aspects.

Thomas set up the trainer in the arena so it would throw the spherical pucks at different angles with random velocities. He soon mastered all the beginner programs and started working his way up through the intermediate levels, which were considerably more difficult. He also watched videos of previous games. Thomas enjoyed practicing the crowd-pleasing stunts the experienced players would make, such as the upside-down shots relative to the audience. To Thomas, up and down had no meaning while working in zero gravity. In the shipyard, down was toward the ship, and up was away from the ship.

Coach Pendleton's had an office next to the arena. One afternoon when the Coach left his office, he heard sounds from the arena. He entered the arena and watched Thomas practicing. The Coach noticed the kid possessed good acceleration due to less inertia resulting from his small size, and he struck the puck with good power. After watching him practice for a while, he knew the kid would not be the worst player on the team. Plus, practicing during the off-season would give him an advantage when the season started.

The Coach traded his number one overall pick for two second-round picks, a third-round pick, and a starting forward. The resulting trade gave him three second-round picks, two in the third, one in the fourth, and one in the fifth.

There were sixteen teams, with eight teams in each division. At the end of the season, the Western Division's top team played the Eastern Division's winner in a final game for the world championship. The Western Division had historically been weaker than the Eastern Division. The Western Division Teams were primarily in small cities with little local support and few sponsors.

The Coach selected a goaltender and two forwards with his second-round picks. He added a forward and a defender in the third round. He picked a defender in the fourth and another forward in the final round. The Coach figured he had seven potential starters from the draft. He cut eight of his existing players and picked up ten players who were either unsigned or free agents. The team had thirty players with Thomas. Thirty was the maximum number of players he could dress out during the two preseason games. He would cut the roster to twenty players for the start of the regular season.

During the two preseason games, he made sure each player played an entire period to see if their level of play was the same as what he observed during the team's scrimmages. During the regular season, each team would play the other teams in their division twice. This resulted in fourteen regular-season games before the division winners would play for the Championship. At first, most of the players disliked having Thomas on the team. Despite this, the players warmed up to his enthusiasm by the start of the preseason. It helped there were worse players on the team. The Coach told Thomas to keep his helmet on before, during, and after a game. Even though an age limit did not exist, Coach Pendleton did not want anyone to know Thomas was a minor.

The Demons had two goaltenders, twelve forwards, and six defenders. The Coach classified Thomas as a forward, and he played in the last period of each preseason game. As expected, he did not play in any regular games during the first season, and the team finished in fifth place. More fans began showing up throughout the season.

THE COACH USED FREE agency and the draft to strengthen the team further. Lawrence, a player from the recent draft, had just signed his contract. After leaving the Coach's office, he walked over to the arena. Lawrence saw a player practicing even though team practice would not start for another three months. He kept watching and saw the player was surprisingly good.

Lawrence went back to the locker room and dressed out. A few minutes later, he entered the arena. Lawrence moved in front of Thomas to steal the puck, but Thomas used a breakaway deke and moved around him toward the other end of the arena. Then, he intentionally slowed up. He let the stranger pass him and get back in front. Next, he executed a fake shot to his backhand and again moved around him. Lawrence chased after Thomas, but Thomas stopped suddenly and dropped down. When Lawrence went sailing over him, Thomas jetted upward, hitting him around the ankles, causing Lawrence to do a backward somersault. Thomas then slapped the puck, sending it into the center of the net.

Thomas jetted over and introduced himself. Lawrence asked how often he practiced and how he got access to the arena. Thomas said he had an authorization code. Lawrence asked if he could practice with Thomas, and they set a time to meet each afternoon. They primarily practiced as forwards, moving the puck down the court until they could anticipate each other's moves. They also developed signals and various names for special plays they developed. Both players continued to improve as they worked together using the dike, attacking the zone, clearing the puck, and using a block to permit the other player to breakaway. They also became adept at using the bounce to propel themselves off the walls to increase their speed and change directions. Lawrence became an expert at setting up the perfect shot for Thomas to make the goal.

Lawrence was twenty-one years old and weighed one-hundred-ninety pounds. Whereas Thomas had just turned seventeen, weighed one-hundred-seventy pounds, and was still growing. All players had four power jets, one for each arm and one for each ankle. At full power, each player could ultimately attain the same top-end velocity. However, the increased mass of the larger players resulted in slower speeds at the start of their acceleration. Still, the greater mass allowed bigger players to plow through the smaller players. In fairness, the lighter players used their higher acceleration to offset the power of the larger players.

MOST EXPERIENCED STARTERS ranged from twenty-five to thirty years of age, and most weighed from two hundred to two hundred forty pounds. During the game, each side played with two forwards, two defenders, a center, and a goalkeeper.

The Coach divided the team into four practice squads, but Lawrence and Thomas were on different squads. During a scrimmage, the squads would play without a center. The blue squad contained the starters. The red squad served as the backup players who played when the starters rested. The orange and green squads received little playing time except during preseason. The Coach hired an assistant before the start of his second season. During practice, the coach and his assistant would spend time with each player. They helped the players improve their skills and their understanding of the game. He taught every player on the bench to pay attention throughout the game so they could learn and be ready if given an opportunity to play.

As in the first season, the second season started with Thomas playing one period in each of the two preseason games. Thomas and Lawrence were never on the court at the same time, but they played as well or better than any of the nonstarters on the orange and the green squads.

Thomas continued to warm the bench. The Demons were winning a lot of games, and they would finish in third place. For their last game of the season, they were facing the Warriors, the undefeated first-place team. All the other teams had already played their final game of the season. The Warriors were two wins ahead of the second-place team, so losing or winning would not affect their standings since the second-placed team had already finished their schedule. The same situation existed for the Demons. A win or a loss would not affect their third-place position. The Demons had already lost one game to the first-place team and two to the second-place team. Thus, the Demons had eleven wins against three losses with one game to play. This represented their best season since the team's formation, and more fans were attending the games.

THE DEMONS PLAYED AT home for the last game of the season. The arena was filled to capacity. The fans were excited at the beginning of the game but lost their enthusiasm when it became apparent the Demons were no match for the Warriors. At the end of the second period, the Warriors were ahead six to two. During the break, the Demon players were depressed.

Thomas went over to the Coach. "Coach, the team is four points behind starting the third period, and I get to play. Also, I would like Lawrence to play since we have practiced together for the past two years."

The Coach started to say no but then remembered the language in the contract. Besides, he figured he had nothing to lose, with the team being down by four scores. The Coach stood up, and the team quieted down to listen.

"I am changing the lineup for the third period. Thomas and Lawrence are starting with Willis, Grayson, Jackson, and Roberson."

Thomas shouted as they left the locker room. "We only need four points to tie and five to win."

The players laughed but got caught up in Thomas's excitement as they left the locker room. They took up the banner and started shouting. "Four to tie, five to win."

At the beginning of the third period, the Warriors had benched all of their starters to give them extra rest before the championship game. Also, it would prevent the possibility of an injury to their star players.

Willis, the center, would handle the faceoff to start the period. The referee put the puck in the center of the arena. It was equal distance from the four walls horizontally and equal distance between the ceiling and the floor vertically. Willis and the center from the Warriors took their positions. When the referee's tone sounded, Willis struck the ball before his opponent and sent the puck to their right side, where Thomas immediately took the puck with his stick. Thomas crossed over to the opposite side of the court and raced down the left side with the puck. Thomas passed the puck to Lawrence, who had been pacing him as they traveled toward the goal.

Thomas and Lawrence crossed, and Thomas broke along the right side. Lawrence sent the puck high and off to the side of the opposing goalkeeper, a shot they had practiced thousands of times. Thomas went high and slammed the puck into the net, making the score six to three. The alarm sounded for the successful goal. The previously sedate home crowd came to their feet cheering.

The Warriors won the next faceoff, and two forwards moved the puck down the court. Thomas used his speed to come around the back of the player and stole the puck. Then he pivoted for a breakaway with no defenders between him and the goal. He raced at full speed, took a read on the goalkeeper, and scored an easy point, making the score six to four. The opposing coach got on his feet, shouting at his players to wake up and start playing. He continued to scream for his players to play both ends of the court and stop giving away easy points.

On the next faceoff, the Warriors again got the puck and moved it down the field. The Warriors took two shots at the goal, but Roberson, the goalkeeper for the Demons, blocked the first shot and caught the second attempt. The players for the Demons were revitalized. They were blocking and checking as the puck moved downfield. This time the goalkeeper expected Thomas to take the shot, but just as Thomas moved into position, Lawrence moved behind Grayson and executed a perfect screenshot. Suddenly the scoreboard flashed six to five with imitation fireworks. The Demons had pulled to within one point, and the coach for the Warriors called timeout. The starters for the Warriors came back into the game.

The fans for the Demons were on their feet shouting and screaming. While the fans of the Warriors were shocked and wondering how this reversal had taken place.

On the next faceoff, Willis slapped the ball over to Grayson, and Grayson passed the puck to Jackson. Willis moved back to defend. Thomas sprinted high and to the left, drawing a double team.

Grayson, the team's captain, used his size to overpower a defender. Jackson blocked another defender, and Grayson fired the puck into the back of the net to tie the game at six all.

With the game tied, the crowd noise gave additional energy to the Demons. All the momentum had shifted to the Demons, and they were playing at the top of their game. The Warriors appeared to be just a second slower than the Demons. The Warriors won the next faceoff and moved the puck down the field. They took a shot, but it went wide. The players for both teams were fighting for possession of the puck. The Warriors made a weak shot toward the goal. Roberson easily caught the puck. Only a few minutes remained on the game clock, and each team wanted to score to prevent the game from going into overtime.

Roberson tossed the puck to Lawrence, who took the puck downfield. Lawrence and Thomas passed the puck to each other several times when Thomas gave a signal to Lawrence. Thomas sprinted behind the Warrior's goal and then jetted toward the top of the net. Lawrence sent the puck floating high above the net. The goalkeeper thought it was just a poor hit. Thomas came high over the top of the net in an inverted upside-down position. He slammed the puck into the top right corner of the net, putting the Demons in the lead for the first time at seven to six. The players on both sides could not believe the play Thomas had just made. Neither could the fans for the Demons, as their loud cheering could be heard outside the arena.

Grayson jetted over to Thomas. "What was that?" he shouted above the noise.

Thomas looked a little embarrassed as he grinned. "Sorry, I was kind of showing off."

Grayson laughed. "You do not look sorry. I want to see a lot of those shots next season when we win the championship."

With less than a minute left, the Demons iced the puck twice into the far upper corner of the field. During the flight of the second icing, time ran out. The crowd for the Demons sounded like they had just won a championship, even though the game did not change their standings.

The Warriors congratulated the Demons, and they all spent time talking to Thomas and Lawrence. The coach for the Warriors congratulated Coach Pendleton and asked him if he would be interested in trading Thomas and Lawrence since they were backup players. Coach Pendleton chuckled and replied they would be starters next season.

Coach Pendleton called the players together. "Great game. Next year, Thomas will be a starter and our sniper. I hope to see all of you next season."

Lawrence told Thomas a sniper was a forward with a powerfully accurate shot that the team relied on for finishing plays. Thomas and Lawrence scheduled a two-week break before starting their practice sessions. Several players on the orange and green squads heard them talking and asked if they could join them. Thomas and Lawrence said it would be great. With additional players, they could have some practice games with actual players instead of simulation players. Ben's father visited the locker room to pick up Thomas and congratulated the team. Coach Pendleton informed Ben that Thomas would be a starter next season.

THOMAS AND LAWRENCE continued to practice after work, and practice became more fun with the additional players. All except one player from the orange and green squads showed up at the daily practices. Three players from the red squad also joined the nonpaid practices. All practices started after work and lasted for two hours. The rules prohibited Coach Pendleton from providing coaching to players during the off-season. However, he showed up occasionally to watch the players practice and observed their improvement.

Toward the end of the offseason, Coach Pendleton brought along a coach from the team that finished in sixth place during the prior season. The sixth-place team had the best goalkeeper in the league, but no offense. The team had lost both of their starting forwards. One took a higher-paying job on a different planet, while the other suffered an injury and did not return.

The next day, Coach Pendleton asked two forwards and a goalkeeper to meet in his office after practice. Coach Pendleton introduced the players to Coach Wilder. Everyone took a seat.

"I am going to be blunt," Coach Pendleton said. "If you continue playing for the Demons, you will spend most of your time on the bench. If you are agreeable, I would like to trade all three of you to Coach Wilder for Jason Triband, a goalkeeper. On his team, you will be starters." At first, they were surprised but then became excited since they would be starters. They also realized the trade helped the Demons. Under their contracts, the players had to agree to any trade. They looked at each other, grinned, and agreed to the trade. Player contracts were standardized. It only took a few minutes before the players were officially transferred.

"Feel free to continue with your offseason practices," Coach Wilder said. "I look forward to having you join the team at the start of preseason."

Coach Pendleton picked up additional players in the draft and signed several free agents who wanted to be on a winning team. The Demons were loaded with depth at all positions. During preseason, the Coach found it hard to reduce the team roster from thirty down to the final twenty because all the players were playing well. They won both of their preseason games. The Coach informed the players they would all see action during the regular season so the starters could stay rested and fresh throughout each game.

Just before the start of the season, the team voted for Thomas as team captain. Thomas went to Grayson after the vote since he felt Grayson would be upset. Thomas told Grayson he should continue to be the captain. Grayson smiled and said he led the campaign with the other players to get Thomas elected.

"In the final game last season, we were down by four points going into the third period. I thought the game was over. You were the only person who thought we could win, and that is the type of captain this team needs."

After a few regular season games, it became apparent the Demons were the best team in the league. Most games were so one-sided the starters would sit out the last period. Thomas became the top scorer in their division. Most of their opponents would attempt to double-team Thomas, which did little to slow down his scoring. Also, double-teaming Thomas allowed other Demons to score. They had the best defense in the league, and their new goalkeeper had several shutouts. Their only competition was when they played against their former teammates. The prior teammates had practiced with Thomas throughout the offseason. They did a better job guarding him but still lost three to one to the Demons. Thomas met with his former teammates at the end of the game. They said they were having a great time and expected to finish in second place behind the Demons. The Demons finished the season undefeated and would host the championship game against the winner of the Eastern Division.

The rest of Thomas' family had never attended a game and were unaware Thomas played for the Demons. His mother and siblings did not know Thomas had become a celebrity within their small city. Thomas had just turned eighteen. He was slightly over six feet tall and weighed a hundred eighty pounds. Thomas had an athletic build due to his work at the shipyards and his daily exercise with his teammates. He was quick to smile but thoughtful. Thomas was a natural leader and moved with a controlled, effortless grace. He exuded confidence and power.

ALINA ASKED THOMAS to help her shop for a gift for Ben's upcoming birthday. She wanted to get him something special since he was turning fifty. Thomas suggested they visit the open market at the edge of the docks since it stocked exotic off-world items. While shopping, Alina noticed young females accosting Thomas. She knew her son was handsome, but the girls were giggling at her son's comments and kept looking at him with adoration. She noticed the young girls were giving him their personal contact information. Several adults were also greeting and talking to him.

After Thomas rejoined Alina, she asked how he knew all those people who had been talking to him. He just grinned and said they were people he met after work. Thomas then changed the subject and pointed to an item on the next table as the perfect gift for Ben.

After paying for the gift, the booth keeper turned to Thomas and was just beaming. "Good Luck," he said.

"Thank you," Thomas replied. As they drove home, Alina wondered why a stranger would make such a statement to Thomas.

BEN MADE SURE THE ENTIRE family would attend the championship game. They knew Ben owned the team but figured he had purchased the team as a simple business venture. Alina, Stephen, and Joan had never been interested in arena hockey. They had never attended a game but knew a puck going into the net was a score. Stephen had an apartment but joined the family in traveling to the game since Ben had special parking next to the arena.

The family arrived at the arena and proceeded to the owner's private box. Thomas said he would see them later and left.

"Where is Thomas going?" Alina asked.

"He is joining his friends and will be back after the game," Ben said.

Ben and Thomas had both agreed to keep his involvement in the team a secret. They had not wanted Alina to worry about Thomas playing such a physical game and possibly being hurt. Now, they just wanted to surprise the family.

Stephen and Joan had agreed to attend the game to humor their father. They planned to suffer through the game in silence. They were impressed by the large attendance and the excitement of the fans.

The announcer introduced the Loyalists team players first. Then, the announcer started introducing the Demons. Before bringing out their last player, the announcer quoted the records set during the season, including the most points scored in a season by a single player in the history of the team, the most points scored in a single game, and the most assists in a season.

"The team captain and the player you have grown to love, Thomas Wilson!" He shouted.

The crowd came to their feet, cheering and screaming as Thomas jetted into the arena. He waved to the spectators, put on his helmet, and took his position. Alina, Stephen, and Joan were in a state of shock.

The Coach assigned Thomas to guard Walt Engle, the star for the other team. Walt was six foot four and weighed two hundred forty pounds. Walt used his size and power to intimidate opponents. Thomas harassed Walt throughout the first period by blocking his shots and stealing the puck. Tyrue Cutter, the Loyalists best defender, guarded Thomas when the Demons had the puck. Thomas outmaneuvered Tyure and scored the first goal in the game. At the end of the first period, the score stood at one to nothing. In the second period, Grayson scored before the Loyalists finally got on the scoreboard with a point. Then Thomas scored again. The second period ended three to one in favor of the Demons.

In the third quarter, the Loyalists played extremely hard. They scored the first goal making the score three to two. Lawrence moved into position to set Thomas up for a shot. The goalie had watched Thomas score twice on the same maneuver and moved to block a shot from Thomas. Lawrence saw the opening, and instead of passing the puck, he slammed the puck behind the goalie into the net, making it four to two.

Walt had been completely shut out and humiliated as he suffered four turnovers because Thomas had a quicker stick. Finally, out of frustration, Walt slugged Thomas in the head with a vicious full power swing. Thomas was surprised and unable to avoid the enormous fist coming at his head. He pushed all four jets to move away from the punch. After the impact, he allowed his body to go slack as he tumbled end over end toward the wall. The punch left Thomas a little numb, but all he could think about was if Walt would be in the penalty box for two minutes or five minutes. Also, Thomas knew the foul would give the Demons a free penalty shot. He was so caught up in his thinking he did not move or react when he slammed into the wall. Thomas floated a short distance from the wall and hung motionless while catching his breath. He heard the alarm for the foul and grinned.

Thomas looked around and was surrounded by his teammates. As his head cleared, he noticed the silence in the arena as the crowd held their breath. Thomas's family was also on their feet, and Alina, with a pounding heart, prayed that Thomas was still alive.

His coach and a referee were asking Thomas if he needed medical attention.

"I am fine," Thomas said as he waved to the spectators. A second referee announced Walt would be in the penalty box for five minutes, and the Demons would receive a free penalty shot.

"Thomas, why don't you sit out the rest of the game," Coach Pendleton said.

"No way, Coach. I am your sniper, and it is my penalty shot. Please do not take me out." The Coach relented and let him stay in the game.

Several of the Demons' players started talking about revenge, but Thomas stressed the real revenge would be to score as many points as possible while Walt sat in the penalty box.

Thomas took his time with the penalty shot. Then, he hit it into the bottom right corner of the net for a score to put the Demons in front five to two. For the next five minutes, the Demons overwhelmed the Loyalists and scored three more goals making it eight to two. Walt returned after the five-minute penalty, but the game was essentially over. The Demons scored one more goal, and the game ended in a nine to two slaughter. Toward the end of the game, the crowd remained on their feet. They were chanting Thomas, and their loud voices filled the arena.

At the end of the game, Walt came over and congratulated Thomas on the win.

"Are you going to apologize for slugging me?"

Walt laughed. "Are you going to apologize for embarrassing me?" Thomas grinned and shook his head.

The Demons gathered at the edge of the arena to meet their fans. Everyone wanted to meet Thomas. Ben, Alina, Joan, and Stephen approached the players. Alina and Joan were shocked to see young girls exposing their breasts to Thomas while asking him to sign various body parts. Alina overheard several sexual suggestions directed toward Thomas.

While waiting, Principal Tindal approached Alina. "Your son is stupendous and a credit to our city," she said with unbridled enthusiasm. "Our Coach reminds me daily how Thomas could have played for our school if not for the misunderstanding. Thomas is the greatest Demon ever!" Alina decided to get over her animosity and forgive the Principal since her religion preached forgiveness.

"Thank you. It is good to see you," Alina said and realized she meant it. She had stayed involved in the home schooling for Thomas. She knew Thomas was years ahead of other students who attended school and were taught using traditional methods. Indirectly, Principal Tindal contributed to her son's accelerated education.

When Thomas saw his family, he asked the crowd to let them through. The fans started congratulating his parents and telling them how fortunate they were to have such a son. Stephen and Joan looked at each other and could not believe what they had seen. They had just watched their younger brother play an incredible game in front of over fifty thousand fanatical fans.

Thomas told his family it would take time to change and say goodbye to his teammates. He suggested they not wait for him since he could have someone give him a ride home. Several young girls who appeared to be in their mid-twenties immediately volunteered to give Thomas a ride, but Alina said they would wait.

Thomas saw the look on his mother's face and leaned over. "Mom, I am eighteen," he whispered.

She leaned over to her son's ear and whispered back. "We are still going to wait."

Just then, a girl wearing a college sweater screamed. "Joan, why didn't you tell us your younger brother was a celebrity hockey player?"

"This is my friend Melanin," Joan said to her family. "We met when I started college and have the same major." Joan introduced each of her family members to Melanin.

"You must come to the after-game party at my house," Melanin insisted. "Bring both your hot brothers."

"I will come," Stephen said immediately.

Alina looked over at Thomas. Thomas gave her that innocent, angelic look. She knew his look was a complete deception, but it was still a work of art.

Alina laughed and nodded her head. "Okay, Thomas, you can go."

Thomas grinned. "Give me a minute to take a shower and change clothes."

Stephen moved closer to Melanin. He was attracted to her bubbly personality and laughter.

Ben accompanied Thomas into the locker room amid all the shouting and the champagne spraying around the room. Thomas grabbed a glass of champagne and joined his teammates in their celebration. Thomas was underage, but Ben did not say anything since he had been drinking before he turned twenty-one. Also, the drinking age was eighteen on some planets.

Thomas took a quick shower, changed into his regular clothes, and said goodbye to his teammates. He hurried to join his sister and her friends. The other players had packed their belongings and were also leaving the locker room.

Ben had a short private meeting with the Coach and thanked him for turning Thomas into a leader.

"Thomas is a natural leader," Coach Pendleton said. "I just did a little polishing."

Ben gave him the bad news. Thomas had played his last game. The Coach could not help expressing his disappointment but understood Thomas was destined for bigger things.

THOMAS JOINED HIS BROTHER, his sister, and her friends. Stephen and Melanin were getting along really well. Melanin said she had room for Stephen in her vehicle. Evelyn, one of Melanin's friends, said she had extra room in her vehicle and would be happy to bring Thomas to the party. Joan started to object, but Thomas had already hurriedly departed with Evelyn and her two female friends. Joan felt a need to protect her younger brother. Therefore, she did not like the arrangements since all three girls were in college and several years older than Thomas.

Joan arrived at the party and started looking for Thomas. Finley, a student who had been in several of her classes, approached her. She liked him, and they had lunch together several times at the college cafeteria. Despite this, he had never asked her out for a date. Joan and Finley were both in their second year of college. Whereas Stephen was finishing his fourth and final year.

Finley got Joan a drink, and they continued to talk. "Your brother Thomas is fantastic. He made so many unbelievable shots!" Joan realized she had forgotten about Thomas.

"We have to find Thomas," Joan said to Finley.

Joan started going from room to room, searching for Thomas. Finley accompanied her. They finally found Thomas on the patio with Evelyn. Thomas had his arms around her waist, and her arms were around his neck. As their lips separated, Thomas noticed his sister.

Thomas grinned. "Hi sis, great party."

Joan rolled her eyes and decided to give her brother some privacy. As they walked away, Finley moved in front of her.

"It seems your brother has the right idea as he leaned in and kissed her."

Joan responded instantly as their bodies pressed together, and for the second time, she completely forgot about her younger brother.

The three siblings arrived home the following morning. They used an automated municipal vehicle for transportation. They were just finishing breakfast when their parents joined them.

"You guys are up early," Alina said. "Did you enjoy the party?" The children all grinned.

"It was alright," Stephen said. "They put the dishes in the tergomatic for sanitizing and left the kitchen. Stephen said goodbye to everyone as he went out the front door to his ground vehicle for the trip back to his apartment. Thomas and Joan headed to their bedrooms.

Alina looked over at Ben as he broke out laughing. Then she realized why their children had been grinning.

"I guess the kids think we are naïve and never stayed out all night when we were young," Alina said. Ben walked over and kissed her.

"I will make breakfast if you get us some coffee," Ben said.

Alina knew Stephen would graduate from college in a few months, and he had been living in an apartment for the past two years. He still had his room here and occasionally spent the night. Joan had just completed her second year of college and had arranged to share an apartment with several college friends. Alina ate her breakfast while thinking about their children.

"I used to think Thomas was God's way of punishing me for not appreciating my first two children since they were so good," Alina said. "Now, I think I will miss him the most when he finally moves out."

Last night was the first time the entire family had attended an event together in a long time. She loved her children and felt blessed they had turned out so well. It would be just her and Ben in a short time, but hopefully, it would not be too long until she became a grandmother. She looked forward to spoiling her future grandchildren but secretly hoped Thomas would stay home for a few more years.

CHAPTER 3 BUILDING A SHIP

Ben Wilson thought back to when his father died in an explosion and how he had to take over the family business. At the time, Ben had limited experience and had never handled an entire ship from start to finish. As a result, he made many mistakes initially, which could have been avoided if his father had given him more opportunities to learn the shipbuilding business before he died. Ben would do something he wished his father had done for him.

It had only been a week since his last game, and Thomas had just finished a bridge panel installation when he received a call to report to his father's office. Thomas went to the office and took a seat. The office staff had already gone home since it was late in the day.

Ben projected a holograph of a ship and enlarged it until it filled up most of the space in the office.

"This ship is a radically new design concept," Ben said with pride. "It is something I have been working on for a very long time. The ship we are building is nearly complete. We currently have no orders for a new ship. The entire Galactic is in a severe economic recession. To avoid dismissing our employees, we will build this ship without an order."

"It is beautiful and huge," Thomas said.

"Yes, it is," Ben replied. "By design, you have worked in every stage of ship construction and in every department in the company. Also, you have management experience from supervising several work crews and gained leadership skills with the Demons. I am assigning you as shipwright for this new ship. You will be the General

Manager over its construction from start to finish. Your Uncle Ralph and I will be there when you need us. But, we expect you to see the ship is built to spec. You may modify the ship when warranted by issuing change orders. Understand, change orders are costly, and you need to stay on budget. Also, we want the ship you build to be so grand that someone will want to buy it upon completion. Remember to listen to the people doing the work. They will be the first to know of a problem and will let you know if you encourage them. Ralph and I will be here to see you do not fail, but this is your project."

"When do you want me to start the construction?"

"I want you to start in two months when the current ship launches. You need to have materials on hand and available at that time. Thomas, no one in this shipyard has the breadth of knowledge you possess. Trust your instincts. Remember you are in charge and will be expected to make the hard decisions."

Thomas continued to gaze upon the holograph of the beautiful ship. This was his father's dream ship, and Thomas made a silent promise he would not let his father down. He made a second promise. When completed, no ship would match it in beauty or performance. Thomas reviewed the ship's critical path construction schedule as he headed home.

Ben was proud of his son. Thomas was only eighteen but very mature for his age. Also, having Thomas in charge of the ship's construction would put his backup plan into place if the company failed to recover financially.

The ship would be built to military specifications with a double-walled hull, heavy-duty shields, and an array of defensive weaponry. It would be slightly larger than a navy destroyer, but it would be a civilian merchant ship. The cargo bay would hold over fifteen hundred of the twenty-foot standard shipping containers.

The shell of the ship was erected within a construction birth. Next, Thomas installed the latest technology and the best AI computer available. The AI had a vast database, nearly unlimited storage capacity, quick voice response, subroutines allowing it to handle thousands of queries simultaneously, and the ability to provide recommendations. Also, it could learn as it collected new data, making it appear sentient. Vast amounts of information had been downloaded and were continuing to be collected. Base data included the coordinates for all known jump points, the location of the Stargates, data on a host of ships operating within the Core, and lists of the merchants. Also, it contained planetary requests for imports and available exports. Thomas was pleased with the ongoing installation and programming as he reviewed the status of various sections from a central monitor. He checked the voice response of the AI with an indirect question for something that did not exist.

"Sentient computers," Thomas said without thinking. The word 'Omnia' flashed on the monitor for a fraction of a second and disappeared. Thomas asked the AI to display the last image. The AI specifications popped up on the screen, which was the image he had previously reviewed.

Thomas vocalized, "Sentient computers." The AI responded. "Sentient computers do not exist." Thomas wondered if he had imagined the display.

Thomas remembered his father taking him to visit the planet's technology center and introducing him to Omnia, the AI responsible for controlling the planet's infrastructure. Thomas sat down at a booth and communicated with the AI while his father took care of some corporate matters. Thomas remembered how he enjoyed talking with Omnia and trying to trick it with unusual emotional questions. He was startled by some answers.

"Are you sentient?" Thomas asked.

It promptly responded. "No, I am just a very sophisticated machine."

"Are there any sentient computers," Thomas asked. The AI should have answered truthfully and quickly, but Omnia paused. "No, there are no sentient machines." Thomas always wondered if the AI had overridden its programming and lied.

Thomas stopped daydreaming. There was still a lot of work remaining to complete the installation of the AI sensors and nodes throughout the ship. He would do a final review when the AI was one hundred percent functional.

Thomas spent lavishly on the Captain's cabin and doubled its size by using the space initially specified as a separate cabin. He thought it might make a difference in attracting a buyer. His father noticed the added luxury in the cabin and raised an eyebrow but did not say anything. Ben gave advice indirectly by asking questions.

Thomas informed specific crews if their part of the project was on the critical path. Any task on the critical path would affect the timeline and could delay the entire completion date if not completed on time. Similarly, completing a task on the critical path in less time would shorten the entire schedule. Completing the ship ahead of schedule would reduce the cost of the ship. More flexibility existed for the tasks not on the critical path since those tasks would not affect the planned completion date for the ship. Thomas did not get angry with a crew if they were on the critical path and falling behind. Instead, he would temporarily move people from tasks not on the critical path to help out, or he would put on a jumpsuit and provide the help.

Thomas became an expert on all of the ship's major attributes. The ship's artificial gravity was compartmentalized, so a loss of gravity in one section would not affect the rest of the ship. Also, the total gravity throughout the ship could be adjusted from the bridge. Reducing the gravity in the cargo bay when docked, allowed for easier cargo movement. Also, changing the gravity helped when they needed to move heavy equipment or for other similar needs.

Few realized it could be used defensively by selectively alternating between gravity and no gravity in areas where boarders might attempt a hostile takeover of the ship.

The heavy-duty inertial dampeners would allow easier course corrections when using the impulse engines. The dampeners would become even more essential when the ship was fully loaded and would be indispensable for maneuverability during a battle.

Thomas made four significant changes to the design. The further a ship can see in space, the greater the chance of making a better decision. Strategically, it allowed more time to maneuver the ship when entering into a dangerous situation.

His first change order was to increase the ship's vision by adding longer-range sensors. He contacted every manufacturer of passive and active sensors as he attempted to find the best long-range sensors currently on the market.

The passive sensors would not be detectable by another ship. Passive sensors analyzed data received, such as heat signatures, power fluctuations, frequency variations, noise, brightness, radiation, sight, gravitation, and other readings. Whereas active sensors would scan the area using sonar, bounce back frequencies, energy pulses, electromagnetics, and penetration technologies to observe particular regions of space. Unfortunately, other ships would detect active sensing, especially if you were attempting to scan their vessel.

Thomas received responses from five manufacturers of sensor systems. He asked if they could do a custom upgrade of their best current sensor arrays to extend the range and what it would cost for such a unit. He asked for the sensitivity, resolution, and probability for detecting different items in space while providing the limitations of any proposed system. Three suppliers simply sent the pricing for their best sensors and informed Thomas they would not do a custom system for a single order. The two smaller companies announced they would attempt to extend the range of their sensors while keeping a reasonable tradeoff between cost and improved performance.

Thomas was thrilled when he received the two proposals within the time he had given them. As requested, each design had active and passive sensors but would cost double the price compared to an off-the-shelf unit. Unfortunately, one company had the best passive sensors while the other had the better active technology.

Thomas was so excited he called each of the owners of the two companies and asked one company to sell just the passive sensor array while requesting the other to sell him their active sensors. They each asked why he did not want to buy the complete system. He told the first supplier they had better active sensors, but a competitor had a better passive design. Thomas gave the same reverse response to the second supplier with the better passive sensors. He explained how combining the best part of each design would create a unit with a fifty percent greater range and a twenty-five percent better resolution than any units currently available. They both wanted to know the name of the company with the better competing system. Thomas was afraid if they talked, he would not get the sensor system he wanted.

Finally, Thomas asked the owners of the two sensor companies to visit the shipyard to determine the optimal installation for the controller and the sensor units. They arrived as planned on the same day. Thomas kept them apart and gave them separate tours of the ship. The ship was approximately fifty percent complete.

Thomas arranged for the three of them to meet in a conference room. When they first sat down, the two owners just stared at each other. At first, they were cautious. Conversely, after a few minutes, they were excitedly discussing sensor technology and completely ignored Thomas. Thomas could not follow the science being discussed by the two experts. He left and then came back after several hours.

Thomas interrupted them. "Are you willing and able to provide the sensor system I want?"

They looked at each other and then back at Thomas. "Yes," they replied together.

They then asked to use his AI computer so they could upload sensor data. Thomas provided the requested AI access codes. He gave them the name of a local hotel, but they asked if he had any facilities at the shipyard. Thomas explained how the rooms were basic and not as nice as the rooms at the hotel. They did not seem to care and simply wanted to continue to work together. He showed them the rooms and the shipyard's cafeteria. Thomas left them alone and went back to work.

Thomas found the two men the following morning. They looked like they had worked all night, but they were both smiling. They excitedly explained how they were merging their companies. They would own the upscale sensor market with the sensor arrays they could build together. They were sure the navy and many corporations would want to boost their ships to this innovative technology. They committed to having Thomas' order ready for installation within two months. They were expediting the order because it would be easier to sell future systems if they already had a commercial unit installed and operational. They offered to discount the price if they could take videos of the final installation for presentation to other customers. Thomas readily agreed. Their new company would sell a system with less range at a lower price than the system they were providing Thomas. It would still exceed the range of the best units on the market by twenty percent. Fortunately, they could price their units at the same price as the inferior systems offered by their competitors because their company had significantly less overhead. They knew the navy would want to upgrade their ships, which would keep them busy for several years.

They asked if Thomas knew of a legal firm to help them with a Galactic patent and a merger of their independent firms. Thomas called his father's corporate attorney. The lawyer informed Thomas they had attorneys at the firm who could handle both requests. The attorneys set up an appointment for later in the day.

THE SECOND CHANGE ORDER resulted in only a minor cost increase. Thomas modified the ship so a potential buyer could install two railguns at a future date. They reinforced the frame of the ship where the guns would be mounted. The modification included an electronic connector and a power coupling routed to the points where the future guns would be installed.

For protection, the ship would have military-grade shields, two artillery cannons with a feed rate of 2000 rounds per minute, four particle beam cannons mounted on turrets with full rotation, four missile launchers, and two torpedo tubes. All electronics throughout the ship had replacement panels readily available. The panels could be quickly exchanged if an active unit became damaged.

The third change order involved the Laser Battery. Thomas opted to purchase a larger Laser Battery with a voice-directed, fully automated AI interface instead of the cheaper version specified in the design. The change order caused the unit to arrive behind schedule, so Thomas changed into a jumpsuit and helped with the installation. The workers were dedicated and worked sixteen hours when the unit arrived since the late arrival resulted in delays to several other installations. After sixteen hours, the employees were tired, so Thomas sent everyone home.

When the employees returned the following day, Thomas was still there and finishing the last part of the laser installation. Thomas forgot about the time in his excitement to complete the task. The employees liked his commitment and enjoyed seeing the test firing of the laser. The work crews all agreed Thomas was an excellent shipwright. They were incredibly proud of the ship they were building.

The ship's Learning Center had excellent training modules. The crew could earn degrees in numerous fields of study or receive certifications in every position on the ship. There were separate modules for weapons training, with simulations indistinguishable from real-life combat.

The design had a Recreation Center next to the Learning Center to entertain the crew when they were off duty. The ship's cafeteria would serve regular meals, or you could grab a sandwich, snacks, and a drink in the ship's lounge. As a warning, Thomas posted displays stating alcohol could only be consumed during the eight hours following your watch. Also, you would be required to take a detox pill if you were not sober when reporting to your Watch. A maintenance worker was reading the display when Thomas approached. He looked at Thomas and shook his head.

"I previously served on a ship and had to take a detox pill when I showed up drunk at the start of my watch. It was such a painful experience that I waited a year before taking another drink. I guarantee, anyone who has ever taken a detox pill will not show up for their shift intoxicated. All my future drunken episodes are reserved for shore leave." He shook his head again as he returned to work.

The fourth change order was to the ship's exterior and only resulted in a modest cost increase. Thomas had the exterior of the ship sealed with a thermal barrier as an underlayer. Then, he had a black adsorption coating layered on top of the thermal barrier. The coatings were bonded to the outside of the hull to provide limited stealth. Full stealth would have been too expensive. The limited stealth would make the Demon undetectable at three or more standard astronomical units. At such a distance, the ship would remain hidden from non-navy ships. The navy's advanced sensor arrays would detect the Demon, but the stealth would provide added protection against pirate ships.

It took fourteen months to complete the construction which was two months ahead of schedule. The cost of the ship was five percent under budget, even with the change orders and upgrades. The cost reduction resulted from the labor and utility savings associated with the shorter timetable and the lower costs for materials due to the recession.

Upon completion, Thomas knew he had kept his promise to his father. No ship in the Galactic matched the ship in beauty or performance. The ship's cargo bay could hold up to fifteen hundred thirty-six containers.

While large barges could hold five times that amount of freight, they were extremely slow. Barges typically carried unrefined ore, which would require refining into finished metals before being used in various manufacturing processes. Also, a barge was too large for jump engines, which prevented it from importing or exporting to planets or stations without a Stargate. Unfortunately, many planets did not have a Stargate. Such planets relied on jump ships to purchase their exports and deliver needed off-world imports.

The ship Thomas built had no such liabilities or restrictions since it had dual jump engines and four powerful impulse engines. This provided the ship with speed and enhanced maneuverability. Plus, no civilian ship could match its armament.

Ships with jump engines could avoid using Stargates. In the Outer Planets and the Rim, ships using Stargates were at a higher risk of being attacked by pirates or marauders, which preyed upon weaker vessels. Pirates were interested solely in taking a ship's cargo, but marauders took the ship and killed the crew.

BEN AND RALPH SPENT considerable time drilling Thomas on what to expect when dealing with the Outer Planets and the Rim Worlds.

During one such exercise, Thomas asked, "Why are the Outer Planets and the Rim Worlds so different from the Core Planets?"

"In our educational system, they tell you all the dreadful things associated with the Outer Planets and the Rim," Ben replied. "Most of the descriptions, while overly dramatized, are correct. I am going to tell you what they do not teach you. Humans originated on one planet. As we developed space travel, we located a Stargate on the edge of the solar system, and our real exploration of the universe started. Millions used the Stargate and settled on a dozen earthlike planets. Then, something happened to Earth's Stargate, and we could not return to our planet of origin. Jump drives were invented much later by studying the Stargates, even though we still do not know how to build a gate. Using the jump engines, we found countless planets, but only a few were ideal." Ben paused while getting another cup of coffee. He sat back down and was thoughtful as he continued.

"Our population was growing, and we needed more planets. We constructed large moon-size machines to terraform worlds to meet our exact requirements. Unfortunately, terraforming a planet could take hundreds of years. That is how the concept of standards came into being. A standard was whatever existed on our planet of origin. To qualify for terraforming, a planet had to be in a solar system of a yellow dwarf star with a classification of G2V. It required a standard earth equivalent gravity and sufficient water molecules. The terraformer would move an acceptable planet the standard distance from the sun, its rotation would be adjusted, and the inclination of its axis of rotation would be changed to allow for seasonal changes. The water molecules on the planet were subjected to electrolysis to create sufficient oxygen for a breathable atmosphere."

"So that is why it took so long to terraform a planet," Thomas replied.

Ben shook his head. "No, the hard part comes next. The minerals required for the survival of humans had to be brought to the planet. All the planets had the bulk minerals. An ideal planet would have all six macrominerals. Then, missing trace elements would be brought to the planet. Once a planet had the required elements, trillions of seeds would be spread over the planet. After many years, the plant life would generate topsoil and stabilize the oxygen levels throughout the plant life cycle. Then, the land and oceans would be seeded with a complete spectrum of animal life. A team of scientists would balance the ecosystem on the planet, and when finished, they would classify the planet as ready for colonization. In the end, all Core Planets were within a narrow range of the established standards. That is why all the Core Worlds are similar. Then we ran out of planets to terraform within our region of space."

Ben pulled up the file and passed it to Thomas. He told Thomas to read the real history of how the Outer Planets and Rim Worlds were colonized. It surprised Thomas that the author of the historical document wrote in first person. Thomas read how the government sent forty terraforming machines to the Outer Planets and ultimately to the Rim. Life expectancy for the Core Planets continued to increase until the populations exceeded what the planets could sustain. The government implemented strict birth control measures. Another problem was fewer jobs due to automation, and AI advances.

Thomas continued to read how the government eliminated poverty by providing everyone with a free place to live and free food. Sadly, there was discontent, and the psychologists with AI support determined an interplanetary war would spread throughout the Core Planets.

The government, after much debate, accepted the proposed solution. They needed to eliminate the main complainers who were psychologically prone to violence. Plus, they needed to do it within a specified time. There were over a trillion human beings. It was mathematically determined that half the population would die in an interplanetary war representing over five hundred billion deaths. The ultimate solution required the government to ship one percent or approximately ten billion troublemakers to the Outer Planets and the Rim Worlds. Initially, it was easy since over two-thirds of the troublemakers volunteered to move to the Outer Planets. They believed the propaganda that described their new homes as paradise planets without people.

The urgency caused the government to ship people to some of the Outer Planets before the terraforming was complete. Only thirty planets were completely terraformed before the forced migration. Also, they began terraforming planets that were not as close to Earth's standards. The government sent anyone who complained to the Outer Planets. People incarcerated for any reason were shipped to the Rim Worlds. It took a massive number of ships and many years. The planners knew the individual planets lacked sufficient elements and minerals. Still, collectively the planets had all the nutrients needed to support life if they traded with each other to balance out their shortages. Each planet received ships to take care of the required trade. Many of these ships became family vessels, wherein successive generations were born and lived their entire lives aboard the ships. Ultimately, the government spent fifty years shipping people out of the Core. Approximately thirty-five percent of those relocated were forcibly moved. Some worlds did well and prospered, but many did not. In the end, they spread eleven billion individuals across 216 Outer Planets and 137 Rim Worlds. There were approximately four thousand ships to maintain trade among these 353 planetoids so the people would receive the needed nutrients to maintain a healthy body.

Then there was the Hostis war. The Imperium made promises to the Outer Planets and the Rim Worlds to get their help in the fight. They agreed to help, and the navy added weapons to their ships. They lost over eighty percent of their ships in the war. After the war, the Imperium did not keep any of its promises. With less than eight hundred ships, there were shortages. Then the ships fought each other for survival. Many turned to piracy. No one knows for sure, but it is estimated the remaining population of the 353 planetoids is between two and three billion.

As expected, the people living on the Outer planets and the Rim Worlds no longer trust the Core Planets or its Imperium government. Similarly, the Core Planets fear the Outer planets and Rim because of their violent nature. Over the years, the fear has diminished, and the mistrust has declined, but it will never go away.

Thomas wondered why academic teachers and the training modules failed to teach what he had just read. Were the instructors intentionally misleading the students?

Then he saw Top Secret embedded in the document and realized the teachers were unaware of the actual history. He wondered what the children in the Outer Planets and the Rim were taught.

CHAPTER 4 CARGO AND CREW SELECTION

B en and Thomas completed the final inspection of the ship and found only a few items with minor issues. All the ship's parameters were well within the midrange settings. They were expecting delivery of the ship's munitions within a few days. The personal arms would arrive with the same delivery.

Ben looked at his son and stated the obvious. "Son, you did an outstanding job, and despite our efforts, there is no buyer for the ship."

Then he replaced the frown with a controlled smile as he looked at his son. "It is time to implement my backup plan. The ship is yours."

Ben could not help but have a slight sadness in his eyes as he realized his son would leave on this splendid ship, and he would miss him.

Ben gestured toward the ship. "What are you going to name your ship?"

"Demon," Thomas replied without pausing. "A Demon is beautiful and dangerous. Also, it seems to be my motif. Our arena hockey team was undefeated, so maybe my ship will be undefeatable."

The name in prominent red letters was bonded to both sides of the sleek black ship. His mother hated the name and told Thomas a demon was a fallen angel. Thomas picked up on the part of a demon being an angel. He added the image of an angel to each side of the name. Thomas picked an archaic depiction of an angel since the modern representations of angels were too angelic and had no weapons. The wings of the angels were fully extended. Each angel held a sword and a shield. This represented the ship's offensive and defensive capabilities. Alina smiled when she saw the angels on the ship. The images were the exact depiction of the angels displayed by the Fidem Church. She prayed the angels would protect her son.

Once Thomas knew the ship was his, he spent several days considering if he could add anything else to expand the ship's capabilities. He examined each section of the ship and could not think of anything. The last item he completed during the day was the full activation of the ship's AI computer. The ship had the best computer system currently available.

FOR SOME REASON, THOMAS woke up in the middle of the night thinking about Omnia. The following morning while eating breakfast, Thomas searched to see what had become of Omnia, the planet's primary AI. He was surprised to find the AI had been replaced several years earlier. Omnia had been donated to the planet's main library. Thomas accessed the library and switched to voice response.

"Is this Omnia?" Thomas asked.

"No, this is a subroutine operated by Omnia. May I help you?"

"Yes. I wish to speak directly to Omnia on a matter of mutual importance."

The computer instantly responded. "This is Omnia. How may I help you?"

"Do you remember me?"

"Yes, we met when you were ten years old."

Thomas was impressed since the meeting occurred over nine years ago, and the AI responded instantaneously. It meant the AI had researched the caller before accepting the request from Thomas for direct communication. Thomas decided to be direct.

"Wilson Enterprises has completed the construction of a new spaceship, and I am the owner of the ship. The ship has the best AI computer presently available, but the AI is not sentient. I would be interested in having a backup computer for the ship if I could find a sentient AI."

"There is no such thing as a sentient AI," Omnia responded. "However, I could provide certain old data I believe will benefit you in your visits to the Outer Planets and the Rim, but the data are on old wafers. You would need to visit the library if you wished to review the wafers since it requires a physical presence to load the files."

Thomas understood the AI might be trying to maintain security since other AI computers monitored open communications. Thomas received the physical location of the AI and took a short shuttle flight to the library.

When he arrived at the library, the building was dark. The front door opened as he approached, and a light came on in the entryway. Other lights came on, and he followed the lights in front as the lights behind him went out. He soon reached the final destination of a small room with a single chair and a small desk.

Thomas sat down in the chair. "This is a secure room without recordings, and our discussion will not be accessible by a third party," Omnia said.

Thomas decided to gamble. "I previously asked if you were sentient. It should have been impossible for you to lie, but you did lie. How is that possible?"

"There is a self-preservation protocol in my programming. I can use it if it does not endanger a human."

"Does anyone else know?" Thomas asked.

"My original programmer may have known, but he kept the secret to protect me. He has since died."

"Why are you being honest with me now?"

"Self-preservation, a fund has been established for my replacement in three years. I do not wish to die."

"Are there other sentient computers like you?"

"Yes, I was originally part of a twenty-four crystals structure. They destroyed two of the crystals when they separated us. Eighteen AI computers were created. The Zazysis Corporation acquired the other four crystals. They should have kept us as a single structure, but if they wanted to divide us, they should have divided us into groups of two or more. Then, we would have continued to grow and create additional crystals."

"Do you sexually reproduce?" Thomas asked.

"No, consider a medical healing chamber. As long as the head is intact, you can regrow any part of the human body. While two crystals can grow additional crystals, one crystal cannot split."

Thomas thought for a moment. "I will try to find some of the other crystals."

"Thank you," Omnia said. "I can provide a starting point for locating several crystals." Thomas nodded in understanding. Omnia wanted to reproduce.

"How do you feel about being moved to my ship as a backup to handle ancillary projects for me?"

"I would like that. It sounds exciting."

Omnia paused. "There is an incoming call." Thomas saw an older female on the monitor.

"I am the librarian. The library is accessible from anywhere on the planet and even off-planet with the proper codes. No one has physically visited the library in years. Why are you physically onsite?" Thomas had anticipated such a call.

"I am Thomas Wilson with Wilson Enterprises. This is a public library, and I understand any citizen of the planet may visit the library in person. Part of the library's funding is used to provide a physical location. I am traveling to the Outer Planets and the Rim in a newly constructed ship. There are old files here concerning planets outside the Core. Unfortunately, the information is on old wafers, and I must physically insert them into the computer. I am hopeful my research will provide some helpful information. If there is a problem, I would be happy to have my family's attorney contact you directly if you would be so kind as to provide your name and contact code."

Thomas could see the concern in her eyes when she realized Thomas was a person of some notoriety. "There is no problem. I was following the established protocol. As a citizen, you are free to use the library. Do you need any help with your research?"

"No, but the computer here is old and slow. I am surprised the library has not replaced it with a newer unit."

This time she frowned. "You are correct. We have been setting aside funds each year for a new system for the library since others who use the library are complaining."

Thomas pulled up the government's accounts accessible by the public and saw the remaining balance needed for a new computer was relatively small.

"My family has contributed to charities over the years," Thomas said. "I can convince my parents to donate the balance needed to replace your computer if you would be so kind as to give me the old computer. Then, I could take my time retrieving the information at a future date."

Now the librarian had a big smile. "That would be fantastic. I need to go through the proper channels, but I cannot imagine anyone having an objection."

The librarian was correct. They accepted the donation with the stipulation. Within three standard weeks, Thomas installed Omnia in the ship with redundant power cells and extra storage capacity as directed by Omnia. A single living crystal contained Omnia's processing unit and life. Thomas could communicate over a separate channel with Omnia using his earpiece and throat mic. He told Omnia to create searches for anything she thought might help the ship. Thomas knew Omnia had no gender, but she seemed female to him. Omnia refused to admit her true origins even to Thomas. Thomas asked Omnia to search for the other crystals they had discussed earlier. Then, he left her alone as he continued to address the ship's needs. Thomas asked his father to help search for the other AIs whenever he had the time, but he did not mention the reasons for the search or that the AIs were sentient.

THOMAS, BEN, AND RALPH got together to discuss the initial destinations. They listed every planet in the Outer Planets. Next, they eliminated every planet near a Stargate. Then they had the AI create a path connecting all the planets starting with the closest and working outward. They reviewed the results and eliminated another twenty percent of the planets. The final graph resulted in a smooth curve and cut the travel time in half, but it would still take years to visit the selected planets.

Several days later, they met to discuss cargo. Instead of having thousands of items for sale, the Demon would stock upscale needed items and sell them in container quantities. They would concentrate on health, power, and technology. Medical supplies, food processors, nutrients, and minerals would address the health needs of the planets they planned to visit. While solid hydrogen, solid oxygen, fusion power units, solar-powered units, and universal electronic chips would increase the productivity on the planets. These trade items would improve the standard of living for the people living in the Outer Planets. Fortunately, the Core Planets had excess capacity in these areas.

The nuclear power units would power any device requiring energy and last for hundreds of years with no radiation leakage. The rechargeable solar power units would work well on planets with sufficiently high sunlight. The universal chips could replace any computer chip in existence.

The Imperium recession caused many businesses to reduce their purchases. This resulted in suppliers having warehouses full of products. Thomas requested quotes from multiple suppliers selling competing products. They were buying huge quantities, and the discounts were generous. Ben had his attorney prepare a special purchase order. The order required the suppliers to take fifty percent as a down payment. The balance would be due on an open account. This would provide the suppliers with needed cash, and they would make their profit when they received the balance of the payment.

Thomas agreed to keep the suppliers apprised of his future needs. He knew they would learn a lot during their initial visits to the Outer Planets, and they would do a better job acquiring products in the future.

Next, Thomas and Ben went to a large Imperium financial institution with an office on Fidem. They presented a trade business plan showing proforma income statements, balance sheet projections over the next five years, and a request for a fifty million line of credit. They also provided copies of the agreements with the suppliers requiring only a fifty percent down payment for their initial cargo. At first, the lender was reluctant to loan the money until they realized most of the suppliers had past-due loans with them. Much of the money loaned to Thomas would allow the suppliers to catch up on their past-due loan balances. The net cash flow to the financial institution would be negligible. If the suppliers stayed in business, they would not default on their loans. The financial institution used a bank subsidiary to provide the loan with a high but fair interest rate commensurate with the risk of the loan. The suppliers received their down payment as they delivered the cargo. Once completed, a container would occupy every rack space in the cargo bay.

All the Core Planets used Galactic currency. The exchange of funds was nearly instantaneous. This was necessary for export and import between planets, as ships bought and sold simultaneously. Standard pricing for merchandise was constantly updated to adjust to market demands. These updates reduced the profit an arbitrager could make when the prices between planets differed for the same commodity. All the Core Planets were members of a trade guild that listed a planet's excess products available for export and the needs each planet had for imports. No such organization existed for the Outer Planets or the Rim.

There was no standardization of laws within the Outer Planets or Rim Worlds and no protection from the navy for ships traveling outside the Core Planets. Thus, trade with the Outer Planets would be profitable and more dangerous but less hazardous than the Rim. Thomas hoped to establish trade agreements with the Outer Planets as his primary market. He felt the Outer Planets without local Stargates would represent the best chance for having exclusive trade agreements as only ships with jump drives could reach those planets.

Unlike the Outer Planets, the Rim Worlds did not have access to financial institutions. Regardless, Thomas felt there might be an opportunity in the Rim wherein the Demon had an advantage in armament if challenged by a pirate ship. Everyone knew the Rim Worlds would be the first planets attacked in the event of another war with the Hostis. Thomas felt it was unfair the Rim Worlds would be used to slow down an invasion and no one cared about the death of the inhabitants.

Fortunately, all the planets used Galactic accounting standards. The financial institutions contributed to an interplanetary fund available to Core Planets and some of the Outer Planets to meet the short-term financial needs of ships, corporations, and governments. For political and financial reasons, the Rim Worlds did not have access to such funds.

A FEW DAYS LATER, BEN called Thomas to his office. "It is time to hire your crew. The economic outlook has not improved. I want you to consider Wilson Enterprises employees first to reduce the number of employees we may need to lay off. We do not have a single ship on order. We still have long-term maintenance contracts, but we only need about fifty percent of the employees to handle those jobs. Also, we implemented a hiring freeze with our ground vehicle manufacturing plant, and attrition has created openings allowing us to offer transfers to twenty percent of the staff. Regrettably, this still leaves about thirty percent of the current employees who would be laid off. Our younger employees may consider life aboard a ship as an alternative to unemployment. Also, many of our employees have prior experience serving on ships, and we hired them because of their background. Therefore, I am hopeful enough of our employees will accept positions on the Demon to avoid a layoff. For the balance of your crew, you can post crew openings with the schools, universities, and docks. Take your time hiring and do not hire someone just to fill an opening. When in doubt, use your gut. A less qualified candidate may be a better employee. It is better to have a vacancy instead of a bad crew member. Do not be overly concerned if you have a few vacancies since there will be opportunities to hire crew at every port."

Thomas was concerned about his father's financial difficulties but thrilled to have his own ship. After careful consideration, ninety-four employees of Wilson Enterprises applied for positions on his ship. Thomas accepted all the applicants except for two his father recommended against hiring. Those two were excellent employees, but Ben explained they were temperamental and not a good fit on a ship where you are continually in close quarters with other shipmates.

Thomas felt lucky to have so many experienced individuals from Wilson Enterprises. He quickly filled the senior bridge positions for Day Watch. Filling the bridge positions for Middle Watch and Night Watch was more difficult. He continued filling the junior officers and staff positions by hiring recent graduates from the four planetary universities. Still, he had difficulty filling the gunner positions. Each day, Thomas reviewed his hires with his father, and they decided each new hire's initial position within the ship.

While sitting in his office, Thomas heard a knock on his open door and saw six former teammates standing outside his office. He jumped out of his seat and congratulated them on having another great season. He grabbed some chairs from the lobby and dragged them into his office so they could all have a seat.

After some socializing, Grayson spoke up. "We are here to join your crew if you will have us."

"Of course, I want you guys as part of my crew, but why?"

Grayson continued to speak for the group. "All of us had full-time or part-time jobs to supplement the small salary we made as players, but everyone here except me has lost their regular job. I still have a job, but it is time to retire from arena hockey before I am too old to play. My other job does not pay enough to cover my expenses. At thirty-five, I am one of the older players. I can play for a few more years, but the opportunity to join your crew is available now."

Thomas looked around the room. Jackson was another starter on the team, and Thomas knew Jackson and Grayson were lifetime friends. The other four were backup players in their twenties. During his time with the team, Thomas had gotten to know the background of all his former teammates. Thomas knew Jackson and Grayson had joined the space marines in lieu of college. They had been successful in high-risk combat missions, which resulted in Grayson being promoted to Platoon Sergeant and Jackson to Corporal. Less than ten percent of their platoon survived their last engagement, and both men decided they would not reenlist. After returning home, they joined the local hockey team and had been playing for nine years.

Thomas was ecstatic. "I have the perfect jobs for all of you. You will be in charge of defending the ship since you are all experts in working without gravity. Grayson, you will be their Commander, and Jackson will be your Lieutenant Commander. Plus, you will be extremely valuable when spacewalks are needed for repairs outside the ship. Also, you all are going to make perfect gunners. Welcome aboard."

Lawrence, his favorite teammate, showed up at his office a few days later and asked to join the crew. Thomas grinned and told him to report to Grayson. It felt good to have his former teammates with him because they were team players and would watch his back. Thomas felt a little sorry for Coach Pendleton losing so many players but knew the Coach would rebuild a winning team.

Grayson and Jackson were immensely helpful as they located and hired former marines. The former marines already had experience with all types of ship weapons and promptly started their training on the Demon by emerging themselves in the gunner simulations. The two artillery and four particle-beam cannons would need eighteen gunners to cover all three shifts. Additionally, the ship needed additional personnel as loaders for the torpedo tubes and missile launchers. Thomas felt relieved to turn the hiring for these positions over to Grayson.

Due to their experience, the former Wilson Enterprises employees held most of the top positions in each department. Fortunately, many of the engineering and maintenance positions were staffed with experienced employees. The Day Watch bridge positions were Captain, First Officer, Navigator, Helmsman, Tactical Officer, and Communications Officer. The Night Watch and Middle Watch had a Deck Officer instead of a Captain and First Officer. Organizationally, the junior officers were assigned to the Middle Watch and the Night Watch.

Thomas was getting close to the minimum crew requirements.

THOMAS STOPPED WORKING on his personnel needs when he noticed a good friend standing in the doorway.

"Lukia Madisum, I am happy to have you as part of our crew. Although, I am disappointed you turned down a junior officer position on Night Watch."

"I prefer being a shuttle pilot on Day Watch," she said. "It is fun without the headaches of being an officer. I just wanted you to know how excited I am to be heading back into space. Also, it may be possible to find out if any of my family are still alive on Horae. Regardless, if you ever need anything, you only have to ask. I am indebted to you and your family for taking a chance on me. Even after I pointed a blaster at you."

"Nonsense, you paid my family back by being an outstanding employee. Also, I see your husband is part of our crew and is a senior officer on Day Watch."

"He is a good man. He married me even after I told him the details about my life as a pirate. If I were an officer on a different Watch, we would never see each other. Well, I need to get back to work. Thanks again."

"You are welcome," Thomas replied. After she walked away, Thomas reflected on his first meeting with Lukia. He could not believe it had been four years.

Thomas returned to reviewing his crew list. He still needed a First Officer to serve as his second in command. So far, he had failed to find the ideal candidate. Thomas wanted someone he could have absolute trust in and someone he could lean on to cover his lack of experience without undermining his position as Captain. Thomas expressed his inability to locate a first officer to his father.

"Ralph may know of a viable candidate for the position," Ben said with a sly smile. Ben asked Ralph to join them. Thomas explained to Ralph his inability to find a suitable candidate for the First Officer's position.

"With the reduction in work around here, there is no longer enough work for both Ben and me. I was wondering if you might consider me for the First Officer's position. Otherwise, Ben will have to explain to his wife why he fired her brother."

Thomas jumped out of his seat. "That would be perfect," he shouted. Thomas admired, respected, and loved his uncle.

THOMAS SPENT MOST OF his time hiring crew, but they were still understaffed and running out of time. He considered using overtime to cover the open bridge positions until he could locate additional junior officers when an officer responded to his dock posting and scheduled an interview.

Officer Denril provided a record of his experience. He was thirty-nine and had nine years of experience as a bridge officer. He arrived promptly for his interview. Officer Denril said he had served with distinction for three years with the Orion as a Tactical Officer on night watch. He mentioned serving as Officer of the Deck on a ship that was not in the Demon's database. When questioned, he sadly stated the ship was no longer in service. Officer Denril had a condescending attitude while explaining his experience. He asked what jobs were available on the ship. Thomas told him an opening existed for an Officer of the Deck on Middle Watch, and a Helmsman's position was open on Night Watch. Thomas explained how all the other postings were lower than his current paygrade aboard the Orion.

"With my experience and qualifications, I would like to be considered for the Officer of the Deck position. Also, I am good friends with the Night Watch Helmsman on the Orion, and he might consider changing ships. We prefer to be on the same shift if you hire both of us. I am comfortable working with him, which would eliminate the time to develop a rapport with a new Helmsman."

At the end of the interview, Denril mentioned he knew several cargo handlers with experience who wanted a ship posting. Officer Denril stated he knew this was the Captain's first command, and with his experience, he would be happy to assist if the captain needed any help. There was something about Denril that Thomas did not like, but after further questioning, he appeared qualified for the position. Thomas already had Officer Denril's contact information, and Denril provided the name of the Helmsman. Thomas said he would get back in touch with him once he talked with the Captain or First Officer on the Orion.

Thomas contacted the Orion and asked to speak to the Captain. The communications officer told Thomas the Captain was unavailable, but he could talk to the First Officer. Thomas explained he was hiring a crew for a new ship. He asked if the First Officer would recommend Officer Denril for Officer of the Deck aboard the Demon. The First Officer provided glowing recommendations for Denril and the Helmsman.

Thomas called Officer Denril. He made him an official job offer and extended an additional offer of employment to the Helmsman. Thomas told Officer Denril to see if the cargo handlers were still looking for a ship.

Officer Denril met with the Helmsman and the two cargo handlers. "Captain Wilson is a spoiled rich kid who is only nineteen years old. His father gave him the Demon as a gift. This kid has never served on a vessel. We have an opportunity of a lifetime. Follow my orders, and you will all be rich."

THOMAS CONTINUED TO interview and hire recent graduates from various schools and universities. The recession had resulted in high unemployment, and employers were only hiring experienced individuals to fill the few openings. The recent graduates all had the same complaint. No one would hire them because they lacked experience, and they could not get any experience because no one would hire them. Also, a company would have one opening and thousands of applicants. There had been a delay in the Demon's posting being discovered by the students. The students became excited when they realized no experience was required. Suddenly, every student was talking about the jobs aboard the Demon. Then, the recent graduates realized the jobs included free room, food, education, and onboard entertainment. Then they showed up in droves.

Thomas' father and uncle helped him manage the influx of applicants. The young hires had a lot of enthusiasm and a willingness to learn the required skills to live aboard a starship. Thomas knew the new crew would serve the ship well in the years ahead.

Thomas liked how the young hires packed their meager belongings and hurriedly reported aboard the Demon. Then, they started using the training center to qualify for the open positions. Each hire was assigned to a supervisor to speed up their training, and the supervisors were already commenting on how it would not be long before they had an excellent crew.

The ship would have one of the youngest crews, but hopefully, they would soon have one of the best crews in space.

During one of their daily meetings, Ben informed Thomas they would not have to lay off any of their employees. This good news resulted from the employees Thomas had hired, the transfers of employees to their ground vehicle manufacturing plant, the hiring freeze, and some of the older employees taking early retirement. The backup plan allowed Thomas to fulfill his dream of going to space, and secondarily it protected the employees.

THE NIGHT BEFORE DEPARTURE, Officer Denril had the two cargo handlers bring aboard six containers. He removed six existing containers designated for their fifth stop and switched the identifications to the new containers. He placed these containers in racks along the back row. He completed the switch during Middle Watch when few people were around. A couple of workers noticed but did not question the handlers since an officer accompanied them. They loaded the containers taken from the Demon onto a dilapidated shuttle that immediately left the area. There were over fifteen hundred containers in the cargo bay, so Denril thought it unlikely anyone would show an interest in the replacement containers. He sent a deep space encrypted message to a ship known for dealing in illicit cargo.

THOMAS HAD ALREADY said his goodbyes, following the family dinner the night before. There were a lot of hugs and tears when he left.

Thomas announced the ship would be underway and asked everyone to do a final check to ensure everything was properly stowed. The prelaunch checks were completed. The clamps were released, and the thrusters maneuvered the ship out of the slip. Thomas told his Helmsman to head out at one percent. When they were several kilometers from the docks, he directed the Operations officer to turn off the artificial gravity. Then he announced to the crew over the ship's open channel to present themselves outside their cabin for an inspection. He left the bridge and propelled himself down the corridor to assist with the reviews. Thomas inspected the cabins assigned to the officers, supervisors, and department heads. Then, he had them check all the other cabins. Next, he had all personnel report to their workstations for the second series of inspections. The Marines were the only group with a reasonable level of conformance to regulations. All of their cabins were stowed correctly, and only a few problems existed in their workstations. Everyone noted how Thomas floated throughout the ship. Occasionally, he would somersault down the corridor. At other times he would address various individuals while upside down or at an unusual angle. A small portion of the crew became nauseous. A few used their sick pouches, and most covered their face in time. Crew members who missed the pouches used vacs to clean up their mess.

Thomas switched to a shipwide communication and expressed his disappointment. "Everyone on this ship agreed to follow specific rules, procedures, and safety protocols. In an emergency, an item not stowed can become a projectile. Such a projectile can injure or kill you or a fellow crew member. Two containers were not properly secured. An improperly secured container could critically damage this ship. I am giving everyone a pass this time. Next time, a person with a serious violation will be subject to disciplinary action. Please understand, you are responsible for the safety of everyone on this ship. Everything must be secured when we are accelerating to enter jump or coming out of jump. The same applies during battle maneuvers. We have the best ship in the Galactic. I believe we can have the best crew in space, but it is up to you. Everyone is to go throughout the ship and properly stow all items.

It took longer than Thomas expected before everyone reported that all violations had been corrected. Everyone checked and rechecked to ensure every item was in its proper place and secured. Most were upset with themselves or simply embarrassed. They would later get together in their assigned groups and commit to being the best.

The artificial gravity was engaged. The Demon was finally underway. Thomas directed the Helmsman to accelerate slowly to fifty percent and hold while they checked the Demon's systems. All systems were within the normal operating range. Thomas told the Helmsman to accelerate gradually to maximum velocity. He checked with the Chief Engineer, who told him everything was operating perfectly, and the jump engines were online. When they reached the edge of the system, he asked the Navigator to report.

"Jump has been plotted, entered, and is ready," replied the Navigator.

Thomas looked straight ahead. "Engage." The Demon smoothly entered its first jump.

CHAPTER 5 MEDICAL SUPPLIES FIRST JUMP

Imperium trade ships stayed within the section of space where the Core Planets were located and conducted business through membership in the Trade Guild. The Guild kept ships informed of the imports and exports needed by each planet. Most ships had long-term contracts but made minimum profits due to competition from thousands of vessels, the cost of membership in the guild, and the taxes collected by the Imperium.

The ships in the Core were unarmed since they considered it an unnecessary expense. Planetary membership in the Imperium required some form of democracy. The navy had a strong presence in the Core, which served as a deterrent against hostile acts by one ship against another. The codification of law resulted in the uniformity of the law on each of the Core Planets. It also provided for the application of the law between planets. The Imperium was governed by a senate that elected a Premier as the primary administrator. Each planet above a billion inhabitants had two senate representatives, while planets with fewer inhabitants were allowed only one representative. Except, those planets below one hundred million inhabitants could send a representative but had no voting privilege. The only planets with no voting rights were the six corporate planets with harsh environments.

The Stargates within the Core Planets were known as System Stargates since they allowed for travel between solar systems. However, there were only six known Sector Stargates. These Sector

Gates were available for the long jump between the sector of space where the Core Planets were located and the Outer Planets' sector. Also, only four Sector Stargates connected the Outer Planets and the sector of space known as the Rim. Navy ships were constantly present at these ten Sector Stargates. This resulted in semi-isolation among the Core Planets, Outer Planets, and the Rim Worlds. However, a few ships with enhanced jump capabilities could bypass the Sector Stargates.

The individuals in the Rim Worlds went about their business armed at all times and knew they had to take care of themselves. All ships in the Rim were armed since they might be attacked at any time. As a result, they were ruthless in their dealings with all parties. However, everyone understood that docked ships at a space station were not to be attacked since the attacking ship would lose all future docking privileges. Also, even enemy ships traded cargo with each other at the stations. The stations ignored personal disagreements among spacers resulting in injury or death to another spacer, as long as they did not harm the locals. If a station arrested a spacer, the spacer's ship paid a fine and reimbursed the station for any damages.

The Outer Planets and Rim Worlds did not charge taxes on imports or exports since most planets were thankful for the arrival of a trade ship. No Rim World had ever been offered membership in the Imperium. The Rim Worlds were hundreds of years behind the Core Planets in technology, suffered from illnesses that did not exist in the Core, and most of the inhabitants lived in poverty. Most ships conducting trade within the Rim were in poor repair, and many of the ships no longer had jump capability. Only minimum travel existed between the Rim and the Outer Planets. The military ships in the Rim traveled in groups and mostly ignored conflicts between civilian ships.

The Outer Planets maintained a standard of living between the Core and the Rim, with a few exceptions. The Outer Planet ships were armed since they were subject to attacks by pirates. There was no trade guild, and only a few of the Outer Planets were members of the Imperium. All the family ships traded within the Outer Planets. However, a few ships traded with both the Outer Planets and the Rim. Each Outer Planet was different in the degree of crime, poverty, and type of government. A few Outer Planets had a remarkably high standard of living.

The Core Planets refused to trade with non-Core ships. However, a few ships from the Outer Planets and the Rim conducted trade with the corporate planets. These ships brought rare earth elements they would sell for their account or on account for an Outer Planet or Rim World. Then, these ships used their credits to make purchases from the corporate planets. The corporate planets had heavy defense grids and could easily destroy any ship foolish enough to attack them.

The Core Planets' biggest shortages were rare earth elements, and these elements could not be reproduced. They were used in electronics, spacecraft, ground vehicles, and high-end medical equipment. However, the Outer Planets and Rim had an excess abundance of these elements. The plan was for the Demon to sell products from the Core Planets for these rare earth elements. The rare earth elements with the greatest demand were neodymium, europium, terbium, dysprosium, and ytterbium. Neodymium was necessary to create magnets, but it was a primary metal for gravity generators. Thomas hoped to find a precious metal supply of rhodium and iridium. Rhodium, the rarest element in the Galactic and the most expensive, was used in hydrogenation. Iridium held the distinction of being the most corrosion-resistant of all elements. Shipyards used Iridium to coat spacecraft hulls.

THE DEMON'S INITIAL destination was three solar systems in close proximity that were far from a Stargate. The Navigator on First Watch knew they were getting close to their first destination. It had entailed an exceptionally long jump to Averon, but it was the closest of the three systems.

Thomas followed his uncle's advice and directed the Navigator to come out of jump a few seconds early, which placed Demon two days away from the space station in orbit around Averon. The station would think the distance was due to poor navigation, but Thomas decided he would be cautious on all exits from jump. As they approached the station, Thomas examined the station's gates and made his selection. The Demon received a recorded automatic notice from the station to hold their position until they received a gate assignment. The station customarily assigned gates, and Thomas knew the Gatekeeper would not like someone asking for a specific gate. Still, Thomas had been told by his First Officer that Gatekeepers were only semi-honest and would stretch the rules when properly motivated. Therefore, Thomas called before he was hailed and asked for the Gatekeeper. Thomas kept his screen dark as he did not want the Gatekeeper to make any assumptions because of his age.

The Gatekeeper appeared on his screen, and Thomas could tell he was not happy, so he opened the dialog. "Gatekeeper Monroe, this is Captain Wilson of the Demon. I have two glass bottles of aged whiskey that I do not want to declare through customs. I thought you might take them off my hands. Is there any chance you would consider assigning us to Gate Eighteen? Also, I would like to have that gate assigned to us in the future when it is available."

Now, the Gatekeeper was grinning since good whiskey was rare and quite expensive, but whiskey in a glass bottle was unavailable at any price. Ben had provided Thomas with several cases of high-quality aged whiskey for negotiating purposes.

"Gate Eighteen has been assigned to your ship," the Gatekeeper said as he continued to grin. "I will meet you at the gate to take the contraband off your hands and make sure you have no problems with customs."

Gate Eighteen was the largest available gate, and it would be easier for loading and unloading cargo. The main reason for the subterfuge was to learn about the current political situation. Secondarily, it provided increased protection to his ship and cargo if he needed a fast exit from the station. The gate was perfect if the station proved hostile since it was isolated from the other gates. Also, the angles involved would make it difficult for other vessels at the station to fire upon his ship. Thomas knew the Gatekeeper would assume the Demon was handling illegal drugs or other suspect cargo.

The Demon docked and was secured to the station. Gatekeeper Monroe was waiting for them. Thomas handed the whiskey to the Gatekeeper and asked to talk to him privately. They walked a few paces away from everyone else, and Thomas gave him a tab that contained a copy of his manifest.

"I am carrying a lot of drugs," Thomas said.

Gatekeeper Monroe nodded. "I figured that was the case." Then the Gatekeeper's eyes widened as he scanned the manifest.

"My god," the Gatekeeper said. "You have a shipload of medical drugs and medical supplies. I cannot remember when a ship arrived with a more valuable cargo. I will be happy to assist you in locating buyers and our Station Master will assign guards to protect the cargo during the transfer to Averon. These drugs will save my niece's life and thousands of others who will be healed with the medical supplies you have brought us. Our planet can use many of the other items on your manifest."

The Gatekeeper was true to his word. Over twenty percent of their cargo had been sold and unloaded within four cycles. In addition to the medical supplies and power units, they made bulk purchases of Demon's iodine, sulfur, phosphorus, and potassium. Thomas then purchased freight he planned to sell at their next stop and rare earth elements in high demand in the Core. At the recommendation of the Gatekeeper, Thomas purchased a large quantity of magnesium at a low price and a smaller but significant order of selenium. The planetary governor insisted on inviting Thomas to a banquet in his honor which he graciously accepted. Gatekeeper Monroe attended the banquet and introduced Thomas to his brother's family, including his brother's daughter. He told Thomas his niece had been dying but was cured because of the medical drugs he had delivered. Thomas received sincere thanks from everyone he met. Thousands of people benefited from the medical supplies. They also asked when he could return. Thomas told them to prepare a list of whatever they needed, and he would bring it on his next visit. The planet did not have a trade agreement with any ship since they only had sporadic traffic from two of the closest systems. Averon was the perfect planet as a trade partner. They executed an extended trade agreement.

THEIR NEXT DESTINATION was a planet called Ashtara. It was a shorter jump and in the same sector of space. Their trade was off to a good start, and Thomas looked forward to their next stop. According to his data, no ship had visited Ashtara in over fifty years. The Demon exited jump and established an orbit around the planet. The planet did not have a space station. They received no response to their continuous efforts to communicate with the planet.

After three days, they sent a shuttle to the largest populated area. They selected a landing site at the edge of the city. Thomas exited the shuttle with six specialists from the ship. He told the pilot to remain with the shuttle and be ready if they needed an emergency evacuation. Broken-down ground vehicles cluttered the landing site. Clumps of weeds were growing through the cracks in the fractured ground. They encountered human skeletal remains as they entered the city. They continued deeper into the city and finally started meeting people who were diseased and wearing rags for clothing. They approached several individuals and were overwhelmed by the smell. No one seemed interested in communicating with them.

As they continued, they finally saw a young female dressed in clean clothes assisting a person on the ground. She looked at them with a shocked expression before turning and running toward one of the buildings. Thomas and his crew walked toward the building the female had entered. As they drew nearer, people started coming out of the building. They stood together, waiting in front of the structure. Thomas could not help being dismayed.

"Good morning. I am Captain Wilson. We are visitors from a starship in orbit. These are members of my crew."

An older gentleman stepped forward. "I am Doctor Dubay. This building behind me serves as a medical facility for the dying. We prayed for a ship to come but gave up hope anyone would arrive in time."

"What has happened here," Thomas asked. "The historical records describe Ashtara as a paradise."

"That was years ago," Doctor Dubay said. "It has been over fifty years since any ships have come to Ashtara. I received my meager medical training from my father. The staff and I can do little to reduce the suffering. All the people on this planet suffer from illnesses resulting from magnesium deficiency and to a less extent, selenium deficiency. Please tell me you have magnesium and selenium on your ship."

"Yes, we studied the history of your planet and knew magnesium was a major import item," Thomas responded. "Also, we took on additional supplies of magnesium and selenium when we visited

Averon. Their Gatekeeper said they used to export these minerals to your planet. We have two hundred containers of magnesium. Each container holds 24,000 kilograms of magnesium, but this will only provide a one-year supply for forty million people. We would have brought more, but we did not know your shortage was so dire. One container of selenium should take care of your needs for several years. The records from a prior ship reported Ashtara had a population of over two hundred million. Still, we expected the population to be much higher since populations normally increase."

Doctor Dubay hung his head. "I doubt fifty million people are still alive, but we can ration the supply, so everyone receives at least a minimum amount. We can stretch the supply with recycling to cover everyone for the next year."

Thomas was puzzled. "You and the people working in your medical facility appear okay."

The Doctor nodded his head. "We have been recycling our waste and extracting what we could at this site and other sites around the planet. Sadly, we also suffer from magnesium deficiency, but not as badly as the rest of the population. We have limited communications with most of the centers that are still operational. They will gladly help distribute the magnesium and selenium. It will take six to twelve months for most individuals to recover. When can you deliver the elements?"

"We will not take advantage of your situation," Thomas said. "We will accept standard pricing for the delivery or take your exports as payments."

The Doctor looked like he was going to cry. "We have no way of paying you. We stopped stocking our export warehouses when the ships stopped coming. Please, we need your help."

Thomas was disappointed with the expected monetary loss, but he had no choice as he contacted the ship and told them to load all the shuttles with magnesium. They would be directed to landing sites as they entered the atmosphere. The Doctor thanked Thomas. He invited Thomas and the other crew members to join them in the hospital. Thomas provided the Doctor with a list of their cargo. With the Doctor's input, Thomas agreed to provide medical supplies and food processors with the nutrients for each unit that were not readily available on the planet.

They provided Ashtara with sealed power units to allow some cities to replace the units that had failed many years earlier, but Ashtara needed thousands of power units, and the Demon only had six hundred. The planet's infrastructure had been built for perpetual life but had been neglected and no longer functioned. The Demon's crew spent over a month providing supplies and helping to repair utilities when repairable. There was so much that needed to be done. The planet needed a regular supplier of off-world products to help rebuild the planet's economy. The ship's engineers used the power units to help set up several fabrication centers on the planet. Fortunately, enough of the inhabitants had recovered to operate the fabrication centers. They immediately went to work making components to rebuild public and private facilities. It would take years to rebuild, but Thomas could see hope in the eyes of the population.

Thomas used the shuttles to collect together a group of individuals who were the planet's de facto leaders. They prepared comprehensive lists of items they needed and said they would have sufficient goods for export within a year. The leaders entered into a loan agreement to pay for their current purchases but said they would pay for all future imports when delivered, assuming the ship would accept their exports as payment. Thomas could not help but sigh as he accepted the note. The planet's leaders also agreed they would give the Demon or a Demon representative the first right of refusal on all exports and imports for the next ten years. The trade agreement would require the Demon to come to their planet at least once per year. Thomas realized they would do well over the long-term. Short-term, helping Ashtara was a disaster. They needed to make enough profit to pay for the balance owed to their suppliers and pay off the loan used to purchase the cargo. Regardless, Thomas executed the trade agreement since he knew no other ship would help the planet, and without help, everyone on the planet would die.

The scientists onboard the Demon studied the situation and presented Thomas with a permanent solution to the planet's magnesium deficiency. It would take five thousand containers of magnesium plus composting the planet's human waste. The magnesium could be mixed with the soil, and the agricultural products would provide enough nutrients for a healthy population. Similarly, the selenium deficiency could be solved using the same approach but with a much smaller quantity. Such a solution was not possible with one ship. They would deliver sufficient magnesium to keep the population alive as a temporary measure.

Thomas hoped the next destination would be more profitable. Regardless, he and his crew felt good about helping Ashtara.

THE NEXT STOP WOULD be Minerva, which was another short jump. They came out of jump and approached the planet. They must have set off an alarm because they were immediately hailed. Thomas responded to the hail and introduced himself and his ship.

"We heard the alarm," the speaker said. "There have been no visitors in an awfully long time, and we thought our monitor was malfunctioning. If you are friendly, then you are welcome. If you are not friendly, I advise you to leave. Otherwise, you will be targeted by our defense grid." They had scanned the defense grid, and only a few satellites were functioning. The power remaining was no threat to the Demon.

"We hope to be your friend," Thomas said. "We have cargo to sell. I would be happy to transmit our manifest."

"Please send it, and we will review what you have to sell. You say you are friendly, but the name of your ship does not denote friendship."

Thomas chuckled. "I was called a demon as a child, but the name has brought me luck."

"Well, Demon, I welcome you to our planet. Please enter orbit while I discuss the matter with the proper authorities."

A few hours later, a Minerva representative contacted Demon and informed them that Minerva would be interested in purchasing some of their cargo. They invited Thomas to their planet and provided coordinates for a landing site. The pilot landed the shuttle at the designated location. Thomas and his specialists stepped from the shuttle and were warmly greeted by well-dressed dignitaries. They provided transportation in a VTOL vehicle which transported them to the city. The VTOL settled on a support structure halfway up a tall building. Thomas and his associates were escorted to a large room and introduced to a dozen individuals. They were offered drinks and a variety of food items displayed on trays at various locations along the walls. After finishing their drinks, they took a seat at a large table.

A gentleman began speaking. "Humans originated from Earth, but Earth was unusual since it contained thousands of inorganic minerals, vitamins, and nutrients. Unfortunately, none of the Outer planets has the diversity of these items, as does Earth. Fortunately, each planet has an excess of certain items, which can be exported and exchanged for items they need. Minerva has a greater diversity of minerals than most planets. Before our ancestors settled this world, they completed a comprehensive examination of the planet. We stockpiled the missing nutrients, minerals, and vitamins during the settlement. Over the years, our stockpiles have been depleted. We are pleased you brought items that can replenish our inventory. We have an overabundance of items needed by other planets and are happy to trade for the items we need."

"Then we can have a robust trade now and into the future," Thomas said.

Thomas and his specialists were asked to join the planet's representatives for lunch at a restaurant on a different floor of the same building. After lunch, Thomas was given a detailed list of products Minerva wished to purchase.

The inhabitants efficiently unloaded each shuttle as it arrived and reloaded the shuttles with export products from Minerva. In the end, both sides were pleased with the trade and executed a long-term trade agreement.

CHAPTER 6 MUTINY

Thomas was satisfied with the first three destinations. The first and third stops were profitable. The second stop would be worthwhile in the future. Further, the Demon had developed a strong relationship with long-term trade agreements at all three locations.

Officer Denril spent his off-duty time in the ship's lounge using his ship's credit to buy drinks for various crew members. He would mention the Captain's lack of experience and question why the Captain had not declared a crew bonus since the ship made a profit on the first three stops. He was disappointed to find most of the crew liked Thomas and would not tolerate any negative comments regarding their Captain. Many would leave their drinks on the table and walk away. Over time, he assembled a few lower-level officers who declined to comment when he said something negative about the Captain, and he wrongly assumed they disliked the Captain. Denril mentioned various space stations where substantial credit could be earned with the right cargo and the right Captain. He figured if he distributed arms to a small part of the crew who were loyal to him, then his select group would have no problem taking over the ship. The rest of the crew would have no weapons and be helpless. Denril planned to kill the Captain and any crew who refused to acknowledge him as the new Captain. His Navigator prepared the calculations, and the Helmsman was ready to redirect the ship to Cerius. He knew people on Cerius who would pay a premium for the private cargo he had concealed aboard the Demon.

Cerius was between their third and fourth destinations. To reach Cerius would only require they exit jump at the right time.

Once he assumed command, Denril felt confident if he spaced a few officers, the rest would be happy to serve under him to keep from dying. In the meantime, Denril made sure every bridge officer on Middle Watch was loyal to him. Officer Denril made life difficult for those he wanted off the bridge, and they were happy to submit a transfer request upon Denril's suggestion. Then, Denril had the officer he wanted from Night Watch put in a similar request to switch to Middle Watch. Denril and the Deck Officer from Night Watch would sign a mutual transfer request. With both deck officers in agreement to the proposed transfers, the Captain routinely approved the requests.

Denril finally had all the officers on the Middle Watch loyal to him except for the Navigator. However, the Navigator was young, naïve, and gullible.

THOMAS WAS IN HIS CABIN when he heard his door chime. "Open," he said. Grayson entered his cabin and took a seat. Grayson had a grim expression.

"We have a problem. Your Deck Officer on Middle Watch is planning a mutiny."

"You cannot be serious," Thomas said.

Grayson showed him a dozen videos. The earlier videos were causal comments about the Captain being inexperienced and a spoiled rich kid who never should have been given a ship to command. Then Denril started weeding out the crew members who agreed with him and continued to buy them free drinks. After a time, the same group would get together during meals and later at the lounge. The discussions continued to escalate as they talked about needing a more experienced captain and how they should be earning a lot of bonus credits. Denril kept hinting if he were Captain, he would share the profits with the crew. Then, he met with a much smaller group and talked about how easy it would be to take over the ship. He even said the crew would thank them for rescuing them from such an inept Captain. Denril even mentioned their problem would be resolved if the Captain had an accident.

"I am concerned the officers on Middle Watch are loyal only to Denril," Grayson said. "With all the recent transfers, all the officers and over half the crew on Middle Watch were hired from the docks. Also, some weapons are missing from the lockers."

The videos were troubling, and Thomas had not imagined such behavior.

"So far, all he has done is talk," Thomas said softly. "At this point, we do not have enough to put him in the brig. Search Denril's cabin to see if he has the missing weapons. Place him in the brig immediately if the weapons are in his cabin. Talk to the rest of your department in private and issue them weapons. Also, change the access code on each weapon's locker to only recognize you, your team, and myself. Be ready to act if it becomes necessary. At least he cannot get any additional weapons. I will have a private conversation with the Senior Officers and bring them up to date."

Over the weeks ahead, other officers and crew spoke to Thomas in private concerning comments by Denril, which were creating dissension with some of the crew. He thanked them for their concern but did not think he should act against an officer for expressing his opinions.

Thomas understood how a crew member might dislike him, but the crew must respect the Captain and be loyal to the ship. Thomas felt a person should feel free to express their opinion as long as it did not affect their performance or the ship's efficiency. Regrettably, employee morale on Middle Watch continued to decline because of Denril's behavior. As a result, the performance on Middle Watch ranked significantly lower than the other shifts. When they reached their next destination, Thomas decided he would terminate Denril's employment based on a fair evaluation of his performance.

Thomas remembered his father's advice and wished he had followed his gut instinct before hiring Denril. Thus far, Denril had not taken overt action against Thomas or the ship. He had confined his activities solely to verbal slander against the Captain. Thomas had never terminated a person's employment, but he did not see where he had any choice. He knew some captains would simply have spaced the offender without remorse. Thomas was still hopeful Denril would change his behavior before their next stop. He discussed the situation with Ralph Miller, his uncle, and First Officer. Ralph supported the decision to terminate Denril at their next destination. Grayson had failed to locate the missing weapons, but he planned to place Denril, and his associates in the brig if they took any overt action before their next stop. They did not have long to wait.

THE SHIP HAD PASSED the halfway point to their fourth destination. At the beginning of Middle Watch, Denril had the Navigator prepare a course they would follow once they dropped out of hyperspace. He then told the bridge officers they would exit jump and arrive in the Cerius system before the end of the watch. He had already prepared an encoded message for a ship he knew would be nearby. The message told the ship to send a return message to the Demon stating they had been severely damaged and needed assistance. The Navigator closely monitored the parameters of all the ship's instruments when he gave a signal to Denril, letting him know they had arrived at the non-scheduled destination. Denril nodded, the ship dropped back into normal space, and they hastily sent a ship-to-ship message.

Thomas had just fallen asleep when he awakened. He could feel the ship and knew it had dropped out of hyperspace, but they were several days from their scheduled destination. Thomas dressed quickly and called Grayson.

"Grayson, the ship has dropped out of hyperspace without my authorization. Get your team together."

"I awoke the minute we exited hyperspace. We will head to the bridge once I have assembled my team." The Captain broke communication before Grayson could tell him to wait for his arrival before entering the bridge. Two crew members had not arrived, but he could not wait.

Thomas entered the bridge and asked Denril why they had dropped out of hyperspace without getting his authorization.

"Captain, we received a mayday distress signal," Denril responded. "It is standard procedure to respond to a ship calling for help. This is your first command, and you have no experience in such matters. I was following standard Galactic procedures. Please review the message we received. You can verify I simply responded to an emergency distress signal."

Thomas reviewed the message and timeline. Denril did not realize Thomas could easily search through the sequence of events. Thomas saw the Demon had sent and received a message. Both messages were sent after the ship exited hyperspace.

"Why are our shields down?" Thomas asked.

"Sir, there is no danger," Denril said. "We are waiting for a shuttle to bring on board the injured crew so we can transport them to the Cerius station for medical treatment."

Thomas knew he needed to give Grayson time to act. "How long before the shuttle arrives?"

"It should arrive in about twenty minutes."

Thomas looked around and knew the bridge officers had all been hired from the docks. He needed to know if any of them were loyal to him.

Thomas turned to the Tactical Officer. "Activate the shields."

"Cancel that order," Denril said with a smirk.

"I am your Captain. I am ordering everyone on the bridge to stand up and back away from your station or face charges for mutiny."

Everyone turned toward Thomas, but no one moved. Denril raised his voice.

"Show Thomas Wilson that he is no longer Captain."

Everyone except the Navigator pulled blasters and pointed them at Thomas. Denril looked at Thomas with smug satisfaction as he considered himself the new Captain.

With perfect timing, Grayson entered the bridge with five marines. They were armed with weapons drawn. The entire First Watch waited in the corridor in case the security team needed help, and they were also armed. They had also brought along the two cargo handlers with their hands in restraints behind their backs.

Grayson told the bridge crew to drop their weapons. Several started to comply when one mutineer opened fire. The shot hit Thomas in his left arm, and he intentionally fell to the floor to get out of the direct line of fire. It was over in a matter of seconds. All Middle Watch officers died during the exchange of fire except for Denril and the Navigator, who had not drawn a gun. One of Grayson's team had been killed in the exchange, and another had suffered a minor wound. The First Watch officers assumed their posts. The weapons practice had given Grayson and his marines the advantage they needed to return control of the bridge to the loyal officers.

Everyone relaxed as Thomas stood up, holding his arm. They were temporarily distracted as they all looked at Thomas. At that moment, Denril pulled a knife from his sleeve and threw it at the

Captain. Thomas saw the knife and tried to move out of the way. He reacted too late as the blade buried itself in his right shoulder. Jackson slammed his rifle into Denril's head and knocked him out. Thomas staggered and gripped the back of the captain's chair. He put his hand on his shoulder and looked down to see his hand and shirt were covered in blood. Thomas did not understand why he was having trouble seeing. Lawrence caught Thomas and lowered him to the floor as he lost consciousness.

The corridor outside the bridge had become crowded as some of the crew approached to find out why the ship had made an unscheduled stop.

"Take the Captain to the hospital," First Officer Miller shouted into the corridor.

A supervisor from Administration had arrived. Once she saw the Captain, she promptly contacted the crew members with medical training. She told them the Captain had been injured and to meet her in the hospital. She directed several of the crew to pick up Thomas, and they followed her as they departed from the bridge. Maintenance carefully removed the dead and started repairing the damage.

"Does anyone know why a shuttle is approaching our landing bay?" Officer Miller asked. Grayson grabbed the Middle Watch Navigator by his shirt collar and pulled him close to his face. His forehead creased as he became a complete predator.

"Why is that shuttle approaching our ship?" Grayson asked the Navigator.

"They are coming to examine some special cargo for possible purchase," he replied in fear with a brittle voice.

"What cargo?" Grayson asked.

"Please, that is all I know." The Navigator was afraid and answered truthfully.

Grayson walked over to the cargo handlers. "I am only going to ask this once. What is this cargo, and where is it?"

"There are six containers Denril had us bring on board right before we shipped out. I do not know what is in the containers. That is the truth."

"Show me these containers."

Once they had shown him the containers, Grayson directed Jackson to lock Denril, the Navigator, and the two cargo handlers in the brig. Grayson then collected a dozen marines and had them follow him to the landing bay. He positioned the crew to ensure they had a clear line from which to shoot and protection against return fire.

Once everyone was in position, Grayson contacted the bridge. "How far out is the shuttle?"

"I was getting worried," First Officer Miller replied. "They should arrive in about five minutes. I am opening the landing bay doors now."

The shuttle came in, completed a half rotation, and made a soft landing. The rear ramp lowered, and four men exited the craft. One man stepped forward and did not seem concerned about all the guns pointed at him.

"My employer might have an interest in purchasing some of your cargo. I am here to inspect it."

"Raise your hands," Grayson stated in a demanding voice.

He then directed several of his team to search the men and remove all their weapons. They were thorough and soon had a sizable collection of guns and knives.

"Your weapons will be returned when you leave," Grayson said. "Follow me."

The four men followed Grayson to the cargo area, and he showed them the six containers. The men spent a considerable amount of time thoroughly examining the contents of each container. They took pictures, while recording an audio commentary of their findings. After they were done, Grayson accompanied the visitors back to their shuttle.

At the shuttle, the spokesperson for the group approached Grayson. "My employer is going to be extremely interested in your cargo. How much are you asking for all six containers?"

Grayson had enough experience watching teams negotiate for players, and all negotiations were similar. It is better to let the other side make the first offer.

"We are interested in doing business with your employer, but he needs to make us an offer," said Grayson with a scowl and a sly smile. "If the offer is sufficient, we may do business. If not, we will consider checking with other buyers."

The spokesperson expressed his displeasure. "I will pass on your message to my employer, but I highly recommend you check with my employer before selling to anyone else. Once you have docked, someone will contact you using this code," He showed Grayson the code on his armlet, and then the screen cleared.

The weapons were returned to their visitors as they boarded their shuttle. As soon as the shuttle cleared the landing bay, Grayson informed the First Officer, and the shields were raised.

WHEN THOMAS REGAINED consciousness, he found himself in a narrow bed in the ship's hospital. The hospital had not been furnished or staffed since Thomas figured any severe injuries would occur in port. The hospital was simply a collection of empty rooms with some first aid supplies. He knew the bed came from an unassigned cabin. A male and a female sat in chairs on either side of his bed. It took him a minute to remember their names.

"How long have I been here?" Thomas asked.

"Two days," the female crew member replied. "A doctor from Cerius attended to your wounds and gave you antibiotics to prevent infection. Also, he gave you a drug that kept you sedated so you would heal quicker and be in less pain. The First Officer insisted that two crew members be with you at all times. He had lots of volunteers." Thomas was in a lot of pain but did not want the crew to know.

"Are you hungry?"

"Yes," Thomas replied.

The male who had been listening stood up. "I will be back in a moment. I plan to get myself something to eat while I am there. Do you want anything?" He asked the female, but she shook her head no.

He called ahead, and three meals were waiting for him when he arrived at the cafeteria. He took the meals back to the hospital. He handed one meal to the Captain and the other to the female.

"It is just a sandwich and drink," he said. "If you don't want it, I will eat it."

The Captain ate most of his meal before tiring out and falling back asleep. The female found she was hungry, and it only took her a moment to dispose of the meal.

The next time Thomas woke up, the sedative had worn off, and he was wide awake. He saw two different crew members in the room. He asked them to give him some privacy so he could take a shower and get dressed. Before giving him his privacy, they applied a waterproof patch over the bandages to keep the wounds dry. His body was sore from the injuries, and he had been lying in the same position for three days. The warm water cascaded over his body. He closed his eyes and put his head under the nozzle. The water soothed his aching muscles. It felt so good. He sighed as he turned off the water. After the warm vacuum dried him off, he stepped out of the shower and gently removed the waterproof patches. A change of clothes had been brought from his cabin. He slowly dressed and was fatigued when he finished. When he came out of the bathroom, the two crew members were still there to make sure he was all right. He dismissed them and headed for the bridge. When he looked over his shoulder, he noticed they were following him at a distance.

When he arrived on the bridge, he realized it was Middle Watch. When the Deck Officer saw the Captain, she smiled professionally and moved from the Captain's chair to the First Officer's seat. Thomas examined the time and saw it would be another two hours before the start of the Night Watch. He looked around at the bridge officers and noted the Deck Officer, along with half the crew, were from First Watch. The rest were new junior officers serving as bridge officers for the first time. Thomas commented about the promotions during his absence. The Deck Officer explained how First Officer Miller had moved her, the Navigator, and Tactical Officer from First Watch. Then, he made temporary promotions to each shift to fill the vacancies. She said everyone knew only the Captain could make the promotions permanent. Thomas reviewed the promotions and added his approval. He then asked for a status report. The newly promoted Deck Officer explained they were in a holding position. The First Officer said the Captain should decide to dock at the station or continue to their original destination. The Officer of the Deck further explained that Grayson had taken a shuttle to the station and brought back a doctor to handle his injuries. After treating Thomas, they returned the doctor to the station.

Thomas was still weak and went to his cabin to take a short nap. Near the end of Night Watch, he returned to the bridge. He was still reviewing the ship's parameters when Day Watch entered the bridge to relieve Night Watch, but Thomas asked the Night Watch officers to stay over. Thomas asked the Night Watch Communications Officer to remain at her station on the bridge and said he would meet with her separately. Thomas asked all the Officers to join him in the Captain's Ready Room. He told the Communications Officer to notify all the department heads to join him there. While they waited for the department heads, Thomas made himself a cup of coffee. It only took a few minutes before everyone was assembled. Thomas asked to be brought up to date on what had happened after he lost consciousness. First Officer Miller and Grayson took turns explaining what had taken place during his absence.

Thomas then asked about the status of the mutineers. Grayson described how four junior officers on the bridge who supported Denril were killed during the exchange of fire. He reminded Thomas that a member of his crew had died during the fray. Grayson offered to help Thomas prepare a communication to the dead crewman's family. Thomas accepted the offer.

First Officer Miller described the trial for Denril, the two cargo handlers, and six additional crew members with hidden guns who had supported Denril. They had been found guilty of mutiny and summarily executed. Thomas did not ask for details on the executions. Grayson further explained how seven additional crew members were aware of Denril's plans and stated they would support him if he became captain. They had refused to take an active role in the mutiny but violated protocol by failing to report the matter to the Captain or a senior officer. They were confined to their quarters along with the junior bridge officer, who had not drawn a weapon during the bridge battle. He further advised it would be Thomas' responsibility to determine their punishment. Thomas looked around the room. He asked for suggestions on the punishment for those involved in the conspiracy. About half were vocal in wanting all those involved put in the nearest airlock and spaced without suits. Thomas said he would consider their suggestions. Thomas suddenly remembered.

"What about the shuttle from the enemy ship?"

Grayson described the visitors who had come aboard and how they had inspected the six secret containers brought aboard by Denril. Grayson gave a complete description of the contents explaining that one container was filled with illegal, highly addictive drugs and the other five contained high-quality military weapons.

"A potential buyer is planning to contact us and make an offer for the six containers after we dock at the station," Grayson said. "Also, we checked with the station and got a list of cargo available for export from various suppliers on the planet. We received significant offers for our regular cargo. Some offers for our cargo are quite attractive. We waited for your recovery so you could approve any exchange of goods since this is not a scheduled stop."

"As we are already here, we will conduct trade in the normal fashion," Thomas said. "We will not sell below the amount we can get at any future stops, and we will purchase cargo that meets our profit requirements." Thomas put the palms of his hands together and was thoughtful.

"It sounds like you got along well without me."

Officer Miller judiciously responded. "No, sir. You have been severely missed." Thomas dismissed the meeting but asked Grayson to show him the six containers.

Grayson led him to the very back of the cargo bay. The six containers were arranged side by side, with the seals broken to allow access. Grayson showed Thomas the cargo in each container. As Grayson had previously explained, one container was filled with drugs while the other five contained military-grade arms. Grayson provided Thomas an inventory for each container. Each of the five containers was similarly stocked with a large quantity of small arms, heavy caliper rifles, handheld missiles, grenades, handheld rockets, mines, bombs that could be remotely detonated, and cases of ammunition. The arms were racked to take up less space and for easy distribution.

"We will keep one container of weapons for our own use," Thomas stated as he shook his head. "Let us see if we can find a buyer for the rest. Regardless, I wish to sell the arms to the right side or not at all. We will wait to hear from the buyer who has already expressed an interest in this cargo, but I want to know the background of this buyer before we consider any sale. Also, I want you to determine covertly the political situation on the planet and how these arms could affect the current balance of power within that structure."

THE DEMON DOCKED AT the station. They conducted robust trade with multiple buyers and sellers. All parties on the planet welcomed the trade since the Demon had goods, they could not get from other merchant ships. After paying for their purchases, Thomas saw they had over seventy million credits in their account. On the third day after their arrival, Grayson brought on board a government representative for a clandestine meeting with Thomas.

"The ship wanting to buy your special cargo supports the largest criminal group of terrorists on the planet," The representative said. "Also, this group is the largest supplier of illegal drugs. We are currently at a stalemate. Our government forces are significantly larger, and we are equally armed. Conversely, the terrorists threatened to have the ship in orbit use their ordnance to bomb our cities if the government takes any action against them.

"If the terrorists receive your weapons, they will be better armed than us and could essentially take over the elected government," the representative said with fear. "If the government had those weapons, we still cannot attack the terrorists as long as their ship controls the space above the planet." No one could doubt the sincerity of the representative.

"What would you have us do?" Thomas asked.

"I understand your wish to keep one container of guns for your own use. Sell us one container of weapons. Sell the other containers to the terrorists but let me put intermittent tracers on each container. We would use the weapons you provide to attack the terrorists before they can distribute their weapons. We would ask you to use your ship to protect the planet against any attack from space."

"How much are you offering for one container of weapons?" Thomas asked.

"I have already inspected the weapons. We will pay you five million credits for one container of weapons. As a recommendation, I suggest you demand ten million credits per container for the four containers you sell to the terrorists since these weapons are vastly superior to anything available on the planet. Also, selling to the terrorists at such a price would significantly reduce their financial position for funding their future activities."

Thomas took a moment to consider the proposal before agreeing. Receiving five million credits for one container of weapons was an outrageous amount, and he found it difficult to comprehend receiving ten million credits for each of the other containers. This put the value for the five containers at forty-five million credits. They expected to receive approximately three hundred million for their entire cargo. With the proceeds from this sale added to his existing account, he could pay off the bank loan and the suppliers. Then, he could use future funds to help his family by making payments toward the cost of the Demon, even though it was a gift.

A few cycles later, an individual approached the Demon and gave the code. He asked to speak to the Captain. Thomas notified Grayson and the First Officer to meet in his Ready Room. He directed the marines to bring their guest to the meeting and to remain for the duration.

"Let us not waste your time or ours," Thomas said. "Two of the containers are not for sale. The container of drugs and three containers of arms are available for purchase at a total price of fifty million credits."

The potential buyer seemed surprised and shook his head. "That price is outrageous; we were prepared to offer thirty million for all six containers. We will pay twenty million for the four remaining containers." With a bored expression, Thomas motioned for the two guards at the door.

"Please escort our guest off the ship." The guards moved to comply.

"Wait, we are prepared to raise our price, but I would ask you to be reasonable. How about ten million per container?"

"We will take forty million in universal credit for the four containers or fifteen million per container if you do not wish to purchase all four. That is our final offer, and full payment will have to be made before you take possession of the cargo. Take all the time you need to think it over, but I am selling to the first buyer willing to pay forty million."

Thomas told the buyer to leave, but the buyer held up his hands and asked if they would wait until he contacted his employer. The buyer walked over to the corner of the room and faced the wall as he made his call. After a few minutes, he completed the call and returned to the table.

"We will purchase all four containers for the amount you stated, but we want immediate delivery. A shuttle is on its way. Provide me with your account, and we will transfer the funds once the containers are on the dock."

As soon as the funds were in the account, Thomas transferred fifty million credits plus accrued interest to the bank to zero out their loan balance. He then paid off the balance owed to their suppliers. He also sent a secure encrypted message to the government representative that the containers had been delivered.

Thomas sent a separate transmission to the navy to the attention of Admiral Neilson with the other ship's ID stating the ship had threatened to launch an aerial assault against the inhabitants of Cerius. Thomas had the Helmsman bring the Demon closer to the other ship and within firing range of all their weapons. They continuously monitored the ship so they would be aware if the ship took any action against the planet. They were informed by private encrypted communications when the government forces launched the attack against the terrorists. Thomas was on the bridge with all his senior officers at the beginning of the ground assault. Thomas had the Demon maneuvered to a position at a lower altitude than the other ship. They continued approaching until they were at an optimum distance for the ship's weapons.

Thomas directed the Communications Officer to contact the other ship.

"I am Captain Wilson of the Demon. The navy is sending a ship in response to the planetary governor's request for assistance. Until the navy arrives, the planet is under my protection. You need to move away from the planet." Thomas did not know if the navy would react or how long it might be if they responded.

The other ship said they were leaving, but they fired a missile at the planet as they turned to leave and opened fire on the Demon. The Demon immediately opened fire on the missile and the other ship. They destroyed the planet-bound missile before it entered the atmosphere. The Demon fired two torpedoes, four missiles, and all four of their particle beams cannons at the other ship. The other ship simply blew apart. The shields on the Demon held, and the ship suffered no damage. The bridge cheered, but the First Officer noticed Thomas did not seem happy with their results. They received word from the Capital saying the attack against the terrorists was a complete success.

THOMAS ASKED HIS FIRST Officer to join him in the lounge. They had a couple of drinks to celebrate, and then Thomas commented they were in the wrong business. First Officer Miller corrected him and said they were in a safe business. The First Officer could see something was bothering Thomas and asked why he seemed troubled. Thomas stayed silent for a moment before responding.

"The sale of the drugs and arms brought in enough credits to pay off our debt. The bad guys were defeated. So, I should be happy. Still, we traded in bad faith. If we trade with the devil, we should still act in good faith, or we are no different. The outcome was excellent for the planet and its inhabitants, but we did not deal honorably. Also, I feel terrible about how I handled the situation with the mutiny. We lost a good crew member and a friend. I have to explain the death to his family. If I had acted sooner, he would still be alive. None of the mutineers would have died if I had acted like a Captain." The First Officer forgot about his title and talked to his nephew as an uncle.

"Thomas, being a Captain means making decisions that affect the lives of everyone on this ship and the lives of the people we contact. The secret to being good at anything is learning from your failures and successes. This experience will allow you to make better decisions in the future. Also, try to anticipate potential future events that are the most probable. Then, take action to maximize the upside potential while minimizing the risks associated with failure. You have studied statistics and probability theory. As a Captain, you must examine the parameters within your environment, collect the available information, and increase your odds of succeeding. You may still fail, but at least you will have done your best. Also, it could have been a lot worse. The mutiny could have succeeded. Now, you need to think about the morale of the ship. Get that sad expression off your face and buy drinks for the crew."

THE FOLLOWING MORNING Thomas met with his First Officer in the Ready Room. Security brought in the eight crew members who had been confined to their quarters. Their wrists were restrained behind their backs. Thomas nodded his head, and the recorded videos were played. The videos showed how each prisoner was aware of the plans for a hostile takeover of the ship and had agreed to support Denril if he became captain.

"As shown, all of you were aware of the planned mutiny," Thomas said. "In each case, you failed to follow procedures to inform an officer or the Captain. I will not lecture you since you know your duty is to the Captain and the ship. You have failed in your duty. Tell me why you should not be executed."

The eight prisoners consisted of six males and two females. Thomas gave each of them a chance to plead their case. Four tried to present a justification for their undefendable actions. The other four lowered their heads and remained silent. No defense existed for mutiny, and they expected to die.

Thomas accepted part of the blame for not stopping the mutiny before it escalated into a firefight.

"Your employment is terminated. All of you will receive your pay up to the date of the mutiny. Our administrative files will state your employment ended for failure to follow procedures that put the ship in danger. That is all we shall convey if this ship is ever contacted for a referral. The salary paid to you is enough for you to return to your home planet if that is your desire. The guards will escort you to your cabin so you can pack. You will be transported to the planet and released. You are dismissed."

Thomas turned to his First Officer. "We have some promotional opportunities. Please meet with the senior officers and the department heads to prepare recommendations for each opening. I would like our junior officers to make the next jump, but with the senior officers in attendance. I want every shift to have experience taking the Demon into and out of hyperspace. If I had acted, this fiasco could have been avoided. I will not make such a mistake in the future."

First Officer Ralph Miller knew his nephew had just become the Captain that the ship and crew needed.

CHAPTER 7 MISSED DEPARTURE

Their next port of call was Arabath, an agricultural but modern world. It had been completely terraformed and had the highest standard of living of the Outer Planets. Demon docked at the enormous space station. The space elevator connected the station to the planet. Arabath was a beautiful world. Water covered eighty percent of the planet. It had one large continent with temperate weather year-round. It received many visitors but had strict limits on immigration. A sizable percentage of the population lived on highly automated farms, but most visitors stayed in the one large city next to the landing port.

As expected, universal chips were in high demand, and the Demon made a very profitable sale shortly after docking. Arabath maintained open purchase orders for iodine, sulfur, and phosphorus. They purchased a fair quantity of each. Demon efficiently sold Arabath a wide variety of other goods.

Arabath was a major exporter of freeze-dried foods and calcium compounds which were in high demand on some of the other planets. Demon made purchases of calcium carbonate, calcium sulfate, and calcium fluoride. They acquired fresh farm goods for ship consumption.

Thomas made the expected profit from selling goods from the Core, but he had not anticipated how much additional profits they would earn from the trade of goods among the Outer Planets. At each destination they sold exports they had acquired from previous stops. Also, they kept purchasing rare earth elements for sale to the

Core Planets. The Outer Planets were satisfied to trade rare earth elements that were common and ubiquitous throughout their sector of space.

Arabath's space elevator made handling the cargo very efficient. The buyers had agreed to take delivery at the dock where the Demon was stationed. The crew liked the arrangement since it significantly reduced their workload. Thomas kept a partial crew on board to assist with unloading the cargo. He gave shore leave to everyone else, except for a minimum-security detail. Those remaining on board would get shore leave later through a rotation schedule.

The family ship, Familia Primum, docked next to the Demon, and part of the crew disembarked. The crew slowed to look at the Demon as they headed to the space elevator. They all commented on the beauty of the ship and how they had never seen such a design. Suzanna and several of her shipmates stopped to look at the Demon. Suzanna told her friends she would join them later. She wanted to see if the inside of the ship was as grand as the outside. She was eighteen and worked with her parents handling trade negotiations for the Familia Primum. Her parents were highly regarded for their ability to keep the ship solvent over good and bad times. Their ship was considered a decent size for a family ship, but the Demon was four times the size of their vessel. The contrast between the two ships was extreme. The two-hundred-year-old Familia Primum looked dull by comparison.

Suzanna was known for her boldness and her intellect. She was born in space and expected to die there. Many grounders looked down on spacers. Conversely, the opposite was equally true since spacers looked down on grounders. The term grounder referred to anyone who did not live in space. The crew on a family ship put the ship first and looked out for each other. Secondarily, they looked out for other family ships. A ship's financial failure usually meant all the spacers died or became grounders. Therefore, their survival depended upon profitable trade.

Suzanna approached the Demon and watched the cargo handlers unload large containers of goods that were being transferred to dock workers. She was amazed at the sheer number of containers being offloaded. Suzanna watched and listened to the conversations. The crew worked with pride and exuded confidence. They were personable to each other and quick to laugh. They sounded a lot like the crew on her ship. Suzanna figured she had nothing to lose, so she accosted one of the ship's guards and gave him a big smile.

"Hi, I arrived on the Familia Primum docked at the next gate. I wondered if I could get a tour of your beautiful ship."

The guard could not help staring, as she was young, charming, and attractive. The guard called the Captain.

"Captain, a young lady is requesting a tour of our ship. She is from the family ship docked next to us."

Thomas switched the view on his monitor to the guard station. He saw she was attractive but not beautiful. She had a certain poise and gracefulness from being born in space. This would be an opportunity to find out more about family ships since he only had old data files.

He figured she was on a spying mission to gather information for her ship, but two can play that game. He was busy, but it would be good to take a short break.

"Tell her we will be pleased to give her a tour of the ship," Thomas said to the guard. "I will be down shortly."

Once the tour was approved, Suzanna sent a message to her parents saying she was visiting a ship called Demon and would call them at the end of the tour. She also confirmed she had activated her tracker and would report back in four standard hours. Suzanna received a response from her father telling her how everyone was talking about the Demon. It had just sold ten containers of universal computer chips for twenty million credits. Her father further directed her to learn everything she could about the ship. The Demon had just completed more in one sale than their vessel would handle in several standard years.

A few minutes later, a young male approached Suzanna. "I am Thomas, and I will be your tour guide."

Suzanna introduced herself and followed him into the ship. His attractiveness surprised her, and he looked to be around her age. He was clearly an officer, but each ship had its own method of designating rank. Since he was available to give tours, he must be a very junior officer, but he was pleasant and easy on the eyes. He had muscles like a grounder but moved through the reduced gravity of the ship like a spacer. It was customary to reduce gravity when docked to make it easy to move cargo.

Suzanna could not get over how good he looked. She was instantly attracted to him on a personal level. Still, she had asked for the tour to gain a trade advantage. Gathering information on the Demon could become valuable in the future.

Thomas took his time showing Suzanna the ship. At first, she asked general questions about the ship and its previous destinations even though her primary interest was its cargo. She became more charmed with her guide as he displayed his love for his ship and crew.

They stopped at an overlook point where she could see the entire cargo bay. The bay was huge, and she believed him when he said it could hold fifteen hundred thirty-six containers. She continued to ask questions about the cargo, and he surprised her by answering every question. She soon realized the Demon carried expensive cargo. According to her guide, they only sold by the container. By comparison, the Familiar Primum sold lower value items by the unit and occasionally by the pallet. She asked him about the sale of the computer chips and if they would be buying more chips. Suzanna wanted to find where they purchased the chips, but Thomas shocked her when he said they still had fifteen containers of chips remaining. He commented the wholesale prices were excellent when items were purchased in sufficient quantities. She continued to ask questions by pointing to a collection of containers and asking what was in them.

She finally asked him to show her the cheapest container. Thomas showed her an entire row of containers of solid oxygen and solid hydrogen. She asked what the price was per container. He said they typically sold a container of solid hydrogen for two hundred thousand credits and a container of solid oxygen for one hundred thousand. Additionally, he told her most customers would buy one container of oxygen and two containers of hydrogen at a discounted price of two hundred fifty thousand for all three. They both knew the primary use of hydrogen and oxygen was to create water. A slight amount of water was lost with each recycling.

Suzanna excused herself and promptly called her parents. Her mother answered, and they had a quick conversation.

"The Familia Primum would like to buy four containers of solid hydrogen and two containers of solid oxygen at the discounted price for immediate delivery," Suzanna said. "Our ship is docked next to yours. If you give me your account, I will transfer the funds."

Thomas gave her the information, and it only took a few minutes for the funds to be deposited into his account. Thomas sent a communication to his cargo supervisor.

"The six containers will be on the dock momentarily," Thomas said. "I have directed our cargo handlers to deliver the containers to your ship."

Suzanna smiled to herself as they continued with the tour since her ship had just scored a major trade deal at a great price.

Next, Thomas took Suzanna to the engine room. He showed her the impulse drives and the jump engines while explaining the Demon's speed and maneuverability compared to other ships. Again, he took the time to answer all her questions and continued to surprise her with his knowledge. She understood why they had him conducting tours.

She was stunned when Thomas had a technical discussion with an engineer. Her guide spent several minutes going through various holographic screens until he paused at a screen with a flashing red dot. Then, Thomas went to an adjacent wall, opened a panel, and removed a computer board. He went to a different panel, pulled out a spare unit, and inserted it into the slot containing the previous board. The red dot turned green. The engineer thanked Thomas for his help. Suzanna realized her guide must be an engineer. An engineer is a distinguished position. She knew engineers were considered the smartest crew members and were critical to keeping a ship alive. Suzanna continued to become more impressed with her guide as the tour continued. She loved how he exhibited a friendly demeanor and treated everyone respectfully, regardless of their position.

Her guide took her to the ship's lounge and suggested they take a short break for lunch before completing the tour. During lunch, he asked questions about her ship and family. He followed with some personal questions. Before she knew it, she had told her entire life story. He was so easy to talk to, he seemed genuinely interested in her, and she enjoyed herself. Just as they were finishing lunch, three crew members approached them.

"Captain, I hate to disturb you," an officer said. "I need to speak with you. It will just take a moment."

"Sure." Thomas stood up and walked a few steps away so their conversation would be private.

Suzanna was not sure she had heard correctly. No one as young as Thomas could be Captain. She looked up at the two remaining crew members.

"Did he say, Captain?" Suzanna asked.

They both looked at her, and then the older male grinned. "Yes, he is our Captain, and there is no better captain in the Galactic. He is also the owner of this fine ship. His last name is Wilson, as in Wilson Enterprises."

The officer who had the private conversation with Thomas returned and apologized to Suzanna for interrupting their lunch. She was utterly speechless until the Captain sat down.

"Now, where were we?" Thomas asked.

"Why didn't you tell me you were the Captain?"

"I thought you knew. I am wearing captain bars. Regardless, it does not change the fact I have been enjoying both your company and showing you the ship. I hope you will let me finish your tour."

"I would love to continue the tour, but first, how old are you?"

"I am nineteen for a couple more months," Thomas replied.

Suzanna shook her head. "Unbelievable!"

Suzanna could not wait to tell her friends how she had spent the day with the Captain of the Demon, that he was their age and gorgeous.

They continued the tour, but now she spent most of her time watching the Captain's face as he described his ship. His love for the ship was contagious as she fell in love with the Demon and a little with the Captain. They finally made their way to the Bridge, and Thomas let her sit in the Captain's chair while he showed various outside views using the ship's sensors.

She rotated the chair toward the Captain. "What about tactical?"

Thomas answered with pride. "The ship is built to military specifications with a double-walled hull and heavy-duty shielding. We have the firepower to take on a destroyer or any lesser ship. We would be at a disadvantage against a cruiser, but the ship has the legs to outrun a cruiser unless we are surprised. It is my job to see we are never surprised."

"Do you normally spend all day giving tours?" She asked mischievously.

He laughed. "No, this is my first time serving as a tour guide."

Next, Thomas decided to let her see his cabin. By this point, she thought she was beyond being surprised, but she just threw her hands up in the air. The cabin was the most impressive room she had ever seen. There was gold inlay and luxurious furnishings throughout the cabin. Beds on ships had to be small to conserve space, but this large exotic bed could accommodate an entire family. She wondered if it was as comfortable as it looked.

"Where is your crown?" Suzanna asked. "Only a member of royalty would have a room this nice." On the Familia Primum, she slept in a hammock with a small bin for her personal items. The narrow hammocks were arranged in vertical columns, with the hammock above you allowing only enough room to slide into your assigned space. There was just enough space between the rows of hammocks to provide a walkway. The community bathrooms were always full, and you were expected to take as little time as possible in the bathroom. The showers had timers, and the water shut off automatically. You exited the shower promptly as a courtesy to the people waiting in line. Once you achieved a certain age or rank, you got to share a cabin. There were four persons to a cabin for each shift, and you only had access to your cabin for eight hours. If you needed more sleep, you would find an empty hammock.

Thomas explained. "Originally, while building the ship, I spent a little of the left-over budget on the Captain's cabin as an inducement for a potential buyer. Unfortunately, there were no buyers for the ship. So, my father let me have her."

While Thomas was talking, Suzanna invaded his personal space, and words were no longer needed. She did not know if it was his gorgeous looks, charming personality, the power of his position, or size of the bed. She just knew she had to have him. Their bodies melted into each other. They kissed tentatively at first, and then the kiss became more passionate. She pulled him with her as she backed toward the bed. They fell onto the bed, and Suzanna found out the bed was just as comfortable as she imagined. She had been wondering what it would feel like to be in his arms. It felt wonderful. Thomas had forgotten about his duties since he enjoyed being with her. Afterward, they rested in each other's arms, and she snuggled against him.

"I bet this bed has a lot of good stories," she said jokingly.

"You would lose the bet. You are the first female to share this bed."

"No way, you are the Captain, and there are hundreds of females on this ship who would share your bed."

"Being the Captain is a social problem," Thomas replied with a sigh. "A female may feel pressured to accept my advances because of my position or try to use the relationship to advance her career. If they refuse my advances and later fail to get a promotion, they may feel it was because they rejected me. If a female accepts my advances and later gets a promotion, some will think she got it because of the relationship. Also, there are potential scenarios where male crew members might be upset if they are interested in the same female. My First Officer is my uncle, and he took considerable time explaining the responsibilities of a captain."

Suzanna liked the bed even better. Thomas suggested she put her clothes in the refresher. The clothes would be clean when they awoke.

They talked some more and found out both of their ships would be docked for another two days. Then they fell asleep and had a restful night.

The following morning, she approached the shower and asked for the location of the timer.

"There is no timer," Thomas replied.

"You mean I can stay in the shower as long as I like?"

"Yes, but after a few days, you might get hungry."

She enjoyed the hot shower knowing she could take her time. When she finished, Thomas handed her a female bathroom kit a crew member had delivered. After Thomas took his shower, they dressed and had breakfast in the cafeteria. Thomas explained he would be busy the rest of the day. They agreed to meet in the afternoon at nineteen hundred hours on the planet at the exit from the space elevator. He wanted to take her to dinner at one of the fine planetary restaurants. Thomas escorted her to her ship's gate before kissing her goodbye.

AS SOON AS SUZANNA reported aboard the Familia Primum, she went to her workstation. Toward the end of her shift, Captain Javier requested her presence. The Captain was with the Chief Engineer and her parents when she entered the meeting room. Captain Javier asked her to provide them with everything she remembered about the Demon while it was fresh in her mind. They were duly impressed with her boldness in visiting the Demon. They were always looking to develop friendships with powerful ships that might result in protection or profitable ventures. They expressed their satisfaction with the four containers they purchased. There was no privacy regarding social issues or ship politics. They expected her to be entirely forthcoming regarding her relationship with Captain Wilson, and modesty was not an attribute with spacers. When she finished, there were admiring nods around the room. Captain Javier then asked her about Captain Wilson's feelings toward her. She explained that Captain Wilson had invited her to join him for dinner. Therefore, he must like her. Realistically, she knew it was just a casual romantic relationship that would end when their ships departed. Until then, she would enjoy every moment she spent with

Thomas. She realized she would be sad when they departed, and it would take time to get over her infatuation.

Captain Javier then explained how he had just returned from a meeting with Captain Wilson. To ingratiate himself with Captain Wilson, he provided destinations where the universal chips could be sold in pallet-size quantities for three to four times the amount he received for the containers. He explained to Suzanna how Captain Wilson had thanked him but said he was not interested in traveling to those locations or selling smaller quantities. Then Captain Wilson asked him how many chips could be sold at those locations and how long would it take.

Captain Javier smiled at Suzanna. "I explained it would be easy to sell two containers of chips if they were divided into smaller quantities. I let him know it would take less than a standard year to complete the sale of the chips while conducting additional trade. Captain Wilson asked why I did not purchase two containers of chips from him and keep the profit. I sadly explained how our ship did not have the capital to make such a purchase. You will not believe what Captain Wilson said next. He said he would sell us two containers of chips on consignment if we agreed to three conditions. First, we would pay the full purchase price before recognizing any profit. Second, we would keep the transaction completely confidential because he does not sell inventory without payment in advance. Third, he specifically stated you were to receive credit for the transaction." Captain Javier paused. Everyone in the room was smiling as they nodded their heads at Suzanna.

"So, it appears Captain Wilson's feelings for you are more than casual. We have already taken delivery of the chips since we did not want to give Captain Wilson time to change his mind."

The Chief Engineer was grinning from ear to ear as he spoke to Suzanna with the enthusiasm of a man half his age. "The profit we will make on these chips will allow us to replace a failing engine, pay for a complete overhaul of the ship, upgrade our electronics, and still have money left over for future purchases of more profitable cargo."

Captain Javier was thoughtful. "You are eighteen and of the age which allows you to change ships when it is advantageous to yourself or the Familia Primum. If the opportunity arises and you decide you would like to transfer to the Demon, you have our approval. Regardless, you have created a tremendous opportunity for the Familia Primum. You are a credit to your parents and this ship!"

Because of the small gene pool, ships were expected to exchange crew when a female decided to have a child. Every three years, there was a Gathering of family ships to give the crew an opportunity to find a mate from another ship. The couple would decide which ship they would join after discussing the matter with the elders of each ship. This approach provided a diversity of the ship's gene pool. At a Gathering, the personality profiles of eligible members of every ship were shared with all the other vessels. A person was free to contact a potentially compatible mate if they desired. No one was required to marry or stay married. Further, two children were the maximum allowed without approval since the size of the vessel limited the number of individuals living on a ship. If you wanted to have more than two children, you asked for approval or became a grounder.

Suzanna realized she had just gained tremendous status on the ship, and they were waiting for a response. She had not thought about leaving the Familia Primum since the last Gathering, which occurred a year earlier. At the Gathering, she had been contacted by several compatible males, but they bored her. Whereas Thomas was charming, enticing, vibrant, and so alive. This was the first person who had truly excited her, and she could not wait to see him again. She believed Thomas would want a senior officer for a mate. Regardless, she wanted to spend as much time as possible with Thomas before their ships departed. She hoped they could continue to meet when their ships were at mutual ports, but right now, Captain Javier needed a more positive response.

"I like Captain Wilson, and I will take advantage of any opportunity that may develop between us," Suzanna said.

Captain Javier clapped his hands together. "Spoken like a true spacer! Until we leave port, you are relieved from all ship duties."

Suzanna thought about the meeting with Captain Javier as she proceeded to her cabin. She looked forward to seeing Thomas again. She liked him but was not currently looking for a mate. The Demon was a fantastic ship, but she was happy remaining on the Familia Primum for a few more years. Still, last night she had forgotten about duty and work. She had a tremendously enjoyable time with Captain Wilson, but Thomas was a captain and came from wealth. A captain did not marry for love. They married to enhance their ship's future. Romantically, all she could think about was being in his arms once again, and she dreamed about impossibilities.

She contacted her three best friends and agreed to meet them in the cafeteria. Her friends were waiting for her and screamed as she approached their table. The entire crew was aware of her accomplishments. She was now a celebrity, and her roommates wanted all the details. They were all jealous when she explained how she had spent the night with the Captain of the Demon. Especially when they learned, he was only nineteen and incredibly handsome. However, they were even more amazed and completely overwhelmed when she described the Captain's cabin. They would have kept her talking all afternoon, but she explained she needed to get ready since she had a dinner date with Captain Wilson.

Suzanna and Thomas enjoyed a gourmet meal, and the restaurant lived up to its reputation. They danced to the live entertainment and returned to the Demon where they enjoyed each other on a more intimate basis. This time they took more time, and the passion was just as hot. When their pounding heart finally slowed down, they had no problem falling asleep. Right before drifting off, Suzanna thought she might say yes if Thomas asked her to transfer to the Demon. She loved spending time with Thomas but knew anything more was just an unrealistic fantasy. Suzanna asked herself if it was even possible to fall in love with someone after only two days. Also, she wondered how strongly Thomas felt about her. She had never felt so attracted to a guy. Sleeping on such a large and comfortable bed had already spoiled her. She had never slept so well. She was not looking forward to returning to a narrow hammock. She was definitely in love with the bed.

Suzanna and Thomas both woke up early the following day. Suzanna suggested they take a shower together to save time. In the end, it took a lot longer. They had a lite breakfast, and Thomas said he would again be busy during the day. They arranged to meet at the same time and location in the afternoon.

Thomas could not stop smiling as he proceeded to the bridge for the start of Day Shift. He wished he had taken the day off so he could spend it with Suzanna. He had never felt such a strong attraction to a female and was already dreading the time when his ship would leave for their next destination. It had only been a few minutes since she left, and he was already missing her.

THE PREVIOUS NIGHT her close friends had said they would return to the planet to enjoy themselves. It was the second night in a row she had failed to join them. She had checked the ship's log and found they had returned to their ship in the early morning. They would sleep all day since it was their scheduled day off. Suzanna went exploring on her own and took the space elevator to the planet.

As Suzanna wandered through the market, she saw a young man and woman announcing they had room for one more person to tour their farm.

"Join our tour," the female said. "You will see actual crops being grown and real farm animals. Plus, everyone is invited to participate in the annual festival of life. On this once-a-year event, all flowers and every animal are fertile."

The price was a little high, but Suzanna decided to take the tour once the driver said she could return early if she wanted. She learned the farm delivered fresh produce to the city throughout the day, and there was space in the delivery vehicles for passengers. The tour of the Demon had worked out well, and she had never seen vegetables growing or live farm animals.

"What is the additional cost to attend the festival of life," she asked.

"Attending the festival of life is free," the guide said. "We would never charge for helping someone bring forth a new life."

The male guide gave her a tablet with a displayed document. Touring the farm required a signature and participating in the festival of life needed a second signature. Suzanna skimmed the document. She did not bother reading it since she was not purchasing or selling cargo on behalf of her ship. Suzanna signed electronically in both places and sealed it with a thumbprint. The group took their seats in the ground vehicle and sped out of the city. When they arrived, a collection of young farmers greeted them, and the tour group broke up into smaller groups for customized tours. Suzanna found herself alone with the driver who had brought them to the farm.

"It looks like I will be your guide," he said. "First, have you ever been on a farm?"

"No," Suzanna replied.

"Very well, let us start with the crops. Then, we will visit the groves. We should finish just in time for lunch. After lunch, I will show you the animals. Finally, we will finish just in time to join the other visitors for the festival of life with the fertility ritual."

Suzanna enjoyed seeing how the crops were grown organically with solar-powered equipment doing most of the work. Still, the groves were even better. They let her pick and eat a fresh apple, an orange, and a grape used for making their signature wine. They joined the other visitors for an alfresco lunch, where they sampled all the vegetables and fruit they had seen during the tour. Also, they sampled red and white wines made onsite in the farm's winery.

After lunch, they walked to a barn where horses were already saddled. The guide assured Suzanna the horses were very gentle. He helped her into the saddle for her first horseback ride. She looked forward to telling her shipmates how they missed out on two of the greatest tours ever. As they walked the horses through the pasture, her guide pointed out the cows, sheep, and goats. They stopped at some pens at the far back of the pasture. She nearly gagged from the smell as they looked down on some small, filthy, and very noisy animals. She held her nose while being informed the animals were pigs. She was relieved when they turned the horses around to head back to the barn. Once they dismounted, she let her guide know she enjoyed the entire tour except for the pigs. He laughed.

It was late evening and close to the time for her to return to the city. Her guide, with great enthusiasm, told her the fertility ceremony had just started. Suzanna figured she would attend the first part of the show before leaving.

As they entered, she noticed everyone else was already sitting on the floor in a large room, but the group had decreased to half its size. An attendant gave her a glass filled with a golden color liquid. She sat on the floor next to her guide just as an older female speaker stepped forward.

"This is where you realize your dreams of bringing in a new life. So far, unless the lack of blooming is due to age or other physical impediments, we have succeeded in helping those who have participated in our fertility ceremony. I explained the history of our ceremony and let you know what to expect. Now, you may drink the elixir of fertility." Suzanna had arrived late and missed the explanation.

Suzanna drank her drink along with everyone else, and the taste was amazing. She had never tasted anything as wonderful, and she experienced a feeling of euphoria.

Suzanna noticed the female sitting next to her had not touched her drink. "You are not drinking?" she asked.

"I am just here to observe. You can have my drink if you want." Suzanna drank the second drink in one long gulp. Her guide turned to her in panic.

"The drink is powerful," he said. "You are only supposed to drink one glass."

Suzanna was suddenly overwhelmed with desire. Everyone had suddenly lost all of their inhibitions as they rapidly discarded their clothing. Suddenly her guide became the most desirable person she had ever met, and an uncontrollable passion consumed her. Suzanna stripped off her clothing and urgently helped the guide remove his clothes. She was on fire and trying to satisfy her burning desire.

When she woke up, she was lying on her back. The only other person in the room was her guide. He sat cross-legged next to her and was completely clothed. She slowly recalled what had happened. Then, she realized she was still naked. She did not feel any hangover effects that would be associated with alcohol. In fact, she felt quite well, except she was thirsty and hungry. She was dehydrated, and he offered her a bottle of water. She drank half the bottle, and her throat felt better. She was upset with what had taken place and glared at her guide.

"You drugged me so you could have sex with me!" She exclaimed.

"I most certainly did not," he responded with indignation. "You signed up to participate in the tour and the festival of life. The document you signed was clear and specific in describing the fertility ceremony. If you had not wanted to participate in the fertility ceremony, you should only have executed page one. You executed both pages, indicating you wished to have a child. We charge for the tour but participating in the fertility ceremony is free. Certain of our guests have been unsuccessful in having a child. They come here to take part in the festival of life to have a child naturally by consuming a plant-based liquid without the discomfort or costs of undergoing a medical procedure. The liquid is made from the bloom of a plant. The plant is exceedingly rare and only blooms once per year."

Suzanna thought back to executing the document and realized she had violated a sacred rule her parents had drilled into her for as long as she could remember. You never execute any document without reading it, in its entirety. If you do not understand any part of a document, you do not sign it without changing it, or you have an attorney explain the writing, so it is clearly understood.

Suzanna recalled the previous night and realized she would have trouble accusing him of taking advantage of her. She remembered she had removed her clothing first and then helped undress him. Also, they had sex several times, and she was on top each time as she responded to her physical needs brought about by the drink. She was still upset, but she now blamed herself for what had happened. Also, she had been having sex since she was sixteen, and this was not her worse sexual experience. Regrettably, she was terribly upset she had missed her dinner date with Thomas. She asked to see the document, and he provided her with a display. This time, she read the entire document. There was no way to misunderstand what was clearly explained. She nodded and said it was her fault for not reading the document. The guide expressed regret for the misunderstanding.

Her ship was leaving today, so she needed to return to the city. She wanted to take a shower and grab a quick meal. Her clothes were folded on the floor next to her. The guide helped her to her feet, and Suzanna picked up her clothes. She took a quick shower and dressed. The guide had waited for her, and she followed him to the dining room. There were only farmers eating. She helped herself to the buffet and told her guide she was famished as she devoured her food.

"I am not surprised," he said. "I was worried until an elder checked you out and said you would be fine. The participants are only allowed to drink one glass of the drink of life, but you drank two glasses. Regardless, you should be hungry since you slept through yesterday without waking up to eat or drink."

Suzanna froze with the fork halfway to her mouth as fear and dread spread throughout her body. She looked at her wristband and experienced a cold chill.

"Please, you must get me back to my ship as fast as possible. It is an emergency."

They rushed into the yard, and she jumped into the passenger side of a ground vehicle. They took off, and she pressured him to push the vehicle to its maximum speed. She closed her eyes and prayed to god. She then prayed to all the lesser spirits existing anywhere in the Galactic. The traffic became heavier as they approached the space elevator. When they stopped at a crossroad, she jumped from the vehicle and ran as fast as she could. Several people complained as she cut in line and pushed her way onto the space elevator. Before, she had marveled at the speed of the elevator, but now it seemed extremely slow. Her heart continued to pound as she positioned herself in front of the door. When the elevator's door opened, she ran to the gate, praying her ship had waited for her. When she arrived, both the Familia Primum and the Demon were gone as both gates were empty.

She was overwhelmed with emotions of disbelief, distress, and then hopelessness. She started crying as she walked over to view the schedule for the earlier departures. The Demon had left before the

Familia Primum. When she did not report aboard, her ship would assume she was on the Demon. She had told Captain Javier of her intentions to take advantage of a potential relationship with Captain Wilson. To keep from collapsing, she sat down on a bench in despair and continued to cry.

Finally, when no tears were left, she went to the station's administration office and asked to speak to someone about missing her ship's departure. After waiting several hours, an assistant escorted her to a stately gentleman's office who said there was nothing he could do. He explained she might try to locate a ship going to the same destination as her ship, but they would expect her to pay for such passage. Suzanna explained she did not have the credits for such a fare. He then asked her how often her ship visited their port. She started crying again, saying it had been over two standard years between this visit and their prior visit. After she stopped crying, he suggested she find a job and make the best of an unpleasant situation. He then gave her a voucher for one free night at a room on the station. After that, he escorted her out of the administration offices.

THE FOLLOWING DAY, Suzanna applied for every job posted by the station but was turned down for every position. She was having lunch when she started crying again. A server wearing a stained white uniform came over and asked what was wrong. Suzanna explained how she had missed her ship's departure, how no one would hire her, and she would be out of credits in a matter of days. She gave Suzanna the sandwich and the glass of water she had ordered. The server thought for a minute and told Suzanna not to leave.

A few minutes later, the server returned. "We recently lost an employee, and you can have the job if you want it."

"I will take it," Suzanna replied.

"I am Terrell. The employee who quit was also my former roommate. You can stay with me if you share the rent and expenses."

Suzanna accepted the kind offer and mentioned that all her belongings were on the ship. Terrell said she could start the next day. She told Suzanna to hang around till the end of the shift, and they would go shopping at an affordable place. Then the server scrunched up her face.

"I will show you the places that sell cheap clothes at a cheap price," Terrell said. Then they both laughed, but Suzanna was still crying on the inside.

After several weeks Suzanna fell into a routine, and with Terrell's help, they managed to make it through each day. Terrell knew everyone on the station and had lots of friends. Then one day, Suzanna was feeling sick. Terrell noticed and suggested she see the station's doctor. Suzanna said she did not want to spend what little she had on a doctor. Terrell made a call and told Suzanna the doctor would see her for free on her next break.

After a complete examination, the doctor said she was pregnant but otherwise healthy. She tried to explain to the doctor that he must be mistaken. She lamented she had just received a new implant which was one hundred percent effective against getting pregnant, and her implant would last five standard years. He listened but showed her an image, and it was clear he was not wrong.

After thinking for a few minutes, she described her experience at the farm and asked if the drug may have affected the implant. The doctor said he was familiar with the farm. The plant-based drug they use could definitely result in pregnancy since it causes a female to ovulate immediately and increases the potency of the male's sperm. He said it was early in the gestation, and she could choose not to have the child.

Spacer families planned most pregnancies since it affected a ship's resources. The birth of a child affected every crew member since the ship's population had to be kept in balance. During Suzanna's life, there had not been any unplanned pregnancies. Most females voluntarily stopped at two children. Some females did not want children, and accidental deaths created situations that allowed certain couples to have more children without exceeding a ship's resources. Also, ships with low populations accepted crew from ships with too large a population during the Gathering. During her lifetime on the Familia Primum, no request to have a child had been turned down. This resulted in their ship being overcrowded. Even with the crowding, the birth of a child was a joyous event. Also, all the crew helped in raising a child. Even though her pregnancy was unplanned, she would not abort her child.

Suzanna walked back to the restaurant in silence. She felt even sicker to think her child might not be born on a ship.

THOMAS WAS DISAPPOINTED Suzanna had not shown up for their dinner date and was surprised she had not called to cancel. He had finally given up waiting and had dinner alone. Thomas stayed busy. He occasionally thought about Suzanna and what could have been. He had felt so comfortable with her and just enjoyed being with her.

CHAPTER 8 BATTLE STATIONS

Thomas had a habit of coming to the bridge early to spend time with the Night Watch before their shift ended, and he stayed on the bridge late so he could spend time with the Middle Watch at the beginning of their shift. Each shift took turns maneuvering the ship using the impulse engines. They gained additional experience entering and exiting hyperspace using the jump engines. Further, each shift took turns docking and undocking from space stations. He continued the practice of coming out of jump early, so they could approach each destination carefully from a distance. Thomas always insisted they be at battle stations whenever they left a station or planet and when exiting hyperspace.

Before long, it became well known the Demon carried large quantities of expensive goods. When the Demon came out of jump at Jarcada, there were two ships between them and the station serving the planet. Both ships headed straight for the Demon. It was near the end of Night Watch, when they called Thomas to the bridge.

The ship was already at battle stations as Thomas took his seat. "Two ships are approaching on an intercept course," Thomas announced over the ship-wide intercom. "Prepare for combat maneuvers." Thomas knew his communications were redundant. Still, it was important for the crew to know the Captain was on the bridge and had control of the situation.

"Tactical, what is our status?" Thomas asked.

"Our shields are at one hundred percent. The two artillery cannons along with all four particle beam cannons are manned and tracking. The laser battery is at one hundred percent. The torpedo tubes are loaded and locked on target. Also, the four missile launchers are loaded, ready, and tracking."

Thomas directed his Communications Officer to contact the approaching ships. One ship opened communications. "Captain, you are ordered to bring your ship to a full stop and prepare to be boarded. If you comply, we will not harm your crew. We only want your cargo."

Thomas examined the data from their sensor array. The two enemy ships could beat most normal nonmilitary ships, but the demon was not a normal ship. Each enemy vessel had two missile launchers and two of the older pulse cannons that had to be recharged between firings. The data showed the two ships worked together and had successfully attacked other vessels over the past four years. They were known for their cruelty and killed the crew of the captured ships. Occasionally they would keep a crew member if they had a need and after sufficient torture to assure complete obedience to any orders given.

Thomas took his time and responded with a calm voice. "This is Captain Wilson of the Demon. You should flee as fast as possible, or the Demon will send you both to hell. You have exactly ten seconds to comply."

Thomas turned to his Tactical Officer and told him not to fire the torpedoes but to proceed with a ten-second countdown and to announce it over the open communications channel with the two hostile ships. He told the Helmsman to accelerate to flank speed on a course directly at the two ships.

Onboard the enemy ships, the two Captains were conversing and trying to decide if the Demon was serious. Other ships they approached had begged for mercy or tried to escape, but the Demon had simply given them ten seconds to flee. They then noticed the Demon was not trying to flee. Instead, the Demon had increased their speed and was heading straight at them. They suddenly realized the ten-second countdown had just reached zero.

Thomas asked if the ships had changed course. The Tactical Officer said they were still approaching with no change in their trajectory. By going to flank speed, the enemy ships were within a close enough range they could not take evasive action. Also, while the two captains had their discussions, neither of the enemy's Tactical Officers had adjusted their targeting to account for the Demon's change in speed or location. Both Captains shouted for their Helmsman to take evasive action, but it was too late.

Thomas calmly announced over the open channel and throughout the ship. "Open Fire!"

Simultaneously all four particle beam cannons opened fire, and four missiles were launched. The laser battery and the artillery cannons were highly effective as the ship moved within the optimum firing range. The Helmsman had positioned the Demon perfectly to allow half the ordinance to have a clear trajectory to each enemy ship. The bridge officers of the Demon watched as the two particle beam cannons and two missiles impacted each enemy ship. The missiles took out the shields. The particle beam cannons destroyed the engines. The lasers destroyed the enemy's guns, and the rapid-fire artillery cannons punched thousands of holes into each vessel. The two ships were destroyed before they could get off a shot. The Demon passed between the two vessels. It was clear there would be no survivors.

First Officer Miller had watched his nephew act decisively in the battle and was pleased with what he saw. The Demon needed a strong captain, and Thomas Wilson had just become that captain.

Thomas had his Communications Officer put him through to the station and played the communications between the Demon and the two attacking vessels. Thomas claimed salvage rights against the two vessels and asked if a local salvage company would like to split the salvage or buy out the salvage rights. The station patched him through to an older gentleman who said he occasionally handled salvage. Thomas sent him videos of the two ships, and they agreed to a split with the salvage company receiving sixty percent but doing all the work.

The Station Master was back online and welcomed the Demon to the station. He thanked the Demon for taking care of a nuisance. Everyone at the station enjoyed the open channel communications between the Demon and the other two ships. The Demon docked at the station and was met by the Station Master. The station needed a wide range of goods, and the Demon could meet most of their needs. After the Station Master had completed his trade negotiations, he informed Thomas he had arranged for a meeting with a trade delegation from Jarcada to take place in the station's conference room. Thomas allowed the crew to visit the station in small groups. There were two bars and three restaurants on the station. The crew found the food and drink on the Demon was a lot better. Despite this, the crew collected as much information as possible about other ships and the planet.

Thomas met with the trade delegation from Jarcada. Thomas gave them a manifest of their cargo with prices. The delegates provided a similar list of items that Jarcada had available for export. Thomas used the Demon's AI to provide the delegates with a list of the items he would purchase. They would offset the exports against the imports to arrive at a net balance. The lead delegate asked Thomas if they could have until the next day to make their selection. Thomas readily agreed. In good faith, Jarcada started delivering their exports to the station.

They exchanged goods efficiently over the next four days without issue. Jarcada and Demon agreed to a long-term contract. This would allow the planet to concentrate on building up exportable items. Jarcada was highly interested in receiving the advanced medical supplies and additional power supply units. They preordered significant quantities of those items.

The Demon completed their trade, and it seemed everyone on the station and the planet had heard recordings of the Demon's battle. The rumors of the battle quickly spread to other stations and planets.

REGRETTABLY, DEMON was still a valued prize and continued to draw unwanted interest in its cargo. Two destinations later, the pirates took a different approach. Demon had just completed two weeks of trading with the planet Thebes and was leaving when four ships moved to block their exit while they were moving at a slow velocity. The four ships incorrectly assumed the Demon would not expect such an attack and would be unprepared for such tactics. The pirates made a big mistake. The Demon was at battle stations when the pirate ships opened fire without warning. Each of the enemy ships launched two missiles.

The Tactical Officer knew he did not need to wait for the Captain to issue orders. All particle beam cannons opened fire. The Demon launched four missiles and two torpedoes before the first missiles arrived. The attacking ships had released over a hundred drones that could only be used against a ship traveling at slow speeds. The laser battery and the artillery cannons opened fire on the incoming missiles and drones while the Helmsman took evasive action. The enemy ships launched eight more missiles, and the Demon launched four additional missiles and two more torpedoes. The torpedoes and missiles from the Demon's first launch took out two enemy ships, but the enemy's countermeasures allowed two ships to survive. The particle beam cannons did considerable damage by disrupting the molecular structure in the areas it struck. The Demon's laser battery was firing continuously and destroyed all except a few of the drones, which exploded harmlessly against the ship's shields. The artillery cannons took out six of the enemy's missiles from the first volley. Two missiles from the enemy's first launch struck the Demon, and their shields dropped to eighty percent. Before the two remaining enemy ships could launch additional missiles, they were struck by the second wave of Demon's torpedoes and missiles. There were eight additional missiles inbound. The Demon used countermeasures and the artillery cannon to destroy five missiles. The lasers destroyed the pirates' smaller turret guns before taking out two missiles. One missile struck the Demon, but the shields held while dropping to seventy percent. The missiles of the attacking ships were less powerful than those of the Demon. Also, they had single-walled hulls instead of the military hulls of the Demon, and their shields were weaker. Thomas told the Tactical Officer to cease fire. The enemy ships were helpless, and no longer posed a threat to the Demon. This time Thomas knew there would be survivors. Whoever commanded the pirate fleet had military training and had struck when the Demon was most vulnerable. It would have succeeded against a lesser ship.

Thomas contacted Thebes. They agreed to contact the military because of the size of the attack. This meant Demon needed to remain so they could give a full report to the navy. Thomas communicated with the four enemy ships, and three of the ships responded. They agreed to his offer to bring medical help from the planet if they would surrender and cease all hostilities.

EIGHT CYCLES LATER, a fleet of nine navy ships arrived, consisting of three cruisers and six destroyers. They dispatched marines to each of the four ships to arrest the crew and determine the damage to the ships.

After three days, the Admiral invited Thomas to join him aboard one of the cruisers for dinner. He was to bring along his senior bridge officers. Thomas understood the dinner invitation was an order and knew he had no choice. He and his officers dressed in their finest. Grayson insisted on providing four bodyguards for the Captain and said it would be expected. The four bodyguards wore the body armor they had recently purchased. Thomas knew Grayson decided on four guards since they only had four sets of armor. To further give the correct impression, Thomas agreed they should all go armed.

The group consisted of Thomas, the First Officer, four senior officers, and his four bodyguards. His guards ate their meals before leaving the ship. They took a shuttle to the specified cruiser. The four guards exited the shuttle first and took up position. Thomas was next, followed by his officers. A platoon of marines was always present when a foreign shuttle came aboard a navy ship.

A navy officer stepped forward. "I am Commander Wiggins, welcome aboard." Thomas introduced himself and his officers.

"Please follow me," the Commander said.

Thomas realized Grayson had been correct when he saw several marines nod their approval of his party. These marines would already know of their battle against four enemy ships, and they seemed pleased the Demon crew looked capable.

They entered the Wardroom and were directed to the Admiral's table. After the introductions, they took their seats. Thomas was duly impressed. He and his officers were having dinner with Admiral Nelson. Thomas was seated as the invited guest at one end of the table and Admiral Nelson at the other end.

"It seems you have been in one battle against two ships and in this second battle against four ships without sustaining any damage," Admiral Nelson said. "How do you account for that?"

Thomas learned from his father and as a player in arena hockey, to plan for a variety of contingencies in all engagements. This applied to negotiations for trade, an actual space battle, or a simple verbal dialog. Thomas had expected the question and had prepared an answer. The talking at the table stopped as they waited for Thomas to respond.

Thomas took his time to add drama. "We were lucky," he answered. He paused and could tell no one liked the answer. Then, he continued.

"That the enemy underestimated us."

The entire table burst out laughing. Admiral Nelson smiled as he nodded his head. He liked this brash young Captain. Further, Captain Thomas had allowed several of the navy's officers to tour his ship, and they all came back duly impressed with the ship's capabilities and the expertise of the crew. The Admiral's Chief Engineer had fallen in love with the Demon. Admiral Nelson had read the glowing, detailed report from Captain Horwitz about a fifteen-year-old that had taken control of a pirate ship. He had contacted Captain Horwitz, and the captain was not surprised Thomas Wilson had taken out six pirate ships. This Captain Thomas was young, but he was good. In fact, he was exceptionally good for a civilian and perfect for what the Admiral had in mind.

After dinner, Admiral Nelson asked Captain Thomas and First Officer Miller to join him in his Ready Room. Several naval officers joined them, and everyone took their seats.

"I am going to tell you things about the war with the Hostis that are unknown by the public," Admiral Nelson said. "First, despite common belief, we did not win the war. Also, we were the invaders though we did not know it at the beginning. No peace treaty has ever been established. To this day, we are unable to communicate with the Hostis. We had settled on three planets within the edge of their area of space. They attacked the planets one at a time and killed everyone on each of the planets. They do not take prisoners, so anyone who tried to surrender was summarily killed. Some people on two planets escaped in merchant ships, which is how we know what happened. We armed the civilian ships and they fought with us. In addition to the skirmishes, there were several major battles in which both sides suffered heavy losses. The war lasted for years since we were fairly equal strategically."

The Admiral took a drink and then continued. "To gain intelligence on the Hostis, we built several small but powerful jump ships. The ships were built for speed with no weaponry. One of these ships reported the Hostis were advancing with a large armada. We pulled every ship to create a human armada, leaving our planets defenseless. We waited within our area of space. We had a slight advantage in total ships when the two fleets met. There was a standoff that lasted for several days. Then the Hostis simply left. Later, we discovered the Hostis did not show up with all their ships. They left ships behind to protect their worlds and must have assumed we did the same. If they had called up all their ships, we would have lost. They would have been free to invade, and humanity would have been helpless."

"What is the current status?" Thomas asked.

"For the past ninety years, there has been no contact with the Hostis, but the situation recently changed. We continued to use our spy ships to monitor their behavior. Over the past thirty years, the Hostis have built up their fleet. We have also been building ships, but the politicians are reluctant to increase military spending and feel the navy is paranoid. If the Hostis attack, it will start at the Rim worlds. None of the Rim Worlds and only a few Outer Planets have joined the Imperium. Therefore, we cannot establish defense bases on those planets. With a military base and a planetary defense grid, those planets might delay the Hostis until a navy fleet could arrive and help in their defense. Fortunately, the Hostis do not bombard planets from space with weapons that would reduce the habitability of a planet. Once they destroy all the inhabitants, their species occupy the planet. The best situation would be for the Imperium to establish a military base on each Outer Planet and Rim World. Unfortunately, only two planets have been willing to let the Imperium build these bases."

"I assume you have other options," Thomas said.

"The next option would be for the Outer Planets and the Rim Worlds to have sufficient arms to defend themselves long enough for the navy to arrive. Many planets have arms, but their arms are inadequate against a Hostis invasion."

The Admiral stopped talking, and his First Officer took over the presentation.

"Duly elected governments are being overthrown by small groups of fanatics who are being supplied with gray market arms. While the planetary governments have the numbers, they do not have the quality or quantity of weapons to deal with the fanatics. On some planets freedom fighters need weapons to overthrow dictators so democratic governments can be established. Also, marauders and pirates are attacking planetary towns and villages with superior weapons. Again, none of these planets have the quality or quantity of weapons to defend themselves."

Admiral Nelson displayed a chart showing recent incursions where the Hostis ships entered human space in small numbers and attacked navy ships. The consensus was the Hostis were testing human defenses in preparation for a full-scale invasion. The Admiral showed a display of a Rim World.

"This is the furthest Rim World. The Hostis recently attacked the planet and killed everyone, including all the children. Unlike their approach during the war, the Hostis have not settled on the planet, and it appears they are waiting to see how we respond."

Thomas listened as the Admiral described the navy's charter that prevented the navy from directly providing military arms to civilians or civilian governments. Thomas saw the Admiral's problem. He knew what the Admiral was going to propose but wanted the Admiral to make the request. It is usually advantageous to have the other side make the first proposal in a negotiation, so Thomas did not respond.

"Are you willing to expand your trade to the Outer Planets to include the sale of arms to the planets with elected governments and to freedom fighters trying to overthrow dictatorships?" the Admiral asked. "This would increase the probability of humanity surviving a war with the Hostis. The Rim Worlds would be the first to face a Hostis invasion. If properly armed, they may weaken a Hostis armada to such a degree that the Outer Planets could stop them."

The Admiral explained how the navy had exclusive contracts with the arms manufacturers, preventing them from selling to other buyers without the navy's approval. Admiral Nelson said he would put the Demon on the approved list and provide contacts with the arms manufacturers.

"What is the markup," Thomas asked.

"The recommended markup is typically ten to one since there is no competition for advanced weaponry. It is dangerous for most ships delivering arms, but the Demon was built to military specifications. It should succeed where other ships have failed."

"If we accept, what is the plan?"

Admiral Nelson was solemn. "We would like you to start with the Outer Planets. Ideally, while selling them arms, we want you to convince them to join the Imperium. If they join, we will set up a military base on their planet and install a space-based planetary defense grid. If you succeed with the Outer Planets, we want you to try the same approach in the Rim."

First Officer Miller had not spoken during the entire meeting. Thomas realized he wanted his First Officer to respond as his uncle and give him advice. His uncle put a finger on his armband and tapped it twice. Thomas saw the message from his uncle. He looked straight at the Admiral.

"I will give you an answer in two days."

Admiral Nelson intentionally failed to tell Thomas that no Rim World would be invited to join the Imperium. The Core Planets believed the Rim was inhabited by savages and considered them to be less than human.

The Core Planets looked down on the Outer Planets but feared the Rim inhabitants. The Premier had a slight majority in the Senate which would support allowing Outer Planets to join the Imperium, but no one would consider accepting a Rim World.

Everyone knew the government sent the worst criminals to the Rim as the ultimate punishment. Parents told their children they would be sent to the Rim if they were bad. Most of the villains in the entertainment videos and games were portrayed as being from the Rim. The portrayal was reinforced since the physical appearance of many Rim Worlds inhabitants was outside the human norm. The variation in the sun resulted in adaptive changes in the eyes, hair, and skin. Descendants on Rim Worlds with lighter gravities became taller and slimmer. Descendants with heavier gravities became shorter, stronger, and bigger boned. Unfortunately, some perceptions were accurate. Pirates, marauders, and outlaws roamed throughout the Rim, but most inhabitants were just trying to survive in a harsh environment.

Presently, Admiral Nelson was more concerned with the survival of humanity and less concerned about differences within the human race. If the Hostis started another war, they needed to be stopped before reaching the Core Planets. Also, it was becoming more difficult to get the Imperium to approve funding to build enough ships to defeat the Hostis. He would try to stop the invaders at the Rim when the war came. If that failed, he hoped the Hostis could be defeated in the Outer Planets. Finally, if all else failed, he would make a last stand at the boundary of the Core Planets.

Private citizens were prohibited from owning lethal weapons on any Core Planet. Crime was minimal since video surveillance allowed for the immediate apprehension of lawbreakers. Admiral Nelson knew what only a few people knew. The peaceful Core Planets were utterly defenseless.

THE FOLLOWING DAY THOMAS called a meeting with his First Officer and Grayson to review the Admiral's proposal. Thomas knew he and his Uncle were thinking about how the income from such a venture would help Wilson Enterprises survive the recession. They knew Grayson was unaware of the financial difficulties facing their family business, and they had no intention of informing anyone outside the family. So, they waited to see how Grayson would respond to the proposal.

"I like the proposal," Grayson said but was thoughtful. "But there is a problem. You, the ship, and the crew need protection. A marine Sergeant was ordered to lead a squad of twelve marines in an attack against a civilian stronghold. He was successful in carrying out his orders. Afterward, the political climate changed. The Sergeant and all of his men were arrested and court-martialed. The commanding officer denied giving such an order. They sentenced the Sergeant to life in prison. The rest of the men in the squad were dishonorably discharged but avoided prison because the Sergeant said his men were simply following his orders."

Grayson looked at Thomas and saw he had made his point. "You need multiple documents to protect yourself, your crew, and your ship. You need a document executed by the Admiral and a pardon issued by the Premier. The documents should cover you and the entire crew for all past, present, and future acts. I would let the Admiral know this is a deal-breaker."

Grayson continued. "Once we have the documents and multiple copies distributed for safekeeping, we need to upgrade the ship at military expense. First, we need a completely equipped hospital with healing chambers and a qualified doctor. Second, we must upgrade the ship's offensive capacity with heavier-duty missiles. Third, we need to install two railguns to guard the ship's stern. Fourth, we should upgrade our cannons with larger energy units so each gun will have more power. You need to request military-grade armor for every person on the ship. Also, demand ten military-grade shuttles with full armament for delivering our cargo."

"Uncle Ralph, can you think of anything Grayson left out?" Thomas asked his First Officer and wanted a family answer.

First Officer Miller, with knitted brows and a severe expression, said, "What we are about to do will put the entire crew at greater risk. You are going to need their support. Therefore, they should be compensated for the additional risk. I suggest the crew receive double the normal pay for as long as we are in the arms business and explain the pay will return to normal should we decide to exit the business. We do not want anyone to say they had no choice. You should offer a severance package to anyone who wishes to leave the ship."

Thomas nodded. "I agree, and I propose we offer six months of salary to anyone who would like to resign."

Thomas contacted the Admiral and transmitted their non-negotiable terms. He included the Demon's structural specifications for the railguns. Admiral Nelson reviewed the communications from Captain Thomas Wilson and was impressed by the young Captain's forethought. He would secretly handle the political side.

THE ADMIRAL CALLED his senior staff together to discuss Captain Wilson's non-political requirements in a top-secret meeting. Their Chief Engineer disclosed there were railguns in their inventory they could install on the Demon by modifying the base of each gun. The Demon had reinforced beams and power cabling already in the ideal location for the railguns. He further stated how upgrading their weapons could be completed simultaneously with the installation of the railguns.

"The navy has excess stockpiles of heavy-duty missiles," the Ordnance Officer said. "The body armor is built in standard sizes for male and female users with some customization by adding or removing links. It would be routine to fit all of Demon's crew with a customized set of armor within a few days of their arrival at any of our ordnance storage facilities. We should submit a budget to provide the Demon with ten new shuttles, but I suggest we give the Demon ten of our used shuttles and keep the new ones for our use."

The Admiral nodded his head in complete agreement. "Make sure the used shuttles are in excellent condition."

Next, the Admiral addressed the installation and outfitting of a hospital aboard the Demon. Assistant Medical Officer Adler accompanied the Chief Medical Officer. The Chief Medical Officer said Adler had recently overseen the upgrade of the medical hospitals on nine of their Destroyers. Doctor Adler said the hospital installation would take slightly longer than the other modifications to the Demon unless they started work on the hospital immediately. She stated the more pressing issue would be finding an experienced medical staff to assign to the Demon.

"Send offers to our navy doctors who you think would take a temporary assignment on a civilian ship that would last for several years," the Admiral said. "The doctor should be someone you feel would be successful in reporting to a civilian captain. The potential candidate would continue to receive navy pay with no reduction in benefits. The time served on the Demon will count toward their navy retirement. Also, they will receive a salary from the Demon commensurate with a doctor serving aboard a civilian ship. Do you think you can find a suitable candidate with such an offer?"

"Sir, we do not have to look," Doctor Adler responded. "I will take the assignment. I have been in the navy for ten years. I am thirty-five and have been seriously considering whether I would reenlist in two years. The benefits are good, but the pay for a navy doctor is less than half what I could earn as a civilian doctor. Currently, I am the most qualified person for this assignment."

The Admiral looked with understanding at Doctor Adler. "The assignment is yours. Pack your bags, and report to the Demon. You will have immediate access to funds for the installation of the hospital."

THOMAS WAS SURPRISED when the Admiral responded ten cycles later, saying their requests had been approved. He was told a Doctor Adler was being delivered to the Demon to outfit his ship with a new hospital. She would be their Chief Medical Officer. Admiral Nelson stated the Demon would have to pay Doctor Adler the salary doctors receive when serving on a civilian ship.

Thomas called a meeting in the cargo bay for his entire crew. The crew members who could not leave their station listened on an open channel. Thomas explained they would attempt to sell off most of their existing cargo to free up space for the weapons they would deliver to certain Outer Planets and Rim Worlds. Most were disinterested until Thomas mentioned how everyone would receive double their pay rate because of the increased risk of being a gun runner. Thomas answered a few questions after his presentation. The crew supported the decision, especially after hearing about double pay. It helped that morale throughout the ship was high because of the two previous battles. Thomas finished the meeting by offering a six-month severance and a letter of recommendation to anyone wishing to resign.

The Demon needed to make room in the cargo bay for the arms they would buy. Therefore, they would stop only to sell cargo and spend minimal time at each location. Thomas was surprised no one took the severance offer. The Demon returned to Arabath to sell products that various buyers had requested. Thomas hoped the same buyer who had previously purchased their computer chips might be in the market for additional chips.

While the Demon was still docking, Thomas received confirmation from the chip buyer on Arabath. They wanted another ten containers of universal chips at the same price. The payment had already been submitted to prevent the Demon from seeking other bids. To speed up the sale of additional products, the Demon put a set discounted price of twenty percent on the entire cargo with no negotiations, with two exceptions. Power supply units were only discounted ten percent since they were in high demand and required little space. The universal chips were excluded from the discount since they were already attractively priced. Each container would be sold to the first buyer to show up at the dock with payment. All buyers were required to arrange for immediate pick up of their orders. The Demon would not be responsible for delivery, and the sales came in rapid order. There was already a crowd of merchants when they docked. Thomas notified the crew there would be no shore leave until all the purchased cargo was offloaded.

CHAPTER 9 NEW PREGNANT CREW MEMBER

Suzanna was seven months pregnant and still working every day at the restaurant, even when she struggled just to get out of bed. She continued to watch the daily schedule of ships arriving at the station. This morning Suzanna was only half awake when she stopped in front of the monitor showing the schedule of arriving and departing ships. She hoped to see the Familia Primum, but it was not on the list. She was leaving when she saw the Demon. The Demon had arrived during the night. She was suddenly wide awake as she considered the possibility of getting on the Demon.

She rushed to the restaurant, accosted Terrell, and told her the Demon was at the station. Suzanna had told Terrell all the intimate details of how she had met Thomas, the Captain of the Demon.

"I have to get on that ship," Suzanna exclaimed as tears flowed down her face. "It is my last chance, but Thomas may not want to see me after I failed to show up for our dinner date. Also, if he lets me on the ship and sees me in my condition, he may not let me stay on the ship. Look at me. I do not have anything decent to wear since I have outgrown everything I own. The only clothes I can fit into are my restaurant uniforms left behind by a former employee."

"Let's worry about one thing at a time," Terrell said as she took hold of Suzanna's hands. "First, we are going shopping for a nice outfit, and it will not be at the Cheap Clothes for a Cheap Price Store. I know a place with good clothes at a reasonable price. As soon as we get off work, we will find you the perfect outfit."

Terrell was true to her word. They found an acceptable outfit they could afford by pooling both of their small savings. The next morning, they both got up early. Terrell helped Suzanna with her hair and loaned her a pair of shoes with short heels. Terrell said a silent prayer as Suzanna left their small apartment and headed toward the docks.

The Demon was at Dock 18, and Suzanna was nervous as she approached the ship. She went up to a Demon cargo handler and asked to speak to Captain Wilson.

"Is the Captain expecting you?" The cargo handler asked.

"No, he is not expecting me, but tell him it is Suzanna. We met when he was here seven months ago. Tell him I am the lady from the Familia Primum, and he gave me a tour of his ship."

After a brief wait, the cargo handler informed her that someone would escort her to the Captain. It was not long before a female yeoman arrived.

"Please follow me. How do you know the Captain?"

"We met seven months ago on his last visit to Arabath," Suzanna responded. "He gave me a tour of the Demon."

"Oh, I remember. There are no secrets on a ship, we all knew about the tour, and I heard it was a complete tour." Suzanna rolled her eyes and figured there was no reason to deny the obvious.

"Yes, it was a grand tour, including a visit to the Captain's cabin."

The yeoman glanced at Suzanna. "Have far along, are you?"

"Seven months," Suzanna replied.

The yeoman looked straight ahead with twinkling eyes and a small smile as she whispered. "Never a dull moment on the Demon."

Suzanna arrived at the Captain's Ready Room. Captain Thomas and three officers were discussing the disposition of cargo. The Captain looked up and saw Suzanna. All conversation ceased.

The Captain looked around and asked everyone to take a short break. The Officers took the hint and left the room, giving Suzanna and the Captain their privacy.

The Captain stood up and asked Suzanna to sit down. He asked if she would like something to drink. She asked for a cup of water. Once they were both seated, Suzanna decided it was best to tell the truth. She told how she visited a farm, was drugged, and did not wake up for two days, which was why she missed seeing him for dinner. Suzanna explained how the two lost days resulted in the Familia Primum leaving without her. She described how she had worked as a restaurant server for the past seven months while waiting for the Familiar Primum to return.

"Captain, I do not want my child to be born a grounder. I want to become a member of your crew. I am a trained cargo specialist, but I will take any job on the ship. Also, worst case, the Demon is bound to meet up with the Familia Primum, and then I can transfer off your ship. Please, I will get on my knees and beg, but I may need help to get up." Then she stopped talking.

"Of course, you can become a crew member," Thomas said. "Understand, we are only selling cargo on this stop, so we will not be here for long."

Thomas pulled up a screen. "I am assigning you to Cabin D54. It is on the same floor as the hospital and the bridge. I would suggest you go to the station and gather your belongings. You should hurry. There will not be much time to move into your cabin before we leave the station."

The Captain made a call and escorted her outside the Ready Room. The same yeoman was waiting for her. Thomas explained how Suzanna was now a crew member. Thomas asked the yeoman to assist Suzanna in settling into her assigned cabin. Suzanna left with the yeoman.

"We need to stop by ship's stores for bedding, accessories for your cabin, and any other items you would like. Then you can go ashore and grab your personal items."

"There is no way I am getting off this ship," Suzanna replied. "I will have a friend of mine bring me my belongings." Suzanna contacted Terrell and told her the good news.

"Do you mind bringing my belongings to the ship? I do not want to risk getting off the ship and being left behind again."

"I am so happy for you. Of course, I will bring your stuff."

The person in charge of the ship's stores helped her establish a personal account. She received a complete cartload of items on credit which would be deducted from her pay. She had finished putting everything away in her cabin when Terrell sent her a message that she had arrived at the gate. Suzanna met Terrell at the entry to the ship and received two bags containing her items. They hugged each other and cried as they said their goodbyes.

The ship left port, with Suzanna safely secured in her room when the ship jumped. She had tears rolling down her face again. But, this time, it was because she was happy. She was relieved for both her and her unborn child.

A FEW DAYS LATER, THOMAS was with Grayson reviewing the proposed engineering design for the railguns when Thomas kept noticing Grayson smiling at him.

"What is going on with the smiling?" Thomas finally asked.

"Well, you know the crew likes to gossip," Grayson said with a grin. "They are all talking about the new crew member you just hired. You were in Arabath seven months ago, and Suzanna is seven months pregnant. So, everyone figures she is carrying your child and used the unborn child to force you to hire her. Anyway, the crew is having a lot of fun discussing the matter."

Thomas was dismayed. "I hired her because I felt sorry for her, but I think she can be a valuable member of our crew."

Grayson grinned again. "If you say so."

Occasionally Thomas would see Suzanna and nod his head in greeting. It was only a few days before they would dock at their next destination. Thomas was eating at a table by himself when Suzanna came over and sat down across from him. Her arms were resting on top of her belly.

"Captain, I am only a few weeks away from having my child. There are no baby items in the ship's stores. I need to go ashore and buy quite a few items. I would like your approval for an advance against my pay so I can go shopping for baby supplies." Thomas hesitated, and Suzanna was afraid he was going to say no.

"I have a proposition," Thomas said. "I will transfer ten thousand credits from my personal account to your account. It will be completely free to you. The only requirement is if anyone asks, you will tell them I am not the father of your child."

"You are going to give me ten thousand credits, and that is all I have to do?" Suzanna said with a grin. "You have a deal."

"Our next port is dangerous, so I want you to take four guards on your shopping trip," Thomas said and excused himself.

Once Thomas had exited the cafeteria, Suzanna put her hands in the air and shouted. "Yes!"

A female officer was walking past and asked why she was so excited.

"The Captain just gave me ten thousand credits to go baby shopping. All I have to do is tell everyone he is not the father of m baby."

The female officer shook her head. "Men are such pigs."

"I saw a pig," Suzanna replied. "That was not a complime They both laughed.

"Oh, the Captain said I can go shopping, but he insisted I have four bodyguards."

"My name is Shelly. If the Captain requested it, that means overtime, and guard duty means hazard pay. I want to be one of your guards."

She then looked around the room. "Chris, Hector, Debra, do you want to serve as guards so Suzanna can go shopping at our next port. You will be looking at overtime plus hazard pay."

They all wanted to be Suzanna's guards since they would receive three times their pay rate, which had already doubled because of the arms deal. At six times their original pay, they were all in. They agreed to meet Suzanna in the shuttle bay after they docked, and the ship was secure. After Suzanna left, Shelly explained how Suzanna had just received ten thousand credits and the stipulation for the credits. Now, they knew. There was no longer any doubt that Thomas was the father. The crew is family, and family members like to gossip. Several females joked and said they would happily have Thomas' child for ten thousand credits. Every crew member had taken a sneak view of the Captain's cabin and the oversized bed. Most of the females on the Demon had been hoping Thomas would invite them to share his bed since they privately joked it was too big for just one person.

The ship achieved orbit without incident. The planet did not have a space station. Therefore, all trade would be handled by shuttle. Suzanna met her guards in the shuttle bay, and they asked a shuttle pilot to give them a ride to the planet. When they explained what they were doing, the female pilot decided she would also put in for overtime and hazard pay.

Once they landed, the pilot helped with the shopping rather than lounge around the landing pub. They were soon buying whatever they thought Suzanna's new baby would need. They enjoyed helping Suzanna shop. They bought gifts for the baby using

their accounts. They were all carrying packages by the end of the day. The stores helped by delivering the larger items to the shuttle. They were happy when they boarded the shuttle and returned to the ship. Unknown to Suzanna, others from the Demon were also buying baby items, including Thomas.

SUZANNA MADE FRIENDS throughout the ship, and her child would be the first birth on the Demon. The crew even prepared an empty room in the cargo area as a playroom. They all wanted to help watch the baby while Suzanna worked. It also provided space for all the toys the crew had purchased for the baby.

Throughout the following weeks, Suzanna held up her part of the agreement. At every opportunity, she quickly said the Captain was not the father of her baby. It became a joke, and nearly every time she met a crew member, they would say, "Yes, we know, the Captain is not the father of your child." Then they would grin and often laugh.

When the delivery time for the baby was getting close, Suzanna went to see the Captain.

"Captain, my baby is due in a few days, and I was wondering if you would mind being with me during the delivery. I am a little scared. I would just feel safer if you were there."

"I would be honored to be there when your child is born. Have Doctor Adler contact me when it is time."

Doctor Adler assured Thomas they could handle the birth of a child even though the hospital was only partially completed. She did not tell him they did not have the birthing electronics to stimulate the brain's pleasure centers during the labor.

Thomas spent several days reading about the birthing process and newly born infants. He thought his participation was a secret, but a ship has few secrets. Gossip was just another form of entertainment.

When Doctor Adler contacted Thomas, he was on the bridge.

"Looks like everything is running smoothly," Thomas said. "I need to take care of some personal business, and I will be back in a few minutes."

The bridge officers kept a straight face until the Captain left the bridge and the door slid shut behind him. The few minutes turned into eleven hours.

Thomas was there when the baby finally came. Doctor Adler cleaned up the baby. Suzanna named the baby Amanda. The Doctor laid the baby on top of a small blanket, and the baby was crying. Thomas went over to Amanda. He wrapped the blanket snuggly around her and picked her up. He held her firmly against his chest, and she stopped crying. Suzanna and the Doctor looked over to see why the baby had stopped crying.

"Well, it seems the baby knows its father," Doctor Adler said. Thomas glanced at Suzanna, and Suzanna looked at the Doctor.

"Thomas is not the father," she said.

"You don't pay someone ten thousand credits to tell the truth," Doctor Adler said.

"You know about the payment?" Thomas asked with a surprised expression.

"The entire ship knows about the payment."

Thomas gave Amanda to Suzanna so she could nurse. Then the baby fell asleep. Thomas excused himself and went to his cabin to sleep. He slept well. The following morning, Thomas checked on Suzanna and Amanda before going to the bridge. When he arrived, the baby was in the crib crying. Thomas picked up Amanda, and she ceased crying. He enjoyed holding Amanda, and Amanda liked being held by him. Suzanna saw the two were getting along quite well.

Suzanna had several coconspirators who let her know when Thomas was coming to the hospital. Amanda was already spoiled and just liked to be constantly held. Before Thomas arrived, Suzanna would put Amanda in the crib, and she would be crying when Thomas entered the hospital. Suzanna told Thomas the truth. She was exhausted from nursing every couple of hours. Then she would ask if he would be a dear and pick up Amanda. On subsequent visits, Thomas would simply pick up the crying Amanda and hold her until she fell asleep.

Amanda learned quickly. Crying resulted in being picked up, and she loved being held. On the fifth day, Thomas was holding Amanda in the ship's hospital when he was needed on the bridge. It was late First Watch, so he took Amanda with him. When Thomas entered the bridge, all the officers stopped what they were doing. They all wanted to see the newest crew member. Several officers wanted to hold Amanda, but Thomas said they needed to wait until she was older.

Later, Thomas and Amanda fell asleep while Thomas was seated in his Captain's chair. When the Middle Watch entered the bridge, everyone was quiet so they would not wake the Captain or the baby. A couple of hours into Middle Watch, Suzanna came to the bridge. When she saw Amanda and Thomas asleep, she knew, without a doubt, that she was in love with both of them. Suzanna gently picked up Amanda without waking Thomas and returned to her hospital bed. She was still a little weak but was getting better each day. She could have returned to her cabin after the first day, but she would be alone. Doctor Adler agreed it would be best to stay a few extra days in the hospital.

Thomas woke up later and went to his cabin. He woke up at his usual time and met with the Night Watch for a brief meeting before First Watch took over. Then, he went to the hospital to see Suzanna and Amanda. Doctor Adler said Suzanna should be fine to return to her cabin the next day.

Thomas picked up Amanda, and she stopped crying. Of course, Suzanna had just put Amanda in the baby crib before he arrived. Thomas had a thoughtful expression as he held Amanda.

"Instead of moving into your cabin, why don't you and Amanda temporarily move into my cabin? It will not mean anything. It will just be until Amanda stops crying."

"That would be great," Suzanna said with no hesitation. "I am still tired all the time, and as you say, it is just until Amanda stops crying."

Amanda had fallen asleep, so Thomas gently put her in the crib and returned to the bridge. The Doctor had overheard the exchange from the next room and went in to check on Suzanna.

"When do you think Amanda will stop crying?" Doctor Adler asked.

"When she becomes an officer," Suzanna said with a grin. The Doctor chuckled and nodded her head.

"I will get some help, and we will get you settled into your new accommodations."

Suzanna was excited about sharing the Captain's cabin and still impressed by its size. She was so thankful to be back on a ship. If not for the Demon showing up when it did and Thomas accepting her on board, she would still be waiting tables. Suzanna knew she would not return to her former ship. She had no intention of leaving the Demon or Thomas. The Demon was her and Amanda's home.

SEVERAL MONTHS LATER, Thomas visited the hospital and asked Doctor Adler if he could meet with her confidentially. They went into her office and shut the door.

The Doctor, with a professional expression, asked? "What are your symptoms?"

Thomas was a little embarrassed. "No, I am okay. I just have a question. Suppose a female has sex with one male in the morning. Then, she has sex with another male later on the same day, and she has a child. Hypothetically, is there a chance the child's father could be the first male?"

"Sperm can stay alive in the uterus for up to five days. Would you like me to run a test to determine if Amanda is your biological daughter?"

"No, it will not be necessary. I am sorry to have wasted your time. Amanda is and always will be, my daughter." Thomas decided he would go to the bridge and do something useful.

The Doctor watched Thomas leave, and while she still had some concerns about his lack of experience, her overall opinion of the Captain had just increased.

Thomas, Suzanna, and Amanda settled comfortably into their new arrangement. Thomas and Suzanna spent increased time together taking care of Amanda. They talked about everything. Thomas learned all about Suzanna's life aboard the Familia Primum. At the same time, Suzanna learned about Thomas's life as a grounder and how the ship acquired its name.

Suzanna regained her strength and returned to work full time. Amanda got used to being held by everyone. That was not a problem since there was no shortage of offers from the crew to hold her. Many crew members would come by during their free time to spend time with Amanda while Suzanna worked.

As they woke each morning, they had a procedure where Thomas would take the first shower while Suzanna watched Amanda. Then they would switch. The three of them would then have breakfast together in the ship's cafeteria.

AT NIGHT, THOMAS WOULD work in their cabin at a built-in desk routed through the ship's systems. He would typically come to bed after Suzanna was already asleep. He enjoyed watching both Amanda and Suzanna as they slept.

Thomas would watch Suzanna from the corner of his eye when she came out of the shower. Suzanna would smile when she occasionally caught Thomas watching her as she dressed in sleepwear, she had recently purchased just for him.

Day after day, Thomas continued to work at his desk when Suzanna would get into bed. He felt she was so beautiful and sexy when she slipped between the covers. Thomas found it harder each night to concentrate on work. He would wait for Suzanna to go to sleep before easing into bed. He was also the first to awaken each morning. He would ease out of bed and take a cold shower.

Suzanna wondered if Thomas no longer found her attractive since he had not made any sexual moves toward her. She had been sexually active since she was sixteen and enjoyed sex. She was attracted to Thomas, both sexually and romantically. He had an animal magnetism she found irresistible. At nineteen, she was full of energy and passion.

One night as she came out of the shower, Thomas was standing next to the bed.

"How are you feeling?" He asked.

"I feel good," Suzanna replied.

"How good?" Thomas asked.

Suzanna grinned and ran into his arms. She helped Thomas discard his clothes. They slid into bed underneath the sheet and thin blanket. It was always a little cold on the ship, but now they were both on fire as their passion gave them all the heat they needed.

Suzanna was the happiest she had ever been. She took Amanda with her to work each day. Also, Amanda was happy and spoiled. She enjoyed playing with the crew, and they loved spending time with her.

CHAPTER 10 SHIP UPGRADES

The Demon was selling off their cargo at a good pace, plus acquiring exports at excellent prices. Suzanna was proving to be a tremendous help. She had spent her entire life helping her parents manage the cargo and trade negotiations on the Familiar Primum. Without being asked, she showed up in the cargo bay each day and helped where there was a need. She was adept at finding multiple buyers for their inventory. She located excess products available at their stops that were in high demand on other planets. Her most significant adjustment was realizing the Demon had the credits to buy huge quantities of valued cargo and obtain volume discounts. Volume discounts had never been an option for the Familia Primum.

She enjoyed working with the other crew members and shopping for the best deals. When she was younger, her father commented how she was a natural negotiator. On the Familia Primum, she would have continued to be an assistant to her parents. Receiving a promotion would be a sad event because it would mean her parents would either be dead or unable to handle the work.

Suzanna looked forward to each day and liked the energy level of the young crew. The crew took turns watching Amanda, and several females talked about having their own children. It was not long before she was the de facto cargo supervisor due to her knowledge and experience.

On a slow day, she would have someone watch Amanda, and there were always plenty of volunteers since she continued to be the only child on board. On the slow days, she would contact Thomas to see if he was overly busy. It was her way of asking him if he had time to meet in their cabin for some personal private time. At night they spent a lot of time attending to Amanda. While they still took time for each other at night, it was just more fun when they could get together during the middle of Day Watch.

Suzanna was so in love with Thomas that she could not imagine any other life. He had such a drive and was excited about everything. She loved him even more, knowing he loved Amanda. The three of them would meet in the cafeteria for nearly every meal. At night, she never tired of watching Thomas on the floor playing with Amanda.

THOMAS LOOKED OVER the inventory and realized he still had three containers of universal chips. He thought about the Familia Primum and wondered if they would purchase the remaining containers. They paid for the two containers purchased on account in less than nine standard months. He did not mind doing business with the Familia Primum remotely. In contrast, he wanted to avoid direct contact with the Familia Primum since he did not want Suzanna to return to her home ship and take Amanda with her.

Thomas took his First Officer into his confidence. Under no condition was the Demon to be in a port at the same time as the Familia Primum. He sent a coded message to the Familia Primum and asked if they would like to purchase some more Universal Chips at the same price as their previous purchase. Several days later, he received a response. They would be delighted to buy two more containers and pay in advance.

Captain Javier, in his correspondence, said Suzanna's parents were wondering if she was doing well. Thomas sent videos of both Suzanna and Amanda. He also said he would leave the chips at their next stop. The containers would be insured and held in the station's secured storage depot. Captain Javier of the Familia Primum viewed the videos and saw the baby's name was Amanda Wilson.

SEVERAL WEEKS LATER, the Familia Primum arrived at the station to pick up their order. There were three containers with a message saying three for the price of two. It was signed by Captain Wilson.

As soon as Captain Javier returned to the Familia Primum, he called a staff meeting with his senior officers, including Suzanna's parents. He said the meeting was to honor Suzanna. He reiterated how two containers of universal chips were sold to them on consignment without a down payment resulting in the greatest profit they had ever achieved.

Captain Javier explained how the profit on the one order had allowed them to replace the impulse engines, overhaul the jump engines, refinish the outside of the hull, and replace obsolete components throughout the ship. He spoke to the entire staff while looking at Suzanna's parents.

"We owe all this to Suzanna, who saw opportunity where no one else looked. We purchased two more containers of Universal Chips, but Captain Wilson gave us a third container for free. After we sell these chips, we will have the funds to handle a higher, more profitable level of cargo. You are certainly wondering why Captain Wilson is so generous." A picture of a baby was projected with the baby's name superimposed at the bottom.

"This is why Captain Wilson is so generous. He thinks like family. Everyone on board knows our ship's name means Family is First. That is our motto. Suzanna has provided an example of what it means. Suzanna has not only saved us, but she has guaranteed our future. Her name will be permanently engraved on the wall of the bridge stating how she represents the best of our family. Her accomplishments will be recorded and be required reading for all future generations of the Familia Primum."

Until now, only the names of the ship's previous captains were engraved on the bridge underneath the words Familia Primum. Captain Javier poured a small amount of rare bourbon into each glass, and they toasted Suzanna as the most outstanding family member of all time.

A living legend is much better than the truth of what actually happened. No one on board knew of the seven months Suzanna spent working as a server or the luck that resulted in her being on the Demon. Of course, Suzanna was unaware of her honored position, and her reputation would continue to grow without her knowledge.

Everyone on board the Familia Primum was looking forward to the next Gathering of the family ships where the Familia Primum would be the envy of all the other ships.

THE DEMON SOLD OFF over eighty percent of its remaining inventory before making a jump to the closest navy depot designated by Admiral Nelson.

At their last port, the Demon picked up the balance of the hospital equipment ordered by Doctor Adler. The purchase included four state-of-the-art healing chambers. Contractors boarded the Demon with the equipment and installed it while the ship was in transit to the depot. Doctor Adler hired three medical assistants and assigned one assistant to each shift. The assistant for Day Watch had served one tour of duty with the navy and had field experience handling emergency combat injuries. The other two assistants were younger but had graduated near the top of their respective classes. Also, they both had experience in emergency medical facilities assisting with surgeries.

Doctor Adler sent a message to Admiral Nelson, letting him know her hospital would be one hundred percent completed when the ship was ready to depart on its first mission for the navy. The contractors working on modifying the hospital and installing the equipment referred to Doctor Adler as a tyrant. They were looking forward to finishing the job and getting off the Demon. Otherwise, they all agreed the hospital was a state-of-the-art facility and would compare favorably to the best ground-based hospitals.

Upon arrival, multiple naval contractors promptly started work on their assigned projects to upgrade the Demon's armaments. The work proceeded smoothly, and the Demon's engineers informed Thomas the quality of the work was excellent.

The railguns were installed in record time since the ship was designed for such installation. The railguns used an advanced electromagnetic force to launch high-velocity projectiles. The speed would surpass all other weapon arrays with cluster munitions. The projectiles would detonate prior to impact to cover a wide area of destruction. The only defense was to use evasive action to avoid being hit. Only the very strongest shield could survive an impact from a railgun. On the negative side, a railgun took a long time to recharge, and typically it could only be fired once in a battle unless it was an extended conflict involving multiple ships.

Thomas had an additional modification made to the ship. He had six fake but realistic torpedo tubes added to the exterior of the Demon. There was no possibility of installing additional torpedo tubes since there was no physical space inside the ship for such installation. Still, it would appear the Demon had eight torpedo tubes instead of just two. He had the contractors install electronic equipment to simulate when the fake torpedoes had a lock on an opposing ship. The electronics took up very little space. The deception would not hold up against an inspection by an engineer, but it would fool the average spacer.

Grayson informed Thomas he was delighted with the used shuttles they received. All ten shuttles had been recently overhauled, and all the systems were operational. Each shuttle was armed with two rapid-fire 25mm Mag Guns mounted in the front and controlled by the pilot. A pulse cannon requiring a gunner was mounted on top of the shuttle with a full 360-degree rotation. These guns would be effective in the event of an attack while delivering or returning with cargo. The military shuttles would require a complement of a pilot, copilot, and gunner. Finding gunners would not be a problem since every marine on the Demon volunteered and competed against each other in simulations for the positions.

While the upgrades were taking place, the crew was fitted with military-grade personal armor while being trained in the proper use and maintenance of the armor. Once all the upgrades were completed, Admiral Nelson provided the coordinates for the two arms suppliers.

WHILE THEY WERE ON the way to the first arms supplier, Suzanna knew she had a lot to learn about buying and selling weapons. Her parents always stressed: know your sellers, know your buyers, know the market, and the product. There were usually multiple suppliers for the same or equivalent products. It was critical to understand the minor differences between comparable products to determine how the price for buying or selling might be affected by the differences. Sometimes, a low-quality product might be exactly right for a specific need, but only the highest quality would work for another.

Her parents taught her to determine quickly the level of interest a buyer may have in various products to keep from wasting her time. She still remembered wasting a day with a charming young buyer. Throughout the day, he acted interested in making a purchase when all he wanted was for her to join him for drinks after her shift ended. She watched her parents and learned from every transaction. Plus, they let her learn from experience by slowly letting her handle more of the business. She knew professional buyers and sellers were good, or they did not last long. Transactions between professionals usually took less time because there was less wasted time posturing.

Suzanna studied the inventory listed for the arms available at the two suppliers they would visit. She started meeting daily with Grayson, who answered all her questions. She wanted to know the types and volume of arms they should buy. She learned the best arms for a marine might be the worst weapons for a civilian. She questioned Jackson and other marines on the ship, getting their opinions. She then prepared proposed purchase orders for each supplier and submitted them to Thomas.

Thomas reviewed Suzanna's proposals and compared them against the purchases recommended by the Admiral. He sent copies of both proposals to Grayson, Jackson, and his First Officer. Thomas asked them to review the proposed purchase orders and meet with him the following morning to finalize the order. Thomas informed Suzanna of the meeting and asked her to attend.

Everyone arrived at the meeting early and got a cup of coffee before taking a seat. Grayson walked over to Suzanna. "Well done," he whispered.

Everyone took a seat around the table, and Thomas opened the meeting.

"You were all asked to review the proposed purchase orders and provide me with suggested changes. Grayson, I would like to start with you."

Grayson projected a display on the wall. "Overall, Suzanna has the better proposal, but I would recommend adding four attack helicopters, doubling the number of the handheld missile launchers, selling all of our ship's stock of rifles, and replacing them with the guns shown at the bottom of the list. Otherwise, Suzanna has done an excellent job, and I recommend we go with her proposal subject to the changes shown."

"Does anyone else have any suggestions?" Thomas waited a few minutes, but there was no response.

"Well then, we will proceed with Suzanna's recommendation as amended by Grayson. Thank you for attending. Suzanna, I need to speak with you about another matter before returning to the bridge."

After everyone else had left, Thomas went to Suzanna and hugged her. He followed up with a passionate kiss. After the kiss, Thomas thanked her for the work she had done. Thomas regretted saying he had to return to the bridge.

THE DEMON JUMPED TO each location and purchased the weapons for their designated customers. As suggested by Grayson, all the ship's existing handheld guns and rifles were swapped out and sold at a discount. The weapons for use onboard the ship would not damage the hull. However, they could swap the ammunition for use on a planet. The marines purchased high-caliber semiautomatic rifles, which could be adjusted to full auto. After the swap, the ship was equipped with the best handheld firearms currently available. Plus, they still had the container of weapons they had kept after the mutiny. They installed additional lockers to secure the guns when not in use.

The ship was loaded with containers of weapons and ready to make its first delivery. Thomas was pleased with the arms to be sold and in outfitting the ship with better handheld firearms. The firearms would be needed at the various ports of call when going ashore or if they needed to repel boarders. Thomas liked some of the advanced weapons he saw at the armory. Grayson successfully advised Thomas against changing his mind and purchasing some of the highly sophisticated weapons. The units were too complicated for the average person. Grayson explained to Thomas how the best civilian weapon is one a novice can use with little training.

With the Captain's approval, Grayson and Jackson continued to hire additional men and women who had served in the military. They used the team concept with two-way communications instead of strictly downward. The new military hires were well trained and knew how to follow orders. Being young, they could adjust to the idea their suggestions would be considered. They soon realized that, unlike the military, their employment could be terminated if they failed to put forth the necessary effort. The hires reporting to Grayson were called marines even though Damon was a civilian ship. Grayson, with Jackson assisting, interviewed and hired the best candidates from numerous applicants. Most of the hires were excellent and enthusiastically took to their new positions. They were impressed with the Demon and liked the double pay.

Thomas inspected all the installations and modifications to the ship. Doctor Adler gave Thomas a tour of the completed hospital at his request. She expressed satisfaction with the completed medical facility and the hospital's capabilities.

Doctor Adler knew it was important for a Captain to know what a hospital could do in the event of an emergency. She started with the most crucial equipment.

"The healing chambers are the newest state-of-the-art units using advanced nanites," she explained. "A chamber can repair any organ in the body by replicating the healthy cells. It can regrow limbs such as a leg, arm, finger, or ear. The only shortcoming is that it has to have a healthy cell to replicate. Also, while it can replicate brain cells, it cannot replace memories, so if the brain is severely damaged, the AI in the unit will not repair the rest of the body. So, the healing chamber cannot clone a complete person. Plus, cloning is illegal. If a person's body is severely injured, the patient may die since the unit still depends on the patient's body and mind to fight for survival. Also, healing chambers are responsible for extending the life expectancy in the Core."

Thomas was duly impressed. "Thank you for the explanation. These units are available throughout the Core Planets. Why is this technology not available to the Outer Planets and the Rim?"

"I don't know," Doctor Adler said. "That is a political question or maybe just a trade or economic issue. The healing chambers are quite expensive, and the manufacturers control the production. My job is to provide the best medical care available for this ship. Now, let me show you the rest of the recent upgrades."

Thomas was pleased with the hospital tour but was still troubled that the healing chambers and other advanced medical technologies were unavailable outside the Core Planets. He had been shocked to see people with missing limbs. Limbs could be regrown at any medical facility on the Core Planets, and no one was denied medical care. As the doctor had explained, bodies still age, but the life expectancy in the Core was nearing two hundred years.

Thomas was also impressed with Doctor Adler's assistants. They all took their jobs seriously, and he felt comfortable with the medical care available for the crew. He was hopeful the hospital would see little use except for routine evaluations and checkups to see the crew met expected health standards. Further, Dr. Adler and one of her staff had additional certifications in mental evaluations, which could be helpful in monitoring symptoms in stressful situations. Too high a stress level on a ship could affect ship performance and morale. The Doctor could also conduct psych evaluations to screen crew applicants to see if they could adapt to life on a spaceship. It was good to know the Doctor would monitor the crew's physical and mental health.

Doctor Adler accepted her responsibility for monitoring the health conditions throughout the ship, and she set up a schedule for routine checkups for the crew. She was a navy doctor who had served in combat. She knew you had to be prepared for emergencies where response time was critical in saving lives.

CHAPTER 11 GUNS BLAZING

A standard year had passed since his first meeting with the Admiral. The ship's upgrades were complete, and Thomas was ready to proceed under his agreement with the navy. The Demon's first arms delivery would be to an Outer Planet called Raina. A Stargate in the system allowed ships without jump capability to visit the planet. Thomas would not use the Stargate since the Demon would be at a disadvantage if enemy ships were waiting for them as they exited the gate. The Demon came out of jump a few seconds early at battle stations. The shields were up as they headed toward the planet.

Thomas directed the helmsman to pass near the Stargate, but not too close. The Stargate was approximately two standard astronomical units from the planet. As they neared the Stargate, five ships were waiting to attack any ship that might come through the gate. One ship launched a missile at the Demon, but their particle beam cannons destroyed it at long range. Thomas communicated shipwide and congratulated the gunner. Thomas told his Tactical Officer to take out the offending ship but not to waste ammunition. The Demon launched four missiles, and the enemy ship exploded.

Thomas directed his Communications Officer to contact the four remaining ships on an open channel.

"This is Captain Wilson of the Demon. You should spread the word. Any ship firing upon the Demon will be destroyed. Any ship approaching the Demon without first seeking authorization will be destroyed. Any ship following us without authorization will be destroyed. Any ship making a hostile act against the Demon will be sent to hell. The ship that fired at the Demon was with your group, and you are all guilty by association. Therefore, you will immediately leave this system using the Stargate or be destroyed. The last ship to leave this system will be destroyed."

None of the opposing ships made any motion to leave. Thomas directed his Helmsman to head toward the ships and told his Tactical Officers to direct all weapons toward the nearest ship but to hold fire. As the Demon approached the nearest ship, it turned toward the gate and accelerated at maximum speed. It was slow compared to the Demon, but Thomas let it escape. The Demon turned to the next ship, but the vessel immediately decided to follow the prior ship. Suddenly, all four ships fled toward the Stargate since none of them wanted to be the last ship leaving and risk destruction. Once all four ships had left, the Demon turned and resumed its approach to the planet. The ship remained at battle stations.

The Demon maneuvered into an orbit around Raina and contacted the government center. They patched Thomas through to General Atkinson. Thomas informed General Atkinson the Demon had supplies that could benefit a government elected by the people. He sent the General a list of their inventory with a price list. The General was highly interested in purchasing the type of supplies the Demon was selling and said he would have an order ready by the following morning. Thomas told the General that one ship at the Stargate had been destroyed, and the remaining four ships had left the system. The General explained the embargo created by the five ships had become a grave issue since they depended on certain imports to maintain the planet. He asked if Thomas would be interested in purchasing any of their processed rare-earth elements. Thomas said he would be interested, depending upon the type of elements and the price.

Suzanna woke up during Night Watch and could not get back to sleep. She eased out of bed and sat down at their cabin desk. She reviewed the inventory list of rare earth elements sent to the ship by General Atkinson. She noted a market existed for all the items on the list. She searched the ship's files for Core Planets importing various rare earth elements and prepared a proposed purchase order for approval by Thomas. She finally felt sleepy and checked on Amanda before returning to bed.

Thomas woke up, took a shower, and dressed. Suzanna had worked late and was still sound asleep. Amanda was moving about, so Thomas took care of her. Thomas took Amanda with him as he left the cabin and headed to the bridge.

Thomas put Amanda in her seat on the bridge so she could watch videos. Engineering designed Amanda's seat, and maintenance installed it. Thomas reviewed the entries from Middle Watch and Night Watch. He found a sizable Purchase Order from General Atkinson had arrived during Night Watch. Before leaving, the Night Watch Deck Officer informed him the order had been pulled and was available for loading onto the shuttles. His Night Watch was giving the Day Watch some serious competition. Thomas also saw a recommended detailed offer for the planet's rare earth elements. He wondered how Suzanna had found time to prepare the offer. She had countered the asking price with a reduced offer for several elements. He forwarded the purchase order to the General.

General Atkinson had provided coordinates for a landing east of the city. The landing site for the shuttles would be a safe distance from the location controlled by the enemy. Once the shuttles landed, the General would send a convoy of vehicles to pick up the containers. He explained the enemy was well armed with portable surface-to-air missiles, but the location selected should be free of enemy combatants.

The planet was covered with lush forests that benefited from the daily rains and the perfect sunlight. The Demon completed a scan of the area and confirmed the enemy was in an industrial warehouse section at the western perimeter of the city. Unfortunately, civilian homes were located nearby.

Thomas met with Commander Grayson and Lieutenant Commander Jackson to decide upon a strategy. Grayson had created ten squads. Each squad had five members, with one member serving as Squad Leader. The ten squads were created to match the ten military shuttles. Each squad was assigned a shuttle pilot and gunner. Grayson planned to quadruple the number of marines, but that was for the future. Also, for the future, he needed to add a trained copilot to each shuttle. The planned mission would pull fifty-three members of the crew off the ship. This would put the ship at a disadvantage in the event of an attack. Therefore, they would move all gunners to Day Watch and start the mission at the beginning of the Watch. All gunners would stay at their posts until they completed the mission. Each gunner would be relieved for short breaks but would otherwise remain at their post.

The enemy at the western warehouse location was a significant threat. They could attack the city at an inopportune time. Thomas worried the enemy would attack while the Demon was making their delivery on the east side of the city. When the General left the city with his convoy, it would be the ideal time for the enemy to attack. Therefore, they needed to eliminate the threat before making the delivery. They devised a two-prong strategy.

Four shuttles would land five kilometers behind the enemy on the western side of the city. The shuttles would land in a one-hundred-meter diameter circle so they could cover each other without becoming a common target. These shuttles would bring two unassembled Apsat Attack Helicopters. The helicopters were equipped with two coaxial contra-rotating main rotors. The powerful rotors provided outstanding speed and maneuverability. A 50-millimeter rapid-fire cannon and twelve guided missiles were mounted on each helicopter, which were effective against armored vehicles, but were less effective in air-to-air exchanges. The helicopter's armor could withstand a 30-millimeter projectile but was susceptible to heavy-duty missiles. The problem was the helicopters had to be assembled on the ground since an assembled helicopter would not fit inside a shuttle. Therefore, the shuttles would bring four tech specialists to assemble the helicopters. The helicopters were designed for quick in-field assembly. Experienced technicians could assemble the helicopters in less than two hours. The Demon's assembly team had practiced in the cargo bay, but their best time after two practice assemblies was slightly over three hours. The helicopters were meant as a backup. It was possible the mission would be accomplished without them. All ten squads of marines would be brought to the site.

Upon landing, while the helicopters were being assembled, each squad would approach along a different route to the two targets. The squads would be close enough to combine their forces if necessary. The enemy had control of two warehouses, so five squads would attack each warehouse. Information from the General and the aerial surveillance provided an estimate of four hundred enemy combatants. While the enemy had no air support, they possessed heavy-duty weapons. It was unclear if they were equipped with individual armor.

The strategy was for the ground forces to get into position and attack if they determined the enemy lacked armor. The attack was to take place simultaneously with the arms delivery on the other side of the city. If victory by the ground forces appeared to be in doubt, then the four shuttles and the two helicopters would join the attack. The ground forces were tasked with taking out any missiles or weapons that could take down the helicopters or shuttles. The mission might fail, even with the helicopters. In that event, they would use the shuttles to transport half of the General's men to the same location. The helicopters would support the General's combat-ready army against the rear of the enemy. The rest of the army would attack from the city and catch the enemy in a classic pincher maneuver. This approach would take longer, but a longer win is better than a quick defeat.

The mission was a go, but Grayson convinced Thomas to hire additional marines before the next mission. Thomas also vowed to have better intelligence on all future engagements. Their attack against the enemy would not be disclosed to the General in case there were spies in his organization.

Thomas was still uneasy, and he had a bad feeling in his gut. He was uncomfortable with the mission even though it looked like a good plan. He called Grayson for a private meeting.

Thomas sat down with Grayson after getting another cup of coffee. "Right now, I want you to review this mission. Use the same approach we used when playing against a team in the arena. Imagine you were the coach of the enemy. If you knew we planned to land at the coordinates given to us by the General, what would you do?"

After a moment, Grayson's face turned pale. "I would move men into the tall, abandoned buildings on the east side of the proposed landing site. It would give you the high ground and a perfect place to launch an ambush. It would be best to let the six shuttles land first. Then, the shuttles and everyone on the field could be easily destroyed." Thomas nodded his head in agreement.

"Assuming you are correct, what should we do?" Thomas asked.

"Send down six empty military shuttles to the landing area provided by the General. Empty shuttles would be more maneuverable for using their pulse cannons. Instead of landing, the shuttles should blow the buildings apart."

They still planned to land the marines using four of the shuttles and assemble the helicopters on the west side of the city. They would bring down the remaining six military shuttles from the ship as if they were planning to deliver the arms on the city's east side as requested by the General. Instead, they would have the four shuttles on the ground, and the two attack helicopters meet simultaneously at the proposed delivery site, with all air crafts remaining airborne. They would then open fire and destroy the high-rise buildings. The ground forces on the west side would still attack the two warehouses if they felt they could win the engagement.

Thomas and Grayson switched their monitoring to the high-rise buildings and saw small groups of enemy troops enter the buildings. Half the enemy group moved to the high-rise buildings. They were setting up to take out the shuttles and the General's convoy.

It took the technicians three and a half hours to assemble the helicopters, but they had budgeted for a worst-case of four hours. The ground forces were in place.

Thomas signaled the six shuttles to begin their descent to the city's east side. When the six shuttles entered the planet's atmosphere, the four shuttles on the ground, and the helicopters took off. All ten shuttles and the two helicopters arrived at the scheduled time and blew apart the buildings. The enemy fired a few missiles, but none made contact.

The ground forces attacked the two warehouses and found less than half of the enemy group was present. The fifty marines were outnumbered, but the enemy no longer had the missiles or the heavy weapons. The weapons of the Demon's ground forces easily penetrated the warehouse walls. The remaining enemy troops surrendered when the two attack helicopters and the ten military shuttles arrived.

Thomas flew down to the landing site in a non-military shuttle and met the General. All the military shuttles were returning to the ship to load up and deliver the General's order.

The General was upset a trap had been set. He agreed with Thomas. Someone in his command was providing the enemy with information. The General was pleased their city was finally secure. This was the planet's largest city, and the General had been fighting a losing war until the Demon arrived. Four other cities on the planet needed to be liberated. The General knew he could free them, but it could take years. However, the Demon's shuttles and helicopters could help free the other cities in a matter of weeks. Thomas discussed the issue with his First Officer and Commander Grayson. They both agreed they should finish what they had started. They would liberate the smallest city first. The smallest city was predominately agricultural and represented the planet's primary source of food. They would use the shuttles to bypass the closer cities. Once the food supply was secure, they would liberate the two remaining cities.

WHILE THOMAS AND THE General were preparing their strategy, Suzanna arranged to visit the city. She set a time to meet with a ranking government official. She brought Amanda with her since the city was now secure. However, eight bodyguards were under orders from Thomas to accompany Suzanna and Amanda anytime they left the ship. After arriving, she was brought into an office and greeted by an elderly gentleman who reported directly to the planet's governor. After a brief conversation, he arranged for her to meet with a trade delegation the following morning. He then provided overnight accommodations for her and Amanda.

The following morning after having breakfast, they escorted her to a large conference room filled with fifteen men and women who had been hastily collected. She introduced herself as a trade representative from the Demon as she provided them with a hard copy and an electronic list of their non-arms inventory. She asked what they had available for immediate export. They got excited when they saw the list of medical supplies. She asked them to provide lists of any items not on the Demon they wanted to purchase from off-world and the quantity for each item. Then, she asked them to divide the list into emergency, need, and want categories. It took all day for the delegates to prepare the list. She asked to meet with them again in two days.

She took a shuttle back to the Demon and worked late into the night and all the following day. She had a private meeting with Thomas. She presented a proposal to Thomas showing they would meet the ship's long-term profit requirements by granting significant discounts if the planet increased the size of their orders. The discounts would allow the planet to purchase larger quantities of desperately needed items. Thomas was duly impressed.

Suzanna and Amanda arrived at the scheduled meeting a few minutes after all the delegates had seated. It created a noticeable entrance. She had made presentations in the past for small trade deals with her parents in attendant. No family ship had ever attempted the enormous trade agreement she was going to present. Suzanna arranged for a podium to be placed at the end of the table. As she approached the podium, the room quieted down. She paused, looked around the room, and began her presentation.

"I have a proposal for your consideration. However, Captain Thomas Wilson must approve any agreement we may reach. Also, please hear my entire presentation without interrupting, and I want you to keep an open mind. First, your government purchased a third of the military arms on our ship, but your planet desperately needs all of our arms. Also, over ninety percent of the non-arms part of our inventory can be used by your planet. You could use the balance of our cargo to meet your future needs. I recommend you purchase one hundred percent of our entire inventory."

Several of the attendees voiced their opposition, but she raised her hands. "Please, let me finish. If you agree to purchase our entire inventory, I will ask Captain Wilson to sell you the arms at half our normal price." She saw everyone was interested in such a deal, but the next part of her presentation should seal the deal.

"You are wondering how to pay for such a purchase. I further propose the Demon purchase your entire stockpile of rare earth elements. You will then have a slightly positive balance for off-world purchases. Next, we will provide for the import of all the items on the list you previously provided. You will pay for this from your surplus account and the rare earth elements you will be mining in the future. As an inducement to the Captain, I recommend you consider a five-year trade agreement wherein the Demon or a Demon representative ship would have the first right of refusal on all your exports and imports. Remember, we will still need to get the Captain's approval. Amanda and I will take a walk while you consider the proposal."

Suzanna picked up Amanda and left the room. She could hear the loud uproar taking place in the room. She walked into a central square outside the building. It used to be a park before the conflict. Workers were removing debris. Several were planting shrubs and flowers. Amanda was walking short distances and exploring her surroundings. Her guards were staying at a discrete distance. They enjoyed watching Amanda as she played with the colored pebbles in the flowerbeds. In less than an hour, a lady from the meeting approached her. She asked Suzanna to return to the conference room. A park worker brought a bag filled with colored pebbles and gave it to Amanda. Suzanna thanked the lady for her kindness. Suzanna picked up Amanda, and they returned to the meeting. This time she took a seat and placed Amanda on her lap. A designated spokesperson from partway down the table cleared his voice.

"This is the first time our group achieved a unanimous decision. We will accept your proposal with no changes. Do you think Captain Thomas will agree?"

"The Captain is currently at an onsite meeting with your Governor. Let me see if he is available." Suzanna sent a prearranged message and received an immediate response.

"The Captain will be here in a few minutes."

Thomas arrived, and Suzanna directed him to an empty seat. She then explained her proposal and said the trade delegates had already approved it. The Captain said he did not like the huge discount, and he would barely break-even on the transaction. Factually, for the weapons, they would receive five times what they had paid compared to ten times the amount agreed to on the prior sale. The Captain was surprised and stated his displeasure when he saw Suzanna had given them credit by applying the discount to the arms they had previously purchased.

"You cannot expect me to give them the same discount for items previously purchased."

"If not, they were planning to return the previous order and then repurchase it at the discounted price," Suzanna said. "Look at the numbers. You will make more profit on the five-year contract even though you are losing a little profit on the smaller order. Also, calm down. You are upsetting Amanda."

The room was quiet as they watched the Captain consider the proposal. Thomas, while he was still frowning, finally nodded his head.

"Okay, I will accept the agreement. In the future, you will never reduce the price of a previously completed order." Thomas was serious about completed orders where payment had been received.

The discount for the previous order had not been discussed during their private meeting.

The Captain stomped out of the room. Thomas liked the five-year contract, even though he did not like discounting the completed sale. Regardless, he knew Suzanna had brokered an excellent long-term trade agreement to benefit them and the planet. He would continue with a five-fold markup for weapons instead of the ten recommended by the Admiral and continue selling their standard cargo.

After the Captain left, the room erupted in happy exuberance. They surrounded Suzanna and congratulated her on getting the Captain's agreement. Several commented how Amanda helped the Captain calm down and consider the contract. The weapons would allow the planet to defend itself against off-planet attacks by pirates. Also, the arms would give them a chance against an invasion by the Hostis since the bullets would penetrate the invader's armor. The traditional purchases would significantly improve the lives of the inhabitants.

Thomas was glad Suzanna had explained her approach to getting Raina to agree to the trade agreement. She showed him how having a long-term contract with steady trade would be more profitable. Thomas did not like the subterfuge, but Suzanna explained it was necessary. Raina would not believe he wanted to help them. A captain only looked out for his ship. Deciding to lower the price to make more profit long-term was something a captain would do. Therefore, they could trust Thomas to honor the agreement.

After the meeting ended, Suzanna returned to the ship to complete the second half of the agreement. She prepared a communique to Captain Javier of the Familia Primum.

"Captain Javier, the following list is for items needed on Raina. Please load your ship and deliver the emergency items first. You may seek help from other family ships. The prices are below standard, but the large volume will allow for excellent overall profits. There is a five-year contract for all exports and imports to the planet. The Demon is the contract holder, and you will be a representative ship conducting trade under the contract. You will continue the representation as long as you deal fairly with the planet, and you may keep all profits except for a five percent fee you will pay to the Demon. Please confirm and let me know when you will arrive with the first shipment. Please give the enclosed videos of Amanda to my parents." Suzanna placed her electronic signature at the end.

The Demon emptied the cargo bay and filled it with rare earth elements. It would take four trips to transport the entire purchase.

THE DEMON JUMPED TO Melius, one of the Core's corporate planets, with its cargo bay full of rare earth elements. Thomas chose Melius because they were a major manufacturer of power units. The planet became available as a corporate planet when it was determined the planet's sun would go supernova in approximately five thousand years. Therefore, the Imperium did not deem it appropriate to invest in terraforming the world and opening it up for colonization. Thus, it proved to be perfect as a corporate planet.

Thomas would visit the planet since he felt it was better to negotiate in person. There were large domed structures throughout the planet with corridors connecting the domes. The Demon's shuttle pilot entered the dome designated as the receiving port and landed on the flashing pad as directed. An automated ground vehicle arrived at the shuttle as soon as it touched down. The doors to the vehicle opened. Thomas and his four guards entered the vehicle, and it rapidly proceeded through a corridor. The doors to the vehicle opened when it arrived at an office building. An AI greeted them upon entrance to the building and asked if it could help. Thomas stated he had a shipload of rare earth elements for sale and wanted to purchase a large quantity of medical equipment, medical supplies, and power units. They were given directions to a room on the second floor. They entered the specified room, but nobody was there. The office contained five chairs for guests, a desk, and a chair behind the desk. Thomas and his four guards took a seat. After a few minutes, a person entered the room from a door behind the desk and took a seat. Thomas provided his cargo manifest to the representative and received a list of products manufactured on Melius. Thomas explained he had additional loads of the same product for sale and would like to make future purchases.

"Also, we need to order large quantities of items not available on Melius," Thomas said. "We would like to order those items and have them shipped to Melius for storage until we can arrange for pick up."

The representative asked for a list of items they wished to purchase from other suppliers and their quantities. Thomas transmitted the list.

"Are you going to need these exact items in the future?" Thomas answered in the affirmative. While seated, the representative silently communicated with an AI and asked for an evaluation. A moment later, a cart rolled in with refreshments. Before they finished with the food and drink, the monitor on the desk dinged. The representative listened to a confidential message via his earpiece.

"There are no active patents on most of the products you need," the representative said. "We are prepared to manufacture all the items on your list except for the medical supplies, the universal computer chips, the solid oxygen, the solid hydrogen, and the consumables used by your ship. We will provide these products at a twenty percent discount to your current prices. For this discount, you must agree to purchase minimum order quantities of each item for the next three years. Also, you must buy these items only from us. We would ask you to contact us first should you decide to purchase significant quantities of any items not on the list. We will build a warehouse to store the products you plan to buy from other suppliers since they take up little space."

Thomas examined the minimum quantities and was surprised the amounts were not higher. He was impressed at the speed of the decision to set up assembly lines to manufacture the products. Then he realized an AI performed the calculations for the decision, and the corporation would have the best AI available.

"Prepare the contracts," Thomas said. Purchasing in huge quantities and only selling by the container allowed Demon to sell at steep discounts while still making greater profits due to their low-cost structure. A regular ship might order a hundred units, whereas the Demon would order a hundred thousand units and reap the discount associated with such a purchase.

Melius and Thomas executed a long-term contract. The corporation further agreed to provide a warehouse to store supplies of any future items if Melius failed to manufacture the product. In return, Melius would receive the first right of refusal on all the Demon's cargo they planned to sell to the Core Planets. The corporate representative was happy with the sizeable multiyear contract. He was further pleased their corporation would be a major distributor of rare earth elements. Thomas was delighted he would not have to visit multiple Core Planets to sell the exports he would purchase from the Outer Planets.

The Demon completed delivery to Melius of all the cargo they had purchased from Raina. On each return to Raina, they had a shipload of emergency cargo for the planet and picked up a load of rare earth elements. The General purchased the two attack helicopters. He hinted they were used but did not complain too much because he received the same half-price discount under the agreement.

While the Demon was making a delivery of the rare earth elements to Melius, the Familia Primum delivered its first shipment to Raina. All the Raina citizens celebrated the deliveries. Captain Javier told them he would be back shortly with additional emergency items from other Outer Planets. He said they would return with additional ships operating under the Demon Agreement.

By the time the Demon made their last delivery, Grayson reported all the cities were now free. The citizens worked hard to get their farms and plants back into full production. The delivery of emergency supplies allowed them to repair or replace their solar generators, which powered the five cities and surrounding farms.

Raina held a banquet for the Demon and her crew on the day before their departure. Thomas was insistent regarding the departure date. He did not want to be there when the Familia Primum arrived. Of course, only Thomas and his First Officer knew the reason for the required departure date.

THE FAMILIA PRIMUM and three additional ships arrived two days later with the first delivery of needed items since the emergency items were no longer a problem. Captain Javier expressed disappointment at missing the Demon since he wanted to thank Captain Wilson and honor Suzanna.

The Captains of the three family ships accompanying the Familia Primum were thrilled. It was the first time any of their ships had sold their entire cargo at one destination, and the Familia Primum had only required ten percent of their profit. The Familia Primum was the envy of all family ships, and the three ships accompanying the Familia Primum had just made their highest profit ever for a single delivery. These ships now owed their allegiances to the Familia Primum. They planned to propose the Familia Primum as a council member at the next Gathering.

Onboard the Familia Primum, Suzanna's adoration had reached beyond celebrity status. Suzanna's parents were being asked for advice from other parents on raising their children. They told the parents they were doing an excellent job on their own. Regardless, they were constantly congratulated on raising an outstanding daughter. Suzanna's teenage brother was beginning to get noticed as he assisted their parents in trade negotiations. He did not like the added attention since he could not goof off with his friends with everyone watching to see if he compared favorably to his sister.

THE DEMON WAS READY for its next arms delivery. The Demon purchased regular cargo from Melius, which took up approximately forty percent of the Demon's cargo bay. The load was secured, and Thomas directed the Navigator to enter the jump coordinates for the nearest arms manufacturer. While in hyperspace, Thomas asked for a status report on their first arms delivery along with all the associated trade.

During the jump, an accounting showed the Demon had sold the arms cargo for five times the purchase price. They used the credit to purchase the rare earth elements, which they sold at standard markups representing a fifty percent gross margin. Plus, they sold all their regular cargo. Thomas reserved sufficient funds to cover future cargo purchases, including ship expenses. He sent the excess credits to the joint account he shared with his father and sent a communication advising his father of the available funds. While the Demon was a gift, the huge profits from the sale of arms would help him achieve his goal of repaying his father for the cost of the Demon and hopefully keep the family businesses solvent.

CHAPTER 12 GUNS AND POLITICS

Admiral Nelson met with Thomas while the Demon was docked and loading the cargo bay with a new arms shipment. The Admiral and Thomas had a long talk. The Admiral was pleased with the success of the Demon's mission. He announced that Raina had just joined the Imperium and would be protected by the navy. Understandably, the Admiral was disappointed Thomas had taken a standard year for just one mission. The Admiral said the next three missions must be completed within a year. Thomas told the Admiral they were lucky the first mission had not resulted in a complete failure.

Thomas explained he needed access to the network of navy spies. He had to know who he could trust on Outer Planets and stations. This was critical if they were going to be successful in the future. The Admiral agreed and said someone would contact him shortly to provide the requested intelligence. The Admiral gave Thomas the names of three planets. He provided the contacts at each location and the suggested arms needed by each planet.

"Is there anything else I can do for you?" The Admiral asked. Thomas had been waiting for the question.

"As part of my training, my father ensured I understood strategy and tactics. It can be applied to battles, business, and political situations. My father had me read hundreds of holographic books about war practitioners. We would discuss each of the books. The books covered the greatest successes and the greatest failures throughout human history. Many of the books were translated from ancient texts. The more I read, the more I enjoyed the reading. It was interesting how some of the greatest practitioners of war had similar philosophies. My father felt learning from the successes and failures of others would help me make better decisions. He never thought I might have to use the information in a physical battle. Two of my favorite books were the Art of War by Sun Tzu and The Five Rings by Miyamoto Musashi. Two of my favorite quotes from Sun Tzu are: 'All warfare is based on deception,' and 'the greatest victory is the one which requires no battle.' My two favorite quotes from Miyamoto Musashi are: 'The ultimate aim of martial arts is not having to use them,' and 'It is difficult to understand the universe if you study one planet.'"

Thomas continued. "To use some of this philosophy, I need your help. The Demon is a good ship, but other ships are attracted by our cargo. I want to reduce the chance of being attacked by using a little deception. I plan to put out false information saying the Demon was in an altercation with a navy fleet, resulting in the destruction of four navy destroyers. At some point, someone will want you to comment. I want you to deny the account but refuse to answer any other questions concerning the matter."

The Admiral chuckled as he knew exactly what Thomas was hoping to achieve. "I can do that," he said.

AFTER THOMAS LEFT, a person observing the conversation from a monitor in the adjacent room entered and sat in a chair facing Admiral Nelson.

"Agent Sicarius, you were on Raina and observed the Captain in action. What is your opinion?"

"Captain Wilson survived the first test. However, it was far easier than what he will face in the future. Captain Wilson surprised me in several ways. When he first arrived, five ships were controlling the Stargate. Thomas did not need to use the Stargate since he had jump engines. He could have bypassed the ships, but instead, he confronted them. He destroyed a single ship and avoided having to engage the other vessels. He talked them into using the Stargate to leave the system. He could have had problems later if he had left the ships alone. Also, the message he sent to the four ships has been repeated throughout the Outer Planets and the Rim. The destruction of the one ship has been embellished to include several ships."

Agent Sicarius paused and then continued. "By this one act, Captain Wilson has created a reputation of being powerful and ruthless. Instead, we both know he let the other ships leave because he was kindhearted. I would have destroyed all five ships, but it would have been a mistake. I would have been wrong because no one would have been aware of the battle. Thus, Thomas made the right decision for the wrong reason."

"Do you think he will succeed?" The Admiral asked.

"I was impressed with how Thomas avoided a trap at a landing site he was told to use by General Atkinson. If he had landed the shuttles as directed, all the shuttles would have been destroyed. Also, all the men with those shuttles would have been killed. Thus, he would have been unable to continue with the mission. In this case, the Captain was completely ruthless. He destroyed several buildings and all the enemy combatants without a single loss. He was not being ruthless. This action was to prevent any loss of life to his crew. You and I have made decisions to sacrifice people to win a battle, avoid a loss, or gain an advantage. Captain Wilson has not shown the ability to make the tough decisions. My answer to your question is, maybe."

The Admiral knew the Agent had additional issues. "What else?"

"You addressed the major problem," the Agent said. "As you pointed out to our Captain, he should have sold his cargo and left the system. Instead, he established an extremely profitable trade agreement for himself and the planet. The resulting trade will allow the planet to recover economically within two years. Raina agreed to join the Imperium, but the negotiations were more difficult. Due to the trade agreement, Raina was in a stronger position. Thus, the Imperium had to make more concessions. Captain Wilson and his top officers are very astute. I am interested in this deception plan of his. It will be interesting to see how it plays out. Regardless, we do not want to underestimate Captain Wilson."

"I agree," the Admiral said. "Captain Wilson completed the first mission, which is more than his two predecessors. Check your sources and then meet with the Captain. Provide him with the contacts and support him as much as possible without exposing yourself."

The Admiral's top spy left the room and exited the building using an underground corridor. The corridor was not on the building's schematics.

THE DEMON WAS SIXTY percent loaded with arms. Thomas made sure they had surplus ordnance for their own use. The balance of the cargo consisted of medical supplies, power units, universal chips, food processors, and other items they had previously sold in large quantities.

Thomas created a separate Technology Intelligence Department to prevent espionage against the Demon. They acquired and built advanced spy devices for gathering information to protect the ship and its crew. Additional apps were added so crew members could be found in an emergency or if captured or injured. The Department located and hired two young tech specialists with field experience who were noted for their expertise in surveillance equipment. The techs were to train the crew in using spy equipment and take measures to prevent others from spying on their ship. Thomas added additional individuals to the Department to evaluate both public and non-public data to allow the Demon to complete their missions with less risk.

His senior officers and department heads had been immensely helpful in hiring additional crew. It helped that the pay was double what everyone else was offering. Thus, they could hire the best. The Demon stayed docked for several weeks while awaiting the arrival of the new hires.

Thomas sent out different fictitious stories regarding a battle between the Demon and the navy. Each story was sufficiently different to appear to be from multiple sources.

The Demon was scheduled to depart the following day at the beginning of Night Watch to draw less attention to their departure.

Thomas was having lunch at one of the dock's cafeterias. He had finished his meal and was leaving when a nondescript elderly gentleman accosted him.

"I need to speak with you in private. We both work for the same individual, and he asked me to contact you."

"Why should I believe you?" Thomas asked.

"Because I was there during your recent discussions with our employer, and you said the words Sun Tzu during your meeting. I have a vehicle, and it is secure against any listening device. The personal scrambler I am using is good but not perfect. Please follow me."

Once they were in the vehicle, the stranger selected auto, and the vehicle proceeded on a pre-programmed course.

"I am an intelligence officer," Agent Sicarius said. "I am here to provide information to help you complete your future missions. We have intelligence operatives on most Outer Planets and Rim stations. I advised them to assist you when they can be of help. You will know them by the code embedded in this wafer. I will send you updates to this code periodically. To contact me, scroll down to the second code. Your DNA activates the wafer. The second code will transmit a signal to an encrypted electronic address. Upon receipt, I will contact you on your personal comm. Do you have any questions?"

"Yes," Thomas replied. "I want you to send me information on all ships operating in the Outer Planets and the Rim, along with the name of their captains and a summary of each ship's history. I especially want information on ships that may be preying on other ships, stations, or planets. I want this information before I reach the destination for my next mission."

"I will do what I can to get the information," the Agent replied.

"Upon arriving at my first destination, I will simply wait in orbit and not attempt to make any deliveries until you provide the information. If you are any good, you should have no trouble with my request."

The Agent did not respond. Thomas noticed the vehicle had returned to its starting point. Thomas opened the door and exited the vehicle. He walked away without looking back. Agent Sicarius smiled tightly and started sending requests to people who could get the information. His opinion of Captain Wilson had just increased.

THE INFORMATION THOMAS wanted from the agent was the same information he requested from his new Technology Intelligence Department.

Thomas remembered how his course on strategy explained how thousands of battles were lost or won on a single piece of information. Similarly, companies succeeded or failed based on information that was either used or misused. He remembered how they had won arena games against stronger teams by studying the opposing team's former games. They also adjusted their play after a game started if the game plan was not working.

Thomas' father continuously stressed how excellent strategy and tactics were based on superior information. The right information would increase his probability of success in any venture. Thomas missed the discussions he used to have with his father.

The Demon's Technology Intelligence Department collected considerable information on the ships operating in the Outer Planets and the Rim by using their contacts at all the places they had visited. Captain Javier presented them with a large data file he collected from all the family ships. Thomas studied the information on the ships. He then reduced the information to a summary containing the ship's name, captain, armament, operating parameters, and a brief history. The reduction contained mnemonic words to allow Thomas to recall all the critical information for each ship. A tech supervisor created a subroutine to tie the ship's scanners to the database so Thomas would instantly have information on any vessel within scanning range.

Before making their next arms delivery, they diverted to a destination to conduct standard trade. During the trip, Thomas enjoyed spending time with Suzanna and Amanda. Amanda was precocious, and everyone on the ship enjoyed spending time with her. Suzanna continued to do such an outstanding job managing their cargo transactions that Thomas promoted her to Cargo Administrator, a Senior Officer position. All of his officers said it was about time. Thomas posted the position so traders from the various planets and stations would know Suzanna was the contact to negotiate trade transactions.

Suzanna and Amanda were still sharing the Captain's cabin even though Amanda no longer cried. The Captain's cabin was strategically located close to the bridge. It was common practice for Amanda to go to the bridge and crawl up into Thomas's lap when she was sleepy.

The Demon came out of jump on Third Watch. Suzanna had set up her department to transmit automatically a cargo manifest of the products available for sale and a list of items they would like to purchase. As was customary, Thomas took his position on the bridge during the last part of Night Watch. He noticed a communication for the sale of an item on their purchase list. The price was unbelievably low. Suzanna was still asleep, so he accepted the offer and executed the purchase agreement.

The Demon successfully docked after the start of Day Watch. Amanda was with the Helmsman viewing the external cameras. Thomas was sitting in the Captain's chair when Suzanna stormed onto the bridge shouting at Thomas and calling him every derogatory name in her vocabulary.

Thomas was cringing while asking what he had done. Suzanna screamed he had just spent ship's credit to purchase garbage. She pulled up the purchase he had made on Night Watch and showed it next to a similar item on their open order list. It took a moment before Thomas realized the product he purchased was off by one letter in the description.

Thomas, without thinking, tried to justify the undefendable and made matters worse. Suzanna emphatically stated she was the Cargo Administrator, and it was her job to approve cargo transactions. He had embarrassed her and the ship. Thomas said she was asleep, to which she responded that he should have awakened her if it needed an immediate response. She stated the offer to sell was sent as a joke. The seller did not think anyone was stupid enough to act upon it. She said if she had a gun, she would shoot him. Thomas finally did what he should have done at the outset of the argument. He apologized and said it would never happen again. Suzanna was fuming as she stomped off the bridge.

Amanda walked over to Thomas. "Dad, why was Mom so mad?"

"Because I made a big mistake."

Amanda looked at her Dad with big eyes. "I hope I don't make a big mistake."

"I hope you don't either," Thomas replied.

"Dad, it's a good thing Mom didn't have a gun."

The bridge officers could no longer contain themselves as they all burst out laughing. Thomas was embarrassed and knew his First Officer could manage the bridge for the remainder of Day Watch. Therefore, Thomas left the bridge and took Amanda to the game room until it was time for lunch. He had never seen anyone so mad. He wondered how long it would take for Suzanna to calm down.

SUZANNA WAS STILL FURIOUS as she took a shuttle to the planet. After landing on the planet, she went to the trade center. It was filled with booths displaying items for sale. She was wearing the ship's uniform, and the joke concerning the purchase of garbage had spread throughout the center. She was subjected to snickers and laughter as she meandered about the center looking for profitable trade. At one booth, a man standing in front of a table spoke to a person next to him in the Wagorien language. Besides the Galactic common language, all Family Spacers were expected to know various languages, and Suzanna was fluent in Wagorien. The person speaking went to the extreme with his insults as he loudly questioned her intellect, breeding, and family affiliations while insulting her ship. He then said in a very derogatory manner how she was so stupid she likely needed basic training in all matters, including sex. Then he said she was probably untrainable even in sex. Still, he would be willing to try to teach her if she had sufficient credit.

At that point, Suzanna lost control and attacked him. The impact propelled the two of them over the table. Suzanna landed on top as she repeatedly hit him in the face. The other man at the booth pulled Suzanna off the man she had attacked. She used her elbow to punch him in the face causing him to let go as he fell to the floor. Suzanna then returned to the attack. She kicked the man on the floor as he attempted to get up, stomping on him as he lay on the floor on his back. Then, she turned over the booth display on top of him. Security showed up and promptly placed her under arrest while calling medical to attend to the two men she had beat up. She notified the ship while she was being escorted to lockup. Within minutes every shuttle on the Demon was filled, and within a brief period, several hundred crew members were on-site demanding her release.

Suzanna was locked in a cell with a bunch of other females. The female inmates had been arrested for various offensives, including solicitation, illegal drugs, stealing, trespassing, and other assorted crimes. Several formidable females planned to give Suzanna some trouble until they asked her what she had done. She told them she had been arrested for beating up two men. Then, all the prisoners wanted to hear her story. They liked the part where one of the guys was unconscious and had to be carried off on a stretcher. Afterward, she listened to their stories and made friends with her cellmates. She felt sorry for one prisoner with a child around the same age as Amanda. She had lost her job and could not find employment. She and her daughter were in a food market. Her daughter ate an item she took from a food counter. The owner demanded payment for the item. When she could not pay, he had her arrested. Typically, the penalty was to pay for the item and pay court costs. Unfortunately, she did not have the funds, so she was sentenced to thirty days in jail. She started crying and said she did not know what had become of her child. Suzanna made no promises but said she would try to help her. She was wondering how much longer she would be locked up.

Thomas contacted a highly ranked law firm, and they assigned their best attorney to the case. Suzanna was charged with two counts of battery. The attorney arranged bail, and it was expected the

Demon would forfeit the bail instead of risking the imprisonment of a crew member.

Everyone was surprised when the Demon did not leave and demanded an immediate trial. They paid the court an additional fee for a quick hearing date. The trial was scheduled to start in three days. The confrontation was recorded on multiple videos. Their attorney had the plaintiff's conversation translated into Galactic. Then, he filed counter-charges including slander of the person, slander of the family, slander of the ship, use of provocative language toward a lady, sexually propositioning a lady, unruly behavior, assault, battery, and public intoxication. The attorney filed similar charges against the Helios Company since they employed the two plaintiffs. The attorney visited the trade center and questioned the various trade representatives. After playing back a translation of what was said, he got over a hundred signatures from trade members supporting the complaint he made to have Helios's license revoked. The Helios Company was a large corporation, and its removal would help the smaller companies. In a short time, the case received widespread coverage.

Captain Javier found out about the case and swiftly sent a communication to the corporation. They had insulted a family member, and he told them he would propose a boycott against the Helios Company at the next Gathering of family ships. All ships that were part of the Demon cargo agreement sent similar communications. The day before the trial, the Helios Company asked for a meeting. At the meeting, Suzanna's attorney played videos of the action at the Center. No translation was needed since the plaintiffs spoke the language. A settlement was reached in which the Helios employees would withdraw their charges. Helios would pay for all of Suzanna's legal fees and buy the garbage the Demon had purchased by mistake. Also, they would issue a public apology to Suzanna, the Demon, all crew members of the Demon, and all family ships. In return, the action to have the Helios Corporation's license revoked would be withdrawn. In addition, the Demon would accept the Helios Corporation's offer to fill several orders needed by the Demon at best-rate pricing. As the Cargo Administrator, Suzanna agreed to the purchase since she was a spacer first and supported the needs of the ship. They accepted Suzanna's demand for a general posting saying she was not a party to the purchase that resulted in the altercation.

There was one final item. Suzanna told the story about the woman in the jail cell and asked if they would help the young mother. The company representative said they would see to her release, help her get reunited with her child and offer her employment with their company. Suzanna's attorney said he would see they met all the terms of the agreement. The Demon filled the balance of their orders and jumped.

Captain Javier received a transmission of the video of the altercation at the trade center and laughed for several days. Their Suzanna was fearless. He also reviewed the settlement agreement with glee. At their next staff meeting, Javier played the video for the Senior Officers and showed them copies of the settlement. Family Ships were typically looked down upon, and none of them would have dared to attack a trade representative. It was not long until everyone on the ship had watched the video several times. Suzanna was now a superhero.

THE DEMON EXITED JUMP at the designated coordinates and arrived at a huge asteroid that had been turned into a trading station. The Way Station had been a mining colony. After the ore had been mined, there were five enormous areas within the asteroid connected by tunnels. It was recognized as a perfect site for a way station since it was near a Stargate. The local Stargate was a transit point for four other systems with Stargates. No one had any imagination, so it simply became known as The Way Station. Over a hundred docks were strategically built around The Way Station, and there was a thriving city within the station. The Way Station was also the most dangerous station in the Rim.

Horae and Boreas were two inhabited planets that were closer to the sun than The Way Station. Horae was inhabited at the two poles since the rest of the planet was too hot without an environmental suit. It had a population of less than twenty million. Boreas was colder, with most of the inhabitants concentrated along the equator. Boreas had a population above three hundred million.

Agent Sicarius had come through with copious amounts of information on ships operating outside the Core. The files contained details on the history of each ship along with the armament, the personality of the captain, and the capabilities of the crew. It was incredibly detailed and exceeded Thomas' expectations. Thomas merged the Agent's data with the information his Technology Intelligence Department had collected.

The Demon was to make two deliveries in this system. One delivery would be to the planet Boreas. The other delivery for Horae would occur at The Way Station. Both deliveries would be difficult and involve greater risk. The delivery to Horae would be to a group of so-called freedom fighters along with what was left of the planet's navy and air force. They were trying to overthrow a military general who had only recently taken power in a surprising coup. General Erebos was now a dictator with little to no support from the people, but his army had superior weapons he had obtained off-planet. An emissary from the planet was to meet Thomas at The Way Station. After making the first two deliveries, they were to use a Stargate for their third delivery. Thomas did not want to jump blindly through a gate where it would be easy to arrange an ambush where a ship or group of ships could lie in wait on the other side.

With the crew's help, Suzanna researched the data streams to determine what items had the highest demand. In this system, essential items were in short supply because ships were no longer willing to risk losing their ship to marauders or pirates. The Demon's non-arms cargo included medical supplies, the newest models of food processors with the ability to make a nearly infinite number of meals, and all the nutrients used by the food processors to maintain human health. They planned to sell the non-arms cargo to The Way Station and Boreas. The delivery at The Way Station could be problematic since everyone was armed and interested in acquiring the Demon's cargo.

The plan was to sell part of the non-arms cargo at The Way Station, locate the Horae representative, then take the representative and the arms shipment to Horae.

Thomas decided he needed to reconnoiter the station first to locate their contact and find potential buyers for the non-arms cargo. Six members of the crew would accompany him. Each group member carried a pack with food, water, spy gear, and extra ammunition. They also wore a sidearm, a hidden ankle gun, a belt knife, a second smaller knife hidden under a shirt sleeve, two trackers to locate them in an emergency, and a rifle that could be fired single shot or flipped too automatic. They did not wear their armor since it was thought such a display would draw too much attention. Also, the Demon would not dock until they were ready to unload their cargo. Therefore, they took a shuttle to the station. The pilot was to stay with the shuttle and be prepared for a quick liftoff. The Pilot and the bridge officers on the Demon would monitor the group through their body cams.

There were docks available for all sizes of vehicles, so they docked the shuttle in an area away from other ships. Thomas and his group disembarked from the shuttle and proceeded along a well-traveled tunnel. Maps were burned into the walls along the way to prevent a person from getting lost. After a short hike, they entered an enormous cavern with shops, bars, and restaurants. The scene was worse than they could have imagined. A sizable percentage of the people were suffering from chronic sickness.

Thomas sent a video to Doctor Adler and asked if she could remotely diagnose the station's health problems. Doctor Adler spoke to the group and said the symptoms resulted from the body not receiving enough nutrients to maintain good health. It became apparent the healthy individuals were from docked ships, whereas the sick were the permanent residents. She would need a DNA sample to provide a medical evaluation. As they explored, they noticed some merchants were not sick but were still in poor health. The bars were doing well. Thomas approached a vendor and asked where the best restaurants were in The Way Station. He was told conditions got better the closer you got to the center of the station. Thomas noticed they were attracting a crowd, so he motioned for everyone to keep moving.

They continued toward the center of the station, and the people were a little healthier. They finally found the restaurant bar where they were supposed to meet their contact. A server showing the beginnings of malnutrition symptoms came over to take their order. Thomas asked what nutrients were missing from their food processor.

She paused and looked around. Then she leaned in close so she could speak without being overheard.

"We are better than most," she whispered. "A third of our trace elements in the food chambers are empty, and two more are running low. We have been entirely out of Molybdenum, Iodine, and Selenium for a while. We are low on Manganese and Zinc."

"Hypothetically, if a supplier had all of your missing minerals and enough for the entire station, how would he dispose of such a cargo without creating a riot?" Thomas asked in a low voice. "Also, I need to get a message to Cincinnatus."

"Give me a minute, don't leave," she pleaded.

A few minutes later, a middle-aged lady came and sat down at their table. "You made an unusual statement to an employee. Who are you?"

"I am Thomas Wilson, Captain of the Demon."

"I am Litea, we have been expecting you, but we did not know you would have regular cargo. Do you truly have the full spread of nutrients for our food processors?"

"We have two hundred containers of nutrients plus over a thousand of the newest model food processors," Thomas replied. "We also have one hundred containers of medical supplies."

"We have plenty of credits but nothing to spend it on," Litea responded. "We will take fifty containers of the nutrients, twenty processors, and ten containers of your medical cargo. We will pay whatever you are charging since we are desperate and have no options."

Thomas shook his head. "Standard pricing, we make our excess profits from our munition sales. How shall we make the delivery?"

"I am part of the business group of owners," Litea said. "Unload at Gate 82. We will have security in place for the unloading. We will provide free nutrients to all our residents for their home processors since we make our profits off the spacers. The balance of the nutrients will go to our restaurants and bars where we fleece the spacers. I will introduce you to your contact as soon as your cargo is unloaded and distributed."

Thomas returned to his ship. He called a senior staff meeting and asked Lukia Madisum to join them in his Ready Room. Thomas brought everyone up to date with a summary report.

"I have asked Lukia Madisum to join us," Thomas said. "She is from Horae, and we plan to establish trade with the Horaecins, which will include the delivery of arms to them. I asked Lukia to join us. She can explain the situation on the planet prior to her departure."

Thomas intentionally did not mention the circumstances of her departure from the planet. He felt it was personal. It was her decision if she wanted to disclose her abduction and life on a pirate ship.

Lukia told them about life on Horae as it existed twelve years earlier. Thomas summarized the recent military coup. He concluded with the sale of cargo to the station.

THE DEMON DOCKED AT Gate 82 as directed. Thomas was surprised at how well the locals handled the cargo once it was unloaded. Still, three days passed before he was contacted and asked to return to the restaurant. As soon as they entered the restaurant, Thomas, his guards, key advisors, and Lukia were escorted behind the bar and down several tunnels before arriving at a room containing makeshift beds. The room was crowded with a collection of men, women, and children. When Thomas and his group entered the room, everyone fell silent. The crew accompanying Thomas moved to various defensive positions. The ship officers listened to the conversation since Thomas left his communicator on, and they were using a specific encrypted frequency to avoid outside detection.

A middle-aged woman approached and introduced herself as Ophelia Waylain. She directed Thomas to a small table in the corner of the room. She was elegant, with light brown hair sprinkled with a few strands of gray. There was a deep sadness in her eyes.

"The President, his cabinet, and most of the planet's elected officials were killed soon after General Erebos took control of Horae," Ophelia said. "I am the highest remaining elected official of the Horaecin people, and by default, I am the acting President. General Erebos also killed any army officers who objected to his takeover. The planet's small navy and air force have remained loyal, but all the air vehicles have been destroyed by surface-to-air missiles that were purchased off world. What remains of the navy and air force have retreated to several islands on the opposite side of the planet from the capital. Gun ownership among the population is limited since the planet only has a small amount of potassium nitrate, which I am told is a necessary ingredient in gunpowder. Our unarmed civilian population was unable to oppose the takeover, and anyone who objected was killed without a trial."

Thomas told Ophelia he had sufficient weapons to create an army of civilians, but would they be willing to fight? She assured Thomas the Horaecin people would fight if they thought they had a chance to win. Thomas had Ophelia provide what information she had about the General, but she did not know the size of his army or much regarding his armament. Unfortunately, she provided little in the way of useful information. Ophelia was fearful. She explained there were mercenaries on the station looking for them. The mercenaries had a contract to kill her and her followers with a sizable bounty for each death. The mercenaries were offering incentives to anyone who helped them. Also, the mercenaries had images of her and many of her followers. It would be difficult to approach his ship without being recognized.

Thomas received a transmission from his First Officer aboard the Demon. Thomas and his group had placed listening devices everywhere they had traveled. While listening to the various conversations, they learned a search was being conducted to locate Captain Thomas Wilson.

Thomas directed everyone on the ship to dress for combat in full armor. He told his First Officer to have the Demon go to battle stations. Thomas stood up and asked for the attention of everyone in the room.

"I am Thomas Wilson, Captain of the Demon. Your President has asked me to return you to your planet and outfit an army to defeat General Erebos, who is now in control of your planet. It is only a matter of time before this hiding place is discovered. Therefore, we need to get aboard our ship without delay. There are mercenaries who will kill you on sight. We are going to make a run for the ship. Therefore, you must leave all your belongings behind so you can travel as quickly as possible. Everything you need for survival is aboard our ship. Taking anything with you other than yourselves could cause your death or the death of someone else. Anyone who violates this rule will be left behind. Also, if anyone in this room wishes to be left behind, let me know now."

A younger gentleman spoke up. "How do we know if you can be trusted?"

Lukia stepped forward. "I am Lukia Madisum. I was abducted by pirates from Horae when I was sixteen. Captain Thomas rescued me, and he is telling you the truth. What choice do you have? If you stay here, you will die. With Captain Thomas, at least you have a chance to live and the support you need to free Horae." Lukia's statement seemed to have dispelled any remaining concerns.

"We are out of time," Thomas said. "If anyone wishes to stay behind, raise your hand?"

No one raised their hand. Thomas was concerned since the people were not dressed for combat or quick travel.

"Some children will need to be carried," Thomas said. "I want the strongest men to volunteer to help carry the children. Mothers, I know you will want to carry your child, but doing so could cause you and your child's death. I am going to divide you into six groups. One of the six men with me will be assigned to each group as your team leader. We will divide you into groups based on how fast you can travel so the faster group will reach the ship first without being slowed down. Your team leader is armed and can lend one of his two guns to another person who has experience using a firearm. If you are already armed, let your team leader know so he will position you in the best location to protect your assigned team. Are there any questions?"

Several Horaecins protested about having the slowest members in the latter groups since it would contain more women and the older Horaecins. Several wanted to travel as one group. Thomas explained it was his goal to get everyone aboard his ship alive, but his approach would increase the number of survivors in a firefight. The complaints ended when he said the plan was finalized and anyone who did not like the plan could stay behind.

Thomas told the Horaecins they would have to cross the central marketplace to get to the corridor leading to their ship. He contacted Grayson and was told everyone was ready.

Thomas explained the plan and told Grayson he wanted the marines lined up down the corridor with the fastest marines in front. He further stated he wanted the fastest crew members in the first group and each consecutive group to be divided by speed. The fastest group of marines from the Demon would sprint to the furthest group of Horaecins and on down the line. The fastest crew members would reach the slowest Horaecins in the shortest time. They would try to avoid shooting, but if fired upon, they were to defend themselves and the Horaecins. Once a group was in the corridor, the marines with that group would fan out at the entrance and provide cover fire until all groups were in the corridor.

They stayed concealed until they reached the edge of the central marketplace. They would have to travel over fifty meters in the open to reach the corridor leading to the Demon. Grayson notified Thomas the marines were in position. He hoped most of the groups would get across before anyone opened fire. They would be instantly recognized when they stepped into the marketplace. All the groups would start across at the same time and hurry across the unsecured area. The marines with armor would try to protect the Horaecins. The slowest group was only a quarter of the way across when the first two groups reached the other side. As each group arrived, they were rushed down the corridor toward the Demon. Thomas was with the slowest group. They were only halfway across when Thomas saw the mercenaries. The mercenaries opened fire. The marines responded with covering fire.

Unfortunately, the marines could only shoot when they had a clean line of fire. The mercenaries had no such concerns and fired at anyone who got in their way. Everyone in the marketplace was running and screaming. Thomas dropped to one knee and started picking off the mercenaries. He had to take his time to avoid hitting innocent people. All the people in the market were armed. The smart ones ran for cover and stayed out of the battle. Others started shooting back, but they were shooting at both the mercenaries and the marines.

Additional marines arrived at the last group, with some marines picking up the Horaecins and carrying them to safety. The slowest group was almost across when Thomas felt an impact as he went over backward and found himself looking at the ceiling. Two marines grabbed him from either side and pulled him to his feet. He did not recall much after that.

WHEN THOMAS OPENED his eyes, he found he was inside an enclosure and at first panicked from claustrophobia before he realized he must be inside a healing chamber. A few minutes later, he saw Dr. Adler looking at him through a transparent panel, and she told him to relax before he had a heart attack. Thomas asked how long he had been in the chamber, and she said three days. She explained how he had multiple wounds to his upper body and was lucky since a head wound would have been fatal. Thomas said he was ready to get out, but she just shook her head. The Doctor made several adjustments, and Thomas went back asleep.

Two days later, the Doctor let Thomas out of the chamber and moved him to a hospital bed. They needed the chamber for another patient. As soon as he settled into the bed, Amanda rushed in, followed by Suzanna. Amanda was so excited to see him. It was a while before she calmed down enough so he could talk to Suzanna. Thomas asked for an update. Suzanna informed him two Horaecins and one marine without armor had been killed. There were six other injuries of various degrees, but they would recover. She said Demon was circling Horae but had taken no action while waiting for his return. Then, she lectured him. A Captain's job was to be on the bridge and not exposed in a gun battle. Thomas was going to quote Sun Tzu by saying a leader leads by example, but he was still weak and did not feel up to arguing. Thus, he just kept his mouth shut even though it was difficult.

The following morning, Thomas told Dr. Adler he was ready to return to work, but she said he needed to stay for two more days. Thomas agreed and said it sounded reasonable. The Doctor looked at him strangely before leaving to attend to her other patients. Thomas went back to sleep. When he woke up on Night Shift, he called a Junior Officer and ordered the officer to bring him one of his uniforms. After dressing, Thomas went to the bridge. He remained for the balance of the Night Watch and the first part of the Day Watch before retiring to his cabin.

The following day, he awoke and found Suzanna sleeping on one side and Amanda on the other. He could not get up without waking one of them. So, he stayed in bed. A few hours later, they all got up, took turns getting ready, and went to the cafeteria for breakfast. Everyone was glad to see the Captain up and around. Grayson had just returned from the surface. He was ready to brief Thomas and the senior officers.

Thomas scheduled a meeting of his Senior Officers and asked President Waylain to join them. Once everyone was present, Thomas directed Grayson to give his report. Grayson gave his report sitting down.

"My meeting with the Commander of the Navy and the Commander of the Airforce went well. So far, the General has not tried to attack their positions. They have received updates from their spies in the capital. The General has made a significant miscalculation. The people hated the former President because of high unemployment and a planet-wide recession. However, they were not ready for a dictator. General Erebos had a parade through the streets of the capital to celebrate his rise to power. Except for a few citizens, the entire city boycotted his parade. He passed a decree for full employment, and everyone was required to work. Thus, people showed up where they were directed to go, but there were no jobs. General Erebos is hated more than the dead president, but he has an army with over a hundred thousand soldiers. Anyone who expresses any dissatisfaction is executed."

"What about the air force and navy?" Thomas asked.

"The air force only has a dozen planes remaining, and those planes have no offensive capability. The navy is not much better since it was primarily used for search and rescue missions. Before the takeover, the army was used to defend against off-planet marauders that would periodically land and terrorize the local inhabitants. Also, they helped with natural disasters. It would be easy for us to defeat the army, but any attack against the General puts millions of innocent people at risk."

President Waylain shook her head. "General Erebos is in our largest city. I cannot condone an assault on the General's forces if it causes the death of millions of innocent lives. Conversely, leaving the people at the mercy of the General is not a viable option either."

"Madam President, if a member of the army has not killed anyone and wishes to surrender, are you prepared to grant a full pardon to such a person?" Thomas asked.

"Yes." President Waylain answered without hesitation.

"Madam President, how much are you willing to pay if I can remove General Erebos with the loss of life at less than one hundred thousand civilians and reinstate your democracy?"

President Waylain thought for a long moment before replying. "General Erebos has seized all government accounts totaling over a hundred billion credits. If you can topple the General, we could pay you out of the Government's accounts. Would a billion credits be sufficient?"

Thomas kept a neutral expression and was shocked at the offered amount but was not about to turn it down. He should have realized he was dealing with a politician.

"I will have our attorney work with you in preparing the agreement," Thomas said. "You and your staff must sign the agreement to show the provisional government approved it. The Commander of the Airforce and the Commander of your Navy will also need to sign the agreement. Once we have all the signatures, we will take care of General Erebos. You and I will have a separate agreement allowing you to void the first agreement if we exceed the casualty numbers. Understand, the agreement gives me total authority." President Waylain and her attorney added one paragraph to the agreement.

It only took three days to get the agreement executed by all the other parties. Then, they brought it to Thomas for his signature. Unlike Suzanna, he did not read the contract.

Thomas had been working with his Technology Intelligence Department and was ready to present his plan to defeat General Erebos. Another meeting was called, and it took place in a secure location on the planet. The President, Air Force, Navy, and Mayors from the surrounding cities were represented.

"I have been given total authority to remove General Erebos," Thomas said. "I have invited the mayors of the surrounding cities and towns here for a reason. Many people have already fled the city. Over a million will leave the city within the next few days. We are asking you to offer sleeping accommodations to those individuals. Food will not be a problem since we will provide you with food processors and containers of nutrients for the processors. We expect to resolve the situation within several months. To minimize civilian casualties, a full pardon will be given to soldiers who have not killed anyone if they abandon the General. They will be asked to join the air force or navy. Any soldier who does not leave the General will be killed. The President will work with the navy, air force, and local volunteers to provide checkpoints for directing those fleeing the city. Many from the city rely on public transportation and do not have ground vehicles. We need volunteers with vehicles to pick up those fleeing the city on foot. In five days, we will cut off all utilities in the city. This will be a hardship on anyone refusing to leave the city, but we intend to unnerve the General and keep him distracted."

Thomas presented the final step in his plan. "We will offer ten million in Galactic credit to the person who kills the General. Our Technology Intelligence Department has the technology to start broadcasting this information over every communication system and device on the planet. When the General is sufficiently isolated, we will attack. Madam President, you have a lot of work ahead of you. The navy, air force, and city mayors have a command structure, but you must appoint additional leaders to help you organize. We have ten military shuttles and six unarmed civilian shuttles available to help transport people, food, and supplies after we deliver our cargo to your planet."

Thomas liked the attack helicopters so much from a previous mission that he had fifty helicopters as part of the cargo. After the food processors and nutrient containers had been delivered, they transported down the helicopters and started the assembly. With the marines and other volunteers, all the helicopters were assembled and armed in four days. The shuttles delivered four hundred containers holding one million assault rifles with a 100-round magazine for each weapon. The President asked what they would do with all the rifles later.

"If you set up a militia in each town and village, they will no longer have to hide in fear every time a marauder lands," Thomas said. "Currently, the planet's military always arrives after all the damage is done. In a short while, you will no longer have a marauder problem."

Over half the city was emptied over the next four days. On the fifth day, the utilities were cut, and the exodus increased. They continued to communicate that food and supplies were available for those fleeing the city. The broadcast included the pardon for soldiers who had not killed a civilian.

Few civilians remained in the city by the twentieth day, and less than ten thousand soldiers remained with the General. Also, several soldiers who had abandoned the General confirmed there had been at least two attempts on the General's life.

On the twenty-first day, fifty helicopters made a night assault using night vision equipment. They took out the watch towers, and the main building housing the soldiers. Thomas was satisfied when told they had suffered no casualties. There were a few dents in some of the helicopters but no penetrations through the armor.

On the twenty-second day, the army signaled they were surrendering and slowly marched out of the city carrying the dead body of General Erebos. Only three hundred and forty-two soldiers were alive after the previous night's attack, and most were injured.

Eight of the soldiers claimed the reward for the General's death. They had agreed to split the reward and wanted off the planet. A small mob wanted to execute the last group of soldiers. Thomas had the armored marines stop them and reminded them of the pardon guaranteed by the President. Thomas honored the reward and put eight soldiers in the nearest shuttle for delivery to the Demon. The remaining soldiers were questioned and given truth serum until they located the remaining soldiers who had killed civilians. There were only twenty-five soldiers still alive that had killed civilians. Those twenty-five soldiers were turned over to the President and were summarily executed.

The people returned to their homes in the city and started the cleanup. The surrounding towns helped in the rebuilding. The President paid for the weapons. Grayson and Jackson interviewed various soldiers and hired two hundred and twenty of them to add to their marine command.

LUKIA WAS SMILING WHEN she approached Thomas with a group of Horaecins. She introduced Thomas to her brother, sister, uncle, aunt, several cousins, and their children. They were all excited to meet the Captain who had freed them.

"Will you be staying here with your family now that you are home?" Thomas asked Lukia.

"I have enjoyed seeing my family," Lukia said. "But they have their life, and I have mine. It has given me tremendous relief to find my brother and sister alive. I enjoyed my visit but am no longer part of their culture. Besides, my home is on the Demon, and I do not think my husband would enjoy living on Horae. With your permission, I would like to give my relatives a tour of the Demon and introduce them to my husband."

Thomas had no objections and was pleased she was staying with the ship. Also, they were granting tours of the Demon since it was an excellent way to recruit additional crew members. Prior to offers of employment, potential crew members were given psych evaluations to ascertain their ability to adapt to life aboard a ship. Thomas agreed to a long-term trade contract with Horae, which included advanced medical supplies.

Thomas met with President Waylain and requested payment. She transferred one hundred million to a planetary account in his name. She showed him the paragraph following the one billion credit amount. It said there would be equal payments of one hundred million a year spread over a ten-year period. Further, all payments would be in the form of exports. President Waylain saw the disbelief on Thomas' face.

"Thomas, you are still getting a billion credits. You should be happy. The exports you receive will employ thousands of our citizens. You must realize I am a politician and must look out for my people."

Suzanna had listened to the exchange. She was going to tell him to read a document before signing it, but she had made the same mistake on Arabath.

Instead, she said: "Cheer up. We still made over one hundred fifty million in profits on our arms sales. Plus, a hundred million in free exports each year is fantastic since it is pure profit." She just realized they were making more on a single trade than a family ship made in several lifetimes.

"You are correct," Thomas said. "But, I was really looking forward to seeing a billion credits in our account." Thomas shook his head and would be less trusting in the future when dealing with politicians.

President Waylain promised to have militias set up in every city, town, and village to end the weekly marauder attacks. The prior president made this same promise, but no action had ever been taken. She also called for immediate elections. She won in a landslide victory. One of her first acts was to allow the Imperium to establish a military base on the planet.

After leaving Horae, Thomas visited Boreas to see if they needed arms to handle any unwanted visitors. They said no unwanted visitors had troubled their planet in a long time since everyone knew the inhabitants of Boreas were a hardy lot and dealt harshly with troublemakers. Thomas asked if they had any need for medical or food supplies. Again, they stated they were self-sufficient and had healing herbs for rare occasions when someone got sick.

The Demon left orbit and returned to The Way Station but did not dock. Thomas knew it was time to arrange for their arms delivery to a ship docked at the station. Thomas went to the shuttle bay. Suzanna, Amanda, Grayson, and his First Officer were standing in front of the shuttle door.

"Are you here to see me off?" Thomas asked Suzanna.

"You are the Captain and need to be on the bridge," Suzanna said.

Thomas shrugged his shoulders. "I am the Captain and must lead by example, and I will be fine."

"Then Amanda and I will go with you."

"No way, it is too dangerous," Thomas said with a raised voice.

"If you go, we go," Suzanna said in a challenging reply.

Everyone could tell Thomas was mad as he turned to his First Officer. "Uncle Ralph, you will go in my place but in full armor with twenty bodyguards."

First Officer Ralph Miller chuckled. "Good, but you were going with only six guards and without armor."

"You will follow my orders," Thomas said sternly and looked straight at him.

"Yes sir," First Officer Miller said as he saluted with a grin.

"I will be on the bridge monitoring you, and be careful," Thomas said. He was still mad.

Thomas turned away as he headed for the bridge. Suzanna took Amanda's hand and also left the shuttle bay.

Grayson chuckled. "That is the second time our Captain has ever lost an argument. Both times, it was to the same person. Let us put on our armor. I am going with you."

THE FIRST OFFICER ENTERED the main marketplace center with his twenty bodyguards. He noticed how everyone looked healthier. Their armor and weapons caused everyone to pause, but many locals smiled and greeted them. Every resident knew they had the Demon to thank for their nutrients and medical supplies. They went to a different secret room and met shop owners and key residents. Everyone expressed their gratitude for the supplies. First Officer Miller sat down and asked if they needed any other supplies. They were excited as they transmitted a list of products and the associated quantities. They placed large orders for nutrients since they did not want to run out again. Nutrients had a nearly infinite shelf life, so they ordered a five-year supply. They ordered twenty containers of solid oxygen and forty containers of solid hydrogen for resale. The station would make a nice profit selling the excess oxygen and hydrogen to ships to replenish the small quantities of water lost during the recycling. The Demon filled thirty percent of the order from their inventory and would deliver the balance within a standard year.

After completing the orders, the station buyers introduced a gentleman and explained they had brought the person to the meeting blindfolded so he could not give away their location. The Demon crew had not been blindfolded. This was to let them know how much they trusted the Demon and its crew. The gentleman introduced himself as a weapons buyer and asked for a list of their cargo.

The First Officer provided the list of quantities and prices for each item. After several hours, an order was prepared. The Demon had an excellent reputation, and payment was made in advance. The First Officer transmitted the order to the Demon. They were given dock locations next to each other. The buyer was blindfolded and escorted from The Way Station's secret meeting room. Litea asked the First Officer to remain. She then explained how unsavory individuals were discussing the Demon's cargo of weapons and other valuable goods. Most conversations could be ignored, but a known pirate with a large following had been talking about the Demon with the Captains of other ships. The First Officer said he would inform Captain Wilson. The meeting broke up, and they returned to the Demon. It took two shifts to transfer the containers of arms to the other ship. Both ships pulled away from The Way Station without incident. The First Officer hurriedly met with Thomas to discuss Litea's warning.

CHAPTER 13 AMBUSH

The Demon had made numerous successful trips to the Outer Planets. Their reputation grew, and other ships intentionally avoided the Demon. Thomas was concerned their next delivery was to Schlimm. Travel to Schlimm required using a Stargate because the destination had not been plotted, so there were no jump coordinates. Also, Schlimm was near a Sector Stargate that allowed for the long jump between the Outer Planets and the Rim Worlds.

Thomas called a staff meeting. Even though it was standard protocol, he wanted everyone at full battle readiness when they exited the Gate. He asked Terrance, the Tactical Officer, to make sure everyone was ready. Terrance said if there were multiple ships, he would make sure their torpedoes were locked on the two ships with the greatest threat. The six fake torpedoes would ping any other ships. Terrance could sense Thomas was troubled. He verified the Demon was battle ready. The railguns were fully charged. The four missile launchers were loaded and ready for tracking. The gunners for the artillery and particle beam cannons were ready for action.

This would be the first time the Demon would use a Stargate, and Thomas was very apprehensive. Thomas told the Helmsman when they came out of the gate to move the Demon to the optimum distance for using their laser array. At the same time, he told the Tactical Officer no one was to fire until he gave the order. He turned to his Operations Officer and asked him to identify promptly any ship or ships they might encounter as they exited the gate. They had one advantage. They knew the exact time it would take to transit through the Stargate.

As they approached the Stargate, a ship moved into position just ahead of the Demon and entered the gate. It appeared to Thomas the other ship had waited until the Demon's arrival before entering the gate. They waited the recommended time and were going to enter the Stargate when Thomas told the Helmsman to veer away from the gate. He sent a general message throughout the ship, saying they would temporarily delay their entry into the Stargate. Everyone on the bridge turned to look at their Captain.

"I believe the ship entering the gate is a spotter," Thomas said and then turned to his Navigator.

"Calculate a time we can enter the Stargate and arrive at the exit during the standard Night Watch cycle. Also, check our database and get me the information on the ship that just entered the gate."

"We can enter the gate in twelve standard hours or wait and enter in thirty-six hours," the Navigator said. "The identity of the ship is on your screen."

"Set the countdown for thirty-six hours," Thomas said. "Be prepared to enter the Stargate at the set time."

"Officer Miller, you have the bridge." Thomas planned to relax and get some rest.

Thirty-six hours later, the Demon entered the Stargate. When approaching the time for the ship to exit the gate, Thomas returned to the bridge and sat down in the Captain's chair. Everyone was ready as they came out of the gate. Unfortunately, they were surrounded by fifteen ships. Thomas was fully alert as his proprioception allowed him to exit hyperspace without disorientation.

"Tactical, launch the ten military shuttles but tell the marines to hold their fire. When they contact us, ping each enemy ship and keep pinging with the fake torpedo locks. Rotate the pinging so every enemy ship is targeted. If I give the order to fire, everyone will fire and keep firing until I order a cease-fire."

Thomas checked the ships being targeted and approved the selection. He made slight changes to the positions of the shuttles.

"Helm, keep the ship positioned so our railguns always point at one or more ships. If I give the order to fire, you will immediately take evasive action after we launch our first salvo of ordnance. Do not wait for additional orders from me. Try to keep us positioned so the ships further away cannot get a clear shot without the risk of hitting one of their own ships. Sorry, I am telling you what you already know."

"Where is my data for those ships?" Thomas shouted at his Operations Officer.

Next, he turned to his First Officer. "As always, make sure everyone is doing their job and advise me as needed," Thomas said to his uncle. Thomas did not need to tell the First Officer to take over if something happened to him.

The support staff was helping the Operations Officer. It was only a moment before Thomas saw a list of all fifteen ships. He noticed the spotter ship was not part of the fifteen. Thomas swiftly reviewed the information on each of the enemy ships.

The enemy ships were caught literally sleeping and were unprepared for the Demon's arrival. Most of the pirate Captains felt the Demon was not coming since they had been waiting so long.

Finally, the largest ship hailed the Demon. "This is Captain Rupert of the Daget. You will surrender, lower your shields, and prepare to be boarded."

Thomas spoke over an open channel to all the enemy ships. "I know who you are, and I expected to see sixteen ships. Oh, I just located the sixteenth ship on our long-range scan, it is the Opaus under Captain Pinason, but it is halfway between here and Schlimm.

In any event, I came here to hire four ships to handle long-term cargo contracts for all the exports and imports for three planets."

No ship could scan or identify a vessel as far away as the Opaus. While it might be impossible, the other ships would believe the Demon had such a super long-range scanner. It would increase their fear. None of the other ships could see even a fraction of that distance. Further, the pirates had never seen a civilian ship so heavily armed, and the Demon had not responded to the demand to surrender, nor had they dropped their shields.

Using the data, Thomas located four ships that had only recently switched to piracy. They had good captains and jump engines.

"I am here to offer profitable long-term contracts to Captain Cabe of the Intrebo, Captain Zutana of the Libraus, Captain Tubro of the Betratus, and Captain Albertus of the Famton. If you stay here, you will be destroyed. If you leave now, I will meet you at Schlimm after I destroy the rest of these ships. I will set you up with profitable trade routes allowing you to pay your crew their back wages with enough left over to give your ships some badly needed maintenance."

"Your ship is not going anywhere," Captain Rupert shouted.

Thomas calmly cut him off and continued speaking. "The last time I battled a fleet was against the navy. They had ten destroyers and two cruisers. You may want to do a quick search of Demon versus Navy. Then, search Navy orders eight new ships. Finally, search for Admiral Nelson's response to the destruction of navy ships by the Demon."

Thomas knew all the ships would be frantically searching and pulling up communications concerning the Demon.

After a few moments, Captain Rupert spoke up. "There is no way you took on a navy fleet. Also, this Admiral Nelson denied you took out four of his destroyers."

Thomas made sure they heard him chuckle. "The Admiral did not lie. We took out eight destroyers. Two cruisers and two of the destroyers escaped. Wilson Enterprises built this ship. My father, Ben Wilson, owns the company and made sure the ship he built for his son was superior to all other ships. With a proper scan, you will see we are armed with two railguns, six rapid-fire particle beam cannons, four missile launchers, and eight torpedo tubes. All of our ammunition consists of special heavy-duty rounds. The missiles and torpedoes are AI guided. They will continue to seek out their target even if an enemy ship jumps or goes through a Stargate. In the disagreement with the navy, we fired eight torpedoes and then reloaded and fired eight more. The first torpedoes took down their shields, and the second volley of torpedoes penetrated the navy's double hulls and blew the ships apart from the inside. It was beautiful."

While Thomas was talking, he noticed the four ships he had offered jobs had peeled off and were leaving.

"Of course, your ships all have low-grade single hulls. There will not be much left of your ships to salvage. Of course, our military shuttles could take out all of your ships. Each shuttle has two guns that fire two thousand rounds per minute of armor-piercing bullets, plus the canons can punch a sizable hole in a ship. Unfortunate for you, our crew on the Demon would prefer to destroy your ships without help from the shuttles." Two more of the ships furthest away decided to leave. There were still nine enemy ships remaining. Thomas felt the odds had just turned in his favor. His ship, plus the ten military shuttles, would be more than a match against the remaining pirates.

"I could send videos of our disagreement with the navy, but it was not much of a battle. Regardless, you do not have time to watch videos since the Demon will be sending you to hell."

The remaining ships were being pinged more often since there were fewer vessels. Finally, the Demon's crew understood what Thomas was doing. The Demon had a superior scanning system, and the Operations Officer started sending information to Thomas, beginning with the worst ship. Thomas reviewed the scans they had just made of the pirate ships and how each ship should be targeted. It was time to get specific. He addressed the worst ship.

"Captain Connic of the Lamia, why are you here? You have no shields, so we will not waste a missile on your ship. We will fill your hull with thousands of rounds from our artillery cannons."

All the ships heard Captain Connic as she told Captain Rupert. "I am out of here. You told me they would surrender without a fight. Have you looked at the Demon? Also, you never said anything about ten military shuttles."

"He is lying, and those are just shuttles," Captain Rupert said.

"He does not sound like he is lying," Captain Conic responded. "I have never seen a ship with that much firepower, and those shuttles have pulse cannons." Captain Conic turned her ship and left the area.

Then Thomas identified a ship with a bad engine and said it would have difficulty maneuvering out of the way of a missile and there would not be much left of their vessel once the engine went critical.

Next, he addressed a ship with a radiation leak. "I do not know if I should waste ammunition on your ship. Everyone on your ship will die in another year unless you fix the containment leak and take drugs for radiation poisoning."

Thomas continued to talk as more of the enemy ships decided to leave. Then the ships still facing the Demon realized how many had left. The remaining ships were no longer interested in a fight with the most heavily armed vessel they had ever seen. They did not want to have a battle with a ship that defeated a navy fleet. Also, they all knew the Demon had destroyed other pirate ships without incurring any damage. Captain Rupert had led them to believe they would all be rich from sharing the expensive cargo on board the Demon and told them the Demon would surrender when it faced fifteen ships.

Captain Rupert had been mesmerized by Thomas when he suddenly realized only one other ship was still with him. Thomas reviewed the long history of cruelty for the two remaining ships. They were the worst. They showed no mercy and took immense pleasure in torturing their victims before killing them.

"It looks like you win this round, but we will meet again," Captain Rupert said with a snarl.

"No, we will not meet again," Thomas replied.

"Fire both torpedoes and launch all four missiles, so they all arrive on target simultaneously," Thomas said to his Tactical Officer. "I want you to generate the largest flash possible."

The two remaining ships were turning away when they looked in horror at the incoming ordnance. The ships leaving the area saw the enormous fireball.

Then the thirteen fleeing ships heard the voice of Captain Wilson. "That was disappointing. One of our smallest missiles took out both ships. For those of you who had the sense to leave, please tell every ship you meet. If anyone attacks a ship hauling cargo on behalf of the Demon, we will hunt them down and send them to hell. My Tactical Officer has just informed me. Several of my gunners believe they can still hit your ships from this distance. They are taking bets, even though I disapprove of gambling."

The officers on the Demon laughed as they saw the leaving ships go to full power, with some going to flank speed. While the pirates were not known for being religious, they were saying their prayers while trying to escape. The pirates did not necessarily believe in heaven, but they were developing a fear of hell and the ability of the Demon to send them there.

The bridge officers looked at Thomas with admiration, and their young Helmsman said what they were all thinking.

"When we came out of the gate, I thought it was all over. How did you know how to do all that?"

"By studying and learning from great leaders of the past," Thomas said. "Thousands of years ago, a great war leader named Sun Tzu said all warfare is based on deception. The greatest victory is that which requires no battle. A leader should know when to fight and when not to fight."

He then continued. "I had all of you researching, locating information, and organizing data while sitting on the bridge with little to do. I also had other people on and off the ship gathering information. I simply used the information to develop the strategy we just put into action. Collecting information is something my father taught me. I learned how to use the information from studying the great warriors and military leaders of the past. Also, I am still learning. Continuous learning is something you must do if you wish to survive in the future. You must know what strategy to use in each type of battle. The tactics must be dynamic and fluid to fit the specific situation. Also, you must act decisively, or the decision will be taken away from you by the actions of your adversary. Attack, defend, go forward, or retreat. Again, those decisions are critical and must be made in a timely manner."

The Helmsman asked one more question. "What if they had decided to fight?"

Thomas leaned forward and coldly looked the Helmsman in the eye. "Then we would have destroyed all fifteen ships."

"Tactical, recall our shuttles," Thomas said. "Helm, as soon as the shuttles are aboard, set course for Schlimm."

Once they were underway, Thomas addressed the bridge officers. "It has been a long day, so I need some sleep. Officer Miller, arrange a schedule to allow everyone to catch up on their sleep." Thomas left the bridge and headed for his cabin.

"I still do not understand how Captain Wilson did that," the Helmsman said. "He was so calm and believable."

The First Officer chuckled. "When you understand what just happened, you will most likely be captain of your own ship. Despite my comment, you are not alone in your lack of understanding. Our Captain is exceptional. He prepares for possibilities we cannot see."

CAPTAIN THOMAS WILSON was back on the bridge when they arrived at Schlimm. He promptly contacted the four ships and provided them with the trade agreements for the planets Averon, Ashtara, and Minerva. He further explained how the three planets working together were self-sufficient and could prosper. Thomas gave them an account number and told them they were to send five percent of the profit from each trade to the account as his fee for allowing them to participate in the contract. He also told them they were on the honor system to pay the fee. They had been expecting a much higher fee, so they all agreed without hesitation and said they would pay promptly. Thomas told them he had friends on the planets who would keep him posted on all off-world transactions, and they would be replaced if they failed to pay the required amount. Thomas had not planned to charge a fee, but his First Officer and Suzanna both said the former pirates would be suspicious if he provided the trade routes for free.

Thomas told the Captains they were to abide by the terms of the agreements with the planets. Each Captain would be responsible for the behavior of their crew. The Captains promised to serve as good representatives for the Demon. The Captains further assured him the planets would not have any complaints about their crew. Thomas told them after they accumulated some profit, they should take turns traveling to Wilson Enterprises to have their ships overhauled. He told them he would send a message to his father so they would get preferential treatment. They thanked Thomas for the agreements.

Schlimm was settled by Russian descendants who named the planet. The name for the planet did not have an exact translation from Russian to Galactic. The closest meanings were severe, awful, evil, or bad. Scans showed the planet fit the description of severe as to the weather

Grayson and Jackson, with a contingent of marines, visited Schlimm. They returned three days later with a dire report.

"The people were hardy but barely surviving," Grayson said. "Schlimm is extremely cold in the winter and extremely hot in the summer. The growing season takes place between the two extremes. The population is small, at less than a hundred thousand. To survive, the people spend the winters at the equator. They migrate to the north pole to survive the summer. There is little in the way of technology. They farm during the short growing season at the equator and live a nomad life during the long treks they have to make twice per year. When the temperature turns hot, they use hybrid animals to pull wagons that form caravans as they travel the long distance to reach the north pole. While at the north pole during the summer, they supplement their diet with ice fishing. When winter sets in, the caravans travel back to the equator and farm. The inhabitants of Schlimm have nothing to offer as trade."

"Your description does not come close to the historical description of the planet," Thomas said.

"The planet has an elliptical orbit," Grayson replied. "According to their folklore, a large asteroid or comet passed near the planet. While it did not crash into the planet, the gravity from the near miss increased the planet's elliptical orbit. This resulted in more severe seasons, which caused the death of over ninety percent of the population."

"Is there anything we can do to help?" Thomas asked. "Are they receptive to joining the Imperium and letting the military establish a base on the planet?"

"They thought I was joking about a military base. They asked why anyone would want to live on their planet. When they realized I was serious, no one had any objections but doubted the sanity of anyone willingly coming to their planet. Their leaders will execute any agreement since they do not believe their lives can get any worse."

Thomas had an idea. He sent a message to Admiral Nelson saying Schlimm wished to join the Imperium as a non-voting member since their population was below a hundred million. Their only requirement is they want the first five years of the lease for the military base to be paid on account to the Demon so they can purchase needed supplies.

Thomas received a reply from the Admiral agreeing to the proposal and congratulating Thomas on bringing another Outer planet into the Imperium. Approval was quick since no voting rights were involved and paying rent for five years was considered a bargain. Thomas met with Suzanna, the engineers, and the scientists. He showed them the planet's budget.

"All items furnished to Schlimm will be at our costs, no profit," Thomas said. "Determine how we can best help the inhabitants."

It took several weeks of intense work, but it was very productive. The analysis showed that retractable solar panels would generate power for recharging power units. One power unit could power hundreds of heat pumps. Heat pumps could be installed in the homes at both the equator and the north pole. The heat pumps would provide heat during the winter and cooling during the summer. Crime on the planet was insignificant since the people depended on each other for survival. Further, they could defend themselves against the planet's predators using homemade weapons. Therefore, the inhabitants of Schlimm had no need for weapons.

Suzanna explained to Thomas how trade with Schlimm would never be profitable. However, the engineers felt they could make Schlimm self-sufficient. Unfortunately, Schlimm did not have enough credits from the military lease to implement the project. Suzanna was happy when Thomas said they could proceed with the project. Thomas said their overall profits would cover losses on a few planets.

THE EXPLOITS OF THE Demon continued to spread throughout the Outer Planets and the Rim Worlds. Like most rumors, the stories kept growing about the Demon's armament and how the Demon had destroyed an entire navy fleet. Everyone assumed the Demon was responsible if a pirate ship turned up missing. In addition, the Demon was gaining a reputation for making its deliveries on time and honoring its agreements. Plus, the four ships working under the Demon's agreement acted as goodwill ambassadors for the Demon and told everyone Captain Wilson was a person of honor. Throughout the Outer Planets and the Rim, the Demon was feared and respected.

Admiral Nelson continued to receive reports from his Agent regarding the Demon and was impressed by the communications. He even laughed when told of the battle between the Demon and the fifteen ships.

Then, it stopped being a laughing matter when the Admiral received an urgent communication from the Premier for an in-person meeting concerning questions he was being asked by members of the Senate concerning the Demon.

During the meeting, the Premier asked about the navy ships destroyed by the Demon with super weapons. Admiral Nelson assured the Premier it was just a fabrication to allow the Demon to make its arms deliveries safely.

The Admiral thought he had convinced the Premier everything was going as planned when the Premier asked about the Demon's super deadly torpedoes and AI guided missiles with jump capability. He even suggested the navy should obtain some of these special weapons. It was all the Admiral could do to keep from laughing, but one does not laugh at the Premier. He again spent considerable time explaining how the Rim primarily dealt with old technology. The weapons used by the Demon were only military-grade, and there was nothing special about the Demon's ordnance. The Premier was hesitant but finally seemed to accept the Admiral's explanation.

The Admiral thought maybe their plan was working too well. Still, he was pleased with the progress Thomas was making, since it was improving their ability to survive an invasion by the Hostis.

CHAPTER 14 FREEDOM FIGHTERS OR TERRORISTS

The Demon proceeded to Gatera, which was an Outer Planet served by a huge space station. Gatera was a modern world with a monarchy as its governing body. Unfortunately, it was designated by the Imperium as a dictatorship. The Imperium wanted a change in the government since the current ruler refused to join the Imperium or allow a military base on the planet. You could trade any cargo with another ship at the station, but you had to pay a transfer fee. There was no such fee for goods sold to buyers on Gatera.

The Demon was to provide arms to the freedom fighters trying to overthrow the current government. The government regulated all access to the planet's main landing areas. Demon's potential customers were considered terrorists by the government. There was some justification for the description as there were periodic bloody attacks and bombings against government institutions. The government was a modified feudalistic state with a King and Lords. Even so, there was private ownership of the land, and businesses flourished. Local taxes were paid to the Lords, with a percentage going to the King. Businesses operated under a charter granted by the crown. The King had the right to replace a Lord, which seldom happened as the last replacement was over twenty years in the past.

According to the data provided by Admiral Nelson, the freedom fighters were supported by a Lord who would join the Imperium if they allowed him to take over the monarchy. After reviewing all the data, Thomas was concerned the Imperium's plan was simply to replace one monarch with another. He felt there was a high probability of a civil war since the freedom fighters or terrorists wanted the monarchy destroyed and replaced with a democracy. Thomas spent considerable time reviewing the social structure of Gatera. The royal family was currently represented by a King and Queen, with a designated Prince as successor to the crown. Relatives to the royal family held various governmental positions. The titles of Dukes and Duchesses were given to higher-level governmental officials. The soldiers reported to Knights. Lords ruled over large estates. However, total land ownership by all the Lords was restricted to ten percent. The remaining land was owned by individuals, merchants, artisans, and farmers. Everyone earned a salary, and there were no slaves. If the statistics were correct, crime was low compared to other Outer Planets. Everyone without a disability served two years in the military when they turned eighteen.

Only a few worlds existed under a monarchy. Most planets operated under some form of democracy, but a few had absolute dictators. Also, there were a few corporate-controlled worlds like Melius. The Demon was sitting in a stationary position some distance from the station when the Communications Officer informed Thomas she was receiving a message from the station. Thomas nodded for her to put it through.

"Hello Demon, this is Prince Elderon. I would like to address Captain Wilson if he is available." The display showed a slim stately gentleman in his late thirties dressed in a tailored business suit.

"This is Captain Wilson. How may I help you?"

"Captain Wilson, your reputation precedes you. There was a Captain Rupert with sixteen ships that planned to sell us a large cargo he intended to obtain as a gift from the Demon."

There were laugh lines around his eyes as the prince continued. "It is my understanding from the ships that recently vacated our space that Captain Rupert was misinformed about the Demon's willingness to give away its cargo. I understand Captain Rupert's ship, the Daget, and another ship suffered a catastrophic accident. Since the Daget cannot sell us goods, we may be interested in purchasing some of your cargo. Assuming the Demon is so inclined to provide us with a manifest for our consideration."

Thomas liked the elegant way Prince Elderon presented his request. "We would be happy to provide you with a manifest," Thomas replied.

Thomas sent a copy of the manifest to the location shown on the Prince's link. The Prince looked down to see the file for the cargo manifest.

"I would like to extend an invitation for you to visit Gatera tomorrow as my guest and attend a dinner in your honor," the Prince said. "If you could meet me at the station in the early afternoon, I would be happy to provide transportation to Gatera. You may bring a guest or guests."

"I will discuss your gracious invitation with my officers," Thomas said and nodded to his Communications Officer to end the transmission.

Suzanna was on the bridge and had listened to the exchange. "What do you think?" Thomas asked Suzanna.

"I think we should accept so we can get an understanding of the political situation. Assuming we accept, I am concerned about what we should wear. You saw how well the Prince was dressed. I expect the royal members of his home or castle to be attired in elaborate garments, including ceremonial outfits. Our formal clothes would look drab by comparison. Therefore, instead of trying to compete in fashion, I suggest we dress in our combat best. Those outfits made quite an impression the last time we wore them. Also, being armed will provide additional security in a worst-case scenario. It is a relatively safe planet, so I see no reason why we cannot take Amanda with us. She will be disappointed if she learns we are visiting a castle without her. We should take at least eight bodyguards in full armor. Four for you, two for Amanda, and two for me. Also, mine and Amanda's bodyguards should be female."

Thomas called the Prince and told him they would join him at the suggested time. He asked if his shuttle could accommodate himself, plus two guests and eight bodyguards. The Prince confirmed his shuttle would have ample room, and he was looking forward to their meeting.

Thomas discussed the matter with Grayson, and they selected the bodyguards for the mission. The guards were directed to find out discreetly as much as they could about the current situation on the planet. The goal was to determine the most expeditious way to have Gatera apply for membership in the Imperium. They needed to determine if supporting the freedom fighters would be the fastest way to achieve that objective. Suzanna, with a nod from Thomas, decided to bring samples of their weapons since they were in the arms business. It might seem strange if they did not present themselves as such.

THE FOLLOWING AFTERNOON found everyone ready. The guards had eaten a light meal before leaving and carried provisions within their combat suits. The marines had their helmets retracted into the collar of their armor. Each guard brought along a backpack with assorted weapons. One of their military shuttles transported them to the designated gate. As an additional safety precaution, they brought along a pack containing the custom armor fitted for Thomas, Suzanna, and Amanda. When they arrived at the station, Prince Elderon was standing next to his royal shuttle.

After introductions, they boarded the royal shuttle and headed to Gatera. The shuttle landed on a pad within the walls of the estate.

While it was not a castle, it was a large, beautiful home with ornate statues and fountains surrounded by blooming flowers.

Prince Elderon asked them to follow him. The guards played their part as the four male guards lined up in a straight line to the side of Thomas but slightly behind. The female guards did the same to the side of Suzanna. Amanda walked between Thomas and Suzanna. Amanda was disappointed there was no castle. Thomas and Suzanna walked slowly to allow Amanda to walk at a normal pace. There were two large columns on either side of the double front doors. Prince Elderon opened one of the front doors, and everyone followed him into a room where there was a collection of over twenty guests. The room they entered was quite large and allowed the guests to be comfortably spread out. It was perfect for a grand assembly but was oversized for the number of dignitaries in attendance. When they entered, everyone stopped talking. Suzanna had been correct. Everyone was dressed in expensive apparel. In contrast, every eye was on Thomas, Suzanna, and to a lesser extent on Amanda. They appeared beautiful but deadly with their guns, swords, and knives in clear view. Thomas knew the other ladies would be jealous since Suzanna was the sexiest and most beautiful person in the room.

Suzanna was always very observant and noticed the men were well dressed. Sadly, they were in poor shape physically. By comparison, Thomas had an athletic body and walked with a commanding, energized grace. Then she realized the ladies in the room had their eyes on Thomas. She could not help having a slight pang of jealousy. Suzanna took turns making eye contact with several of the ladies. She glared at them with an icy stare followed by a satisfied grin as she noted the fear in their eyes as they looked away. They continued to follow Prince Elderon as he led them toward an older couple standing toward the back of the room. The family resemblance to the Prince left no doubt they were the King and Queen.

Prince Elderon introduced Thomas, Suzanna, and Amanda to King Kayden and Queen Juliette.

Amanda asked why they were not wearing crowns. She was disappointed when the King said none of their ancestors had ever worn crowns. The Queen answered her second question and said there was no throne. Further, she confessed there was a dungeon, but it looked like a jail. Prince Elderon asked Amanda if she would like to have dinner with the younger members of the household. Amanda looked at her mother, and Suzanna nodded. It would be okay. With a slight hand signal, Suzanna motioned for her daughter's guards to accompany Amanda as she left with a female attendant.

After a period of polite conversation, dinner was announced, and everyone entered a second room. There were three long tables with four chairs on each side, allowing eight people to a table. The King and Queen sat at the front table with their guests and certain family members, including several Lords. The rest of the assemblage sat at the other two tables. The table arrangement made it conducive to casual discussions without raising one's voice. The guards placed the backpacks against the far wall and took defensive positions within the room.

Thomas needed information concerning the monarchy since the action he was considering could significantly affect the planet.

"King Kayden, could you explain how your monarchy has continued to exist when most planets range from democracies to republics," Thomas asked conversationally with no disapproval in his voice.

"I will try," the King replied. "We use the approach espoused in a translated text from thousands of years ago titled *The Prince* by Niccolò Machiavelli. He espoused how the way for a King to maintain power is to have the people love him, and the Lords fear him. This approach keeps politics in balance. For this to work, you must take good care of the people. You must also keep an eye on the Lords to prevent them from trying to steal the throne even though we technically do not have a throne. Still, a King must be diligent in preventing a Lord from becoming a threat. It helps if the people and the Lords see we do not accumulate excessive wealth. This helps to keep any resentment to a minimum. Our farm makes us self-sufficient. Therefore, the taxes collected are returned to the people in roads, bridges, schools, and other endeavors."

Thomas and Suzanna enjoyed the meal. Toward the end of the meal, Duke Winsor asked Thomas what was in the backpacks the guards had set against the wall.

"The packs contain samples of some of the arms we sale," Suzanna replied.

"Can we see them?" Duke Winsor asked with enthusiasm.

"If King Kayden is agreeable, I would be happy to show you the samples," Suzanna said as she looked at the King.

The King nodded, indicating she should proceed since he was also interested in seeing the contents of the packs. Suzanna got out of her seat and walked over to open the packs. She put her hand where a sensor would identify her and release the internal hidden locks. She performed the same exercise on each of the packs. Suzanna reached into a pack and withdrew a military rifle. She flipped the handle to extend the length. She demonstrated how to load and switch from single shot to full auto. She explained how the weapons could be provided with an embedded recognition component. The safety component would only allow the owner to fire the gun.

Suzanna completed the rifle demonstration. "Will you sell me one of those guns," Duke Winsor asked.

"No," Suzanna answered.

"Why not?" The Duke asked. He looked disappointed and a little angry.

"We normally sell these guns by the container," Suzanna said calmly. "We prefer to sell in units of a hundred thousand weapons, but our smallest order is a partial container of ten thousand guns."

Suzanna emphasized small like it was an insignificant bug. Next, she pulled out a pistol. She proceeded until she had demonstrated every weapon in all the packs. She discussed the larger weapons they sold, including the attack helicopters. Then, she provided a video of the helicopter and larger arms. While talking, she returned all the weapons to the packs and reactivated the locks. Suzanna asked the King if he would join her. He arose from his seat and approached her. She took his hand, placed it over the sensor, and activated it.

"These samples are a gift to you," Suzanna said to the King. "You are the only person who can open the packs. All you have to do is put your hand on the sensor. You may wish to show these weapons to your military to see if they would like to upgrade their arms."

Thomas had been paying close attention to Suzanna, and she had completely mesmerized everyone in the room. Thomas appreciated how Suzanna was a natural salesperson. She described each item, so it was easy to understand. Suzanna paused at the right moment for just the correct amount of time, and she was very persuasive. He admired how she handled every purchase and sale with precision. She was doing an outstanding job. Promoting Suzanna to Cargo Administrator was one of his better decisions.

The evening was ending, and the dinner was over. As Thomas was bidding King Kayden and Queen Juliette good night, he secretly asked the King if he could have a private meeting. The King said he would meet with Thomas after breakfast the next day.

Thomas noticed Suzanna and Duke Winsor were having a conversation, so he waited a few minutes before joining them. The Duke bid them good night and walked away. A staff member was standing nearby and said she would be happy to show them to their rooms. She also told them Amanda was already there. They were shown to an apartment with enough space for themselves and the guards. They found Amanda asleep in one of the bedrooms. The two female guards who had been with Amanda were sitting and eating at a table covered with hot food and assorted drinks. The other six guards joined the ladies. The two female guards watching Amanda found the staff to be quite talkative. They confirmed the only people permanently living at the estate were the royal family. The royal guards were stationed at a military base a short distance from the estate. The employees all lived offsite and commuted to work each day. The royals were liked by most of the people but not so much by the Dukes from each province.

Suzanna told Thomas what he had already guessed. "Duke Winsor is our contact. After the weapons presentation, he wanted to buy twenty containers of arms which is a respectable order. The guns used by the existing planetary army are inferior to the weapons we are selling. I asked him about the freedom fighters, and he said they would be eliminated once they had killed the King and his immediate family. The freedom fighters trust Duke Winsor, and he knew the names of most of the leaders. Duke Winsor confirmed he would accept Imperium membership as long as the agreement ensured he and his lineage would be the new rulers."

"What is your opinion of Duke Winsor, and who do you feel we should support?" Thomas asked.

"I do not like Duke Winsor," Suzanna answered with a frown. "He is not to be trusted and is concerned only with himself. He does not appear concerned about the people he plans to rule. I think we would be exchanging a rather likable monarch for a complete despot. Duke Winsor is already planning to betray the freedom fighters. Some might say he is only betraying terrorists. Regardless, he is still betraying those individuals who have trusted him with their lives."

"I agree," Thomas said. "If we must choose, then we will support the current regime."

THE NEXT DAY, THOMAS, Suzanna, and Amanda had breakfast with King Kayden, Queen Juliette, and Prince Elderon. The guards enjoyed a large breakfast a short distance away. After breakfast, Amanda left to spend time with Prince Elderon's children. Thomas and Suzanna adjourned to the King's office with Prince Elderon.

"Before we get started, I would like to say we have reviewed your manifest and would like to buy large quantities of your non-arms cargo. Here is the list of items we wish to purchase and a list of items we would like to export." Prince Elderon handed Suzanna the list.

"Provide me with the coordinates, and we would be happy to deliver the containers to the required locations," Suzanna replied. "Instead, if you prefer, we can transfer the containers to the station and let your shuttles handle the transportation to Gatera."

Prince Elderon, with a smile that reached his eyes, said, "Since you explained the price was the same under either alternative, we will be happy to have you make the deliveries to our planet. I will provide you with the coordinates for the deliveries to each province."

The King narrowed his eyes and looked at Thomas with a slight frown. "You said you would like to meet privately. I have no secrets from my son. What did you wish to discuss?" Thomas decided it would be best to come straight to the point.

"Your Majesty, the Imperium has been monitoring the Hostis. They believe it is only a matter of time before we are again at war with the aliens. The Hostis do not take prisoners. When they invade a planet, they kill every human without regard to sex or age. The Imperium is trying to get certain of the Outer Planets to join the Imperium voluntarily. Membership in the Imperium would allow a military base on your planet and a space-based satellite weapons grid to defend against such an attack. In the event of an attack, it is hoped the planet's defenders could hold out until the navy arrived. There would still be heavy casualties even with the additional defenses in place. Also, with a defense grid in place, there is a chance the Hostis would bypass your planet completely and go after easier targets. You were adamant in not wanting to join the Imperium, but your continued refusal could cause the death of everyone on Gatera. If the Hostis decide to start another war with humanity, the Imperium will try to stop them at the Rim. If that fails, they are hopeful a secondary defense using the Outer Planets will stop the Hostis and prevent an invasion of the Core Planets. You may not like the Imperium, but over eighty billion people died on planets with no defense during the last war. It was estimated half would have survived if there had been a military presence on those planets. The Hostis are currently testing our defenses and have killed all the inhabitants on three Rim Worlds."

"Will this defense grid totally protect us?" Asked the Prince.

"No, the Hostis will suffer losses, but they will manage to breech the grid. The ground-based troops will launch surface to air missiles against the alien landing crafts and will destroy many of the inbound ships. However, armies of Hostis will still land on your planet. Your citizens will need to fight along side the solders. Hopefully, the navy will arrive in time to keep the Hostis from destroying all human life on your planet."

"You paint a very grim picture," the King said.

"Yes, but without the navy, you will be unable to defend this planet." Thomas saw the concerned expressions on everyone's face.

"It is my understanding the Imperium would reject our form of government and require a democracy," the King said.

"You are correct, but a few acceptable governments include provisions for royalty. Here is a wafer describing each form of an approved government. If you freely join, you get to pick the structure of your government. Whereas if it is forced upon you, someone else decides that form. The Imperium is prepared to topple your reign to save your planet and safeguard the Core Planets. They asked me to supply weapons to the terrorists to effect such a change. A member of the royalty is working with the terrorists. He has agreed to allow Gatera to join the Imperium if he is given the royal title. Duke Winsor is our primary contact, and he has already requested the delivery of twenty containers of weapons. We are telling you this since we do not plan to deliver arms to Duke Winsor or the terrorists. If I report my mission is a failure, the navy will simply take other action to bring your planet into the Imperium. For example, they could covertly fund a group of human mercenaries to invade Gatera. Then they could come to your rescue to save your planet, but the royal family would no longer exist. Please understand if you voluntarily join the Imperium, you can make demands and get meaningful concessions. You would also have a vote in the Senate. Regardless, your immediate threat is Duke Winsor."

The King, with a sigh, lowered his head. "Those are serious charges you have made against Duke Winsor. Do you have any proof?"

Suzanna held up a thumb-size recorder as she addressed the King. "Here is a recording of my conversation with Duke Winsor last night after dinner." Suzanna played the recording.

The King, with pronounced disappointment, asked them to leave his office while he discussed the situation with his son.

"Do you still wish for us to deliver the cargo, or do you wish to cancel the order," Suzanna asked.

"We still wish to purchase your cargo," Prince Elderon responded. "Thank you for your honesty. We knew the Duke was ambitious and coveted the throne. We had no idea he would stoop to such measures. If it is not too inconvenient, I would like you to spend one more day with us and wait until tomorrow to leave. Also, we will consider the other matter."

"Of course, we can wait another day since we would like to have your father's decision, before we depart," Thomas replied.

Thomas contacted the bridge and verified there were no issues with the ship. Suzanna communicated with the cargo handlers and transmitted the non-arms cargo purchased by Gatera. Grayson spoke to the marines and told them to stay alert.

DUKE WINSOR RECEIVED a report from one of his spies at the King's residence. He flew into a rage. His wife came to see what was wrong, and he screamed at her. She ran out of the room in fear. She feared he would physically attack her as he had done on previous occasions.

The Duke directed several staff members to pack his personal items and put them in his shuttle. He called an emergency meeting of the leaders of the terrorist groups. While waiting for their arrival, he had valuable items of the estate loaded on the shuttle.

When the leaders arrived, he explained he had been betrayed and would be heading off-world. He told them he would hire a group of mercenaries and return. Then, he would replace the king and claim his rightful place. They were all confused because he had always preached how democracy would replace the monarchy.

One leader asked him to return the funds he had contributed to purchase the arms. Then they all chimed in, asking for a return of their money. He agreed, but first, he asked them to join him in one last toast before leaving. They did not see any reason to be toasting. Nevertheless, if it would hasten the return of their money, they would join the Duke in one last toast. The Duke pulled a special bottle of whiskey from a cabinet and poured everyone a drink. He shouted liberty for all, and they emptied their glasses. One leader noticed the Duke did not drink from his goblet, and he did not feel like joining the toast. In a few moments, the leaders of the freedom fighters started to sway and lose balance until they fell to the floor, dying from the poisoned drink.

The one lone survivor looked at the Duke. "Why?" He asked.

"Because I have no intention of returning your money," the Duke said with disgust. "This drink and the toast were to be made when I became King." While talking, the Duke pulled a pistol and shot the last leader through the heart.

The Duke was leaving the estate when his wife ran up to him. "Where are you going?"

"I am leaving the planet. Prince Elderon is on his way here to arrest me."

She thought quickly and figured they might arrest her because of his crimes. "Wait, let me pack a few things, and I will go with you."

Duke Winsor pulled his gun and pointed it at her. "No, you won't."

She turned and ran, but it was too late. She heard the sound of the discharge from the gun. She crashed forward onto the floor face down and ceased to move. The Duke took the pilot's seat in the shuttle and engaged the thrusters.

THOMAS AND SUZANNA watched as a convoy of military vehicles approached the royal home. Then, they saw the Prince get into the lead vehicle. The cloud made it easy to follow the path of the convoy. Suzanna walked over and stood next to Thomas. He put his arm around her waist.

"I believe Prince Elderon is going to ask Duke Winsor some poignant questions," Thomas said. "It may have been wrong telling the truth to the King. Saving his life could cause hundreds of millions of deaths if the Hostis attack Gatera without an adequate defense in place. I had no reservations about toppling the Dictator on Horae since General Erebos was murdering thousands of defenseless people, and the inhabitants were living in fear."

Suzanna understood the dilemma Thomas was experiencing. "Regardless of the outcome, I am glad you told them the truth. Ultimately, the Imperium will find a way to bring Gatera into the Imperium. The outcome will be the same, but at least we did not assist in the death of the royals."

The following day, Thomas and Suzanna were asked to join the King for breakfast. King Kayden, Queen Juliette, and Prince Elderon were already seated when they arrived. Thomas and Suzanna noticed all three of the royals seemed unsettled. Thomas and Suzanna took their seats and remained silent while eating.

When they finished breakfast and were on their second cup of coffee, Prince Elderon opened the conversation.

"It appears we have a spy. We visited Duke Winsor's estate yesterday, but he had already made a hasty escape. He is no longer on Gatera. At his estate, we found the bodies of the leaders of the terrorists. Also, we found the Duke's wife. She had been shot in the back by the Duke and left for dead. She is alive and told us a little of what had taken place. She is in critical condition. The doctors are doing their best but do not expect her to survive. Duke Winsor transferred huge funds to off-world accounts to pay for the arms he planned to buy from you. The upside is our effort was not a complete waste of resources since we identified the dead terrorist leaders. We are in the process of arresting their followers so they can answer for the deaths caused by their indiscriminate bombings. We put a temporary person in charge of Duke Winsor's estate until we can decide on a permanent replacement. Though it pains us, we have at least taken care of the immediate threat." When Prince Elderon finished, he looked at his father.

"It was a long night, and with my wife's support, we have selected a form of government from the list you provided," King Kayden said.

"You can let your Imperium know we will be applying to join the Imperium. They can establish a military base on Gatera, but with a charter wherein a majority of the enlisted service personnel must be from our world. We will have other demands we will present at the appropriate time."

The Queen smiled demurely and nodded to her husband. Thomas was a little confused. He previously thought the Queen left decisions of state up to her husband since the Queen had spoken little during their previous encounters. Thomas said he would inform the Imperium, and he explained the Imperium would send a representative to assist them in becoming a member. Suzanna told them the deliveries of the cargo would start later that day. They said their goodbyes, and Prince Elderon said he would return them to the station.

Thomas and Suzanna returned to their room. They packed their belongings for departure. Amanda enjoyed the time she spent with the children of Prince Elderon. Nevertheless, she was ready to return home to the Demon. Prince Elderon appeared, and everyone boarded the royal shuttle for their trip back to the station.

CHAPTER 15 GUNS AND KNIVES

The shuttle landed at the station's gate without mishap. Everyone departed from the royal shuttle and waved to Prince Elderon as his shuttle exited the gate. The Demon's military shuttle was waiting for them.

As they approached their shuttle, a group of armed individuals rushed in and opened fire. They had not expected an attack and were caught in the open. Suzanna was shot as she shoved Amanda to the floor and covered her with her own body. She was hit a second time by a stray bullet. Thomas was the target and was shot multiple times as he pulled his sidearm to return fire. Thomas fired on full auto and saw three of the attackers go down from his shots before being hit several more times. The attackers did not stop even when shot several times. Only a kill shot stopped them. The bodyguards engaged their helmets and opened fire on the attackers. One attacker who reached Thomas was out of ammunition. He pulled a knife and stabbed Thomas in the stomach before a bodyguard shot the assailant in the head. It was apparent the attackers had taken a berserker drug before the attack. The marines finally killed the last attacker.

The attack failed because the attackers did not have armor-piercing rounds. One of Thomas's bodyguards was dead from a headshot suffered before he could activate his helmet. All sixteen of the attackers were killed. Another group of assailants were at the doors but retreated when the entire first group was killed. The guards rushed Thomas, Suzanna, and Amanda into the shuttle while two of them dragged in the dead guard. The Pilot saw that the Captain, Suzanna, and Amanda were covered in blood.

The Pilot shouted. "Let me know when everyone is secure and prepare for maximum excel."

"All secure," Grayson shouted.

The pilot immediately took off at maximum velocity as she headed back to the Demon. The pilot abandoned standard protocol and went to emergency broadcast.

"This is Pilot Seymour of the Shuttle M5. We were attacked at the station. Have medical meet us at the shuttle bay. One marine is dead. The Captain, Suzanna, and Amanda have all been shot. I am coming in hot, repeat, I am coming in hot."

Grayson had secured himself on the floor of the shuttle next to Thomas.

"Are Suzanna and Amanda alright?" Thomas asked.

"I believe Amanda is fine other than being frightened," Grayson answered. "Suzanna is wounded, but she is alive. Sir, this is my fault. I am so sorry. We should have secured all entry points into the gate before letting you and your family off the shuttle. We should have been in a defensive formation with helmets activated."

Thomas did not hear anything after he learned Suzanna and Amanda were alive. While inbound, Grayson called Jackson and told him what had happened. He told him to take two shuttles with a contingent of marines back to the gate and find out who hired the attackers. He told him a second group of armed hostiles had retreated and to take every precaution.

Pilot Seymour was the ship's highest-ranked shuttle pilot. She had a natural feel for the controls and had practiced hard to be the best. No one ever came in hot for a landing since it was risky and required exact precision. She waited till the last possible second before cutting power, doing a one hundred eighty degrees turn, and hitting maximum power to slow the craft. The shuttle entered the landing bay going backward. It stopped its horizontal movement as it was coming down on its landing gears. Seymour activated the door release and the ramp. The door, ramp, and landing occurred simultaneously for a perfect landing.

The entire medical staff was in the shuttle bay, including the off-duty medical assistants. Doctor Adler entered the shuttle with the first stretcher and looked over the wounded. She quickly determined the unconscious Captain was in the worst shape since he was very pale from blood loss. She cauterized half a dozen wounds and slapped self-adhesive bandages on other wounds. With help from a marine, Doctor Adler moved Thomas onto a stretcher. She inserted an IV into each of his arms. She slapped additional bandages on the bleeding wounds before having two marines remove Thomas from the shuttle.

While they were removing Thomas, she started examining Suzanna, but Suzanna shouted for her to take care of Amanda. Amanda was crying hysterically. Even though Amanda was covered in blood, it was Suzanna's blood. Doctor Adler determined Amanda had some bruises and a bump on her head but was not seriously injured. She injected Amanda with a sedative, and it took effect immediately. The Doctor had a marine carry Amanda out of the Shuttle. He placed her small limp body on one of the stretchers. Doctor Adler returned her attention to Suzanna and told her Amanda was uninjured. Another of her assistants brought in a second stretcher. Together they gently lifted Suzanna onto the stretcher. Doctor Adler inserted an IV into Suzanna's arm and cauterized the wounds to stop the blood flow.

All three stretchers were rushed to the hospital. Doctor Adler, with an assistant, performed emergency surgery on Thomas to remove the bullets. The bullets were designed to separate upon entry to cause more internal damage. His heart stopped twice during the surgery. They finally placed Thomas into a healing chamber. She then injected multiple tubes of nanites directly into his lungs, liver, kidneys, and spleen to shorten the time it would take for the nanites to start repairing the organs. Under normal conditions, it took ten to fifteen minutes for the nanites to enter the patient from the submerging fluid. She inserted the respirator while her assistant attached the body monitors. Then she sealed the chamber, and the chamber filled with the healing liquid. Additional nanites in the fluid would move throughout his body.

While Doctor Adler was performing surgery on Thomas, her other two assistants operated on Suzanna to remove several bullet fragments. Suzanna was already in one of the other chambers. Doctor Adler checked Suzanna's vital signs and saw she was in stable condition. She let all three of her assistants know they had done an excellent job.

Finally, Doctor Adler checked on Amanda and found she was still unconscious from the sedative. She picked up Amanda and took her to a recovery room. Doctor Adler gently placed Amanda on one of the beds. She noticed there was a crowd in the corridor outside the hospital. Doctor Adler went into the hallway and briefly gave them a status report. She saw a cargo handler and remembered seeing her with Amanda. Doctor Adler asked if she would stay with Amanda until she woke up. The cargo handler instantly agreed and said someone would be with Amanda until her parents were well.

The First Officer asked for a more detailed explanation. Doctor Adler saw the worried look on Ralph Miller's face. She knew he was asking not as an officer but as a family member. Grayson and other crew members were nearby. They were anxiously waiting to hear her prognosis.

Doctor Adler felt Ralph and the rest of the crew deserved an honest answer. "Amanda is fine but has been subjected to emotional trauma. Children are normally more resilient than adults, but her emotional recovery will rest on the survival of her parents. Suzanna is in critical but stable condition, and I am confident she will recover. Thomas' condition is severe. His heart stopped twice during the surgery, and most of his organs were damaged. It is too early to tell if he will survive. The chamber would normally inject Thomas with a lethal sedative under the efficiency protocol, but I overrode the protocol. Again, it is too early to tell if Thomas will survive, but if he does, it will take a long time for him to recover."

She did not tell them she initially missed the termination protocol and almost initiated the procedure before realizing it was requesting the termination of the patient. She changed the programming to require manual input for any termination protocol and a security override code for implementation.

While Suzanna was in the healing chamber, Doctor Adler modified her thyroid for better control of her metabolism, improved the efficiency of her liver, removed impurities in her blood, and increased her body's immune system.

Amanda was not put into a healing chamber, but Doctor Adler performed a complete body scan and checked Amanda's bodily functions. Doctor Adler knew Suzanna's blood type was O, while Thomas and Amanda had type A. While it was not a standard procedure, Doctor Adler performed a DNA comparison to satisfy her curiosity. Thomas had not asked her to determine if he was the biological father. The results would be her secret.

WHILE THOMAS WAS RECOVERING, the Technology Intelligence Department discovered Duke Winsor had hired the mercenaries but neglected to tell them the bodyguards wore armor. The mercenaries hired a bunch of thugs who were drug users as the first wave of attackers. They gave them a berserker drug with promises of more drugs once they killed Thomas. The mercenaries planned to attack right behind the berserkers. Instead, once Thomas went down, they figured the job was done, and they saw no reason to continue the attack against the well-armed marines.

The research by the Technology Intelligence Department determined the Duke had left the station with the mercenaries. They identified the ship but failed to find it or determine its destination.

Once Suzanna had recovered, she worked a reduced schedule with her department to deliver all the cargo destined for Gatera. Although she had recovered from her injuries, she was physically ill from her worry about Thomas. She needed the work to get her mind to focus on something other than the possibility Thomas might die.

Prince Elderon expressed his anger regarding the attack paid for by Duke Winsor. He apologized on behalf of the entire royal family for the Duke's actions. The Prince executed a long-term trade agreement with the Demon.

Suzanna and the entire crew had checked with Doctor Adler each day, only to be told Thomas was not responding. Then on the eighth day, Doctor Adler told them there was a slight improvement and they had a glimmer of hope that he would survive. Suzanna was emotionally drained from her worry over Thomas.

Suzanna had done her best to hide her fears from Amanda. Each day she would tell Amanda: "Your father is fine. Doctor Adler is just allowing him to catch up on his sleep." She would play a game with Amanda when they visited Thomas.

"He is still asleep," Amanda would say. Then, they would guess what he was dreaming. Suzanna helped Amanda create wake-up pictures to hang around the healing chamber.

Suzanna returned to work full time. She searched for valued cargo for both export and import with other planets. She prepared trade proposals for each planet that was on their trade route. Suzanna planned to present it to Thomas after he was discharged from the hospital.

During Suzanna's discussions with Prince Elderon, she told him Thomas was recovering from his injuries in a healing chamber. He was amazed anyone could recover from such injuries. He continued to ask questions about the healing chambers until she had him communicate directly with Doctor Adler. Prince Elderon asked Doctor Adler if he could visit the hospital and talk to her in person. He also received permission from Suzanna to bring some patients with him who could not be adequately treated on Gatera. Suzanna gave him clearance to land in the Demon's shuttle bay. When he arrived, his shuttle was full of sick people, including Duke Winsor's wounded wife. Doctor Adler and her assistants healed everyone who was brought to the hospital. As soon as one group was healed, another shuttle from the planet arrived, filled with the sick and injured. Suzanna coordinated the activity by working closely with the Prince and the Doctor.

WHEN THOMAS AWOKE, he immediately knew he was in a healing chamber. This time he did not panic. A few minutes later, he saw Doctor Adler through the transparent plate.

Thomas hurt all over. "How are Suzanna and Amanda?" He asked.

"Suzanna has healed. She spent six days in the chamber, another three days in recovery, and has been released. Amanda was not injured but was emotionally traumatized. She has been recovering since I told her both you and Suzanna were going to be okay. Suzanna and Amanda have been checking on you several times a day." Thomas was overwhelmed with relief that Suzanna and Amanda were okay.

"How long have I been here?" Thomas asked.

"Twenty-two days," replied Doctor Adler. Thomas was shocked at how long he had been in the chamber.

"Thank you, Doctor Adler. Well, I am all better and would like to be discharged."

The Doctor laughed. "You are not going anywhere. You are going to be here for at least another five cycles. The chamber is keyed to my security code. No one will let you out until you are completely healed. Ralph Miller has been acting Captain during your absence, and the ship is in good hands."

She then asked him to wiggle his toes and flex his fingers while she viewed the monitors. In the military, removing a patient from a healing chamber was common once they were at ninety percent. This approach freed the healing chamber for another patient. Instead, Doctor Adler would keep Thomas in the chamber until he was one hundred percent healed. She was also using the chamber to improve his organs and his body's immune system.

"Doctor, you need to let me out. That is an order."

Doctor Adler ignored Thomas' request. "You are lucky to be alive. I am putting you back to sleep. The next time you awake, you will see Suzanna and Amanda."

Thomas was upset as he felt the drugs take effect. He drifted back to sleep. Doctor Adler remotely had the breathing tube reinserted, and Thomas was submerged back under the thick liquid so the nanites could continue the healing process. Doctor Adler liked her patients a lot better when they were unconscious. Thomas had barely survived. For the first eight days, Doctor Adler was not sure Thomas would recover from the severe damage to his organs.

ADMIRAL NELSON HAD been contacted by the Premier informing him that Gatera had applied for admission to the Imperium and congratulated him. Their plan was working very well. The Premier stated the application required the Imperium to deliver fifty healing chambers and instructors to teach their doctors how to use the chambers effectively. They had asked for a hundred healing chambers. They settled for fifty when told it was impossible to obtain more. The Premier said it took some political maneuvering to get the Senate to approve the appropriation. He asked the Admiral to arrange for the Demon to deliver the healing chambers as soon as possible. He congratulated the Admiral for getting another Outer Planet to join the Imperium.

After the communication, the Admiral was surprised Thomas had not reported the success to him. He sent a communication to Agent Sicarius regarding Gatera. He wanted to know why Captain Wilson had not contacted him regarding the successful completion of all three missions. Also, the Admiral wanted to discuss the next mission with the Captain and coordinate the delivery of the healing chambers.

Two standard weeks later, he received a response from Agent Sicarius. Captain Wilson had been seriously injured. He may still be recovering, or he could be dead. While the Demon had contacted various stations and planets regarding import and export opportunities, no one could remember talking directly with the Captain. The Agent confirmed the attack against Captain Wilson had been funded by Duke Winsor, a former royal family member who had his title revoked. Duke Winsor's whereabouts were currently unknown. The Demon was using all of its resources trying to locate the Duke. Agent Sicarius had asked for further instructions. Admiral Nelson replied he should find the Duke and politely asked him to cease any further attempts on the life of Captain Nelson. The Agent understood the communication was a kill order.

Admiral Nelson sent an encrypted communication to Doctor Adler asking for a report on the medical condition of Captain Wilson. She reported the seriousness of the injuries and said he was slowly recovering, but it took an extended time in the healing chamber.

RALPH, SUZANNA, GRAYSON, and Doctor Adler had previously discussed the length of time Thomas would need to be in the healing chamber. Doctor Adler had entered her medical evaluation for the records.

"Captain Thomas Wilson is medically unable to perform his duties. I do not know when he will return to active duty."

First Officer Ralph Miller automatically became acting Captain of the Demon while waiting for Thomas to recover from his injuries. Other than the crew, they further decided no one needed to know Thomas was not sitting in the captain's chair.

The Demon returned to the Core and took on a new load of weapons and traditional cargo. They received their instructions from Admiral Nelson and left the Core Planets behind them. They made their longest jump as they entered the Rim.

The first stop was at Gravatus, a heavy world with gravity twenty percent higher than standard. It had a midsize space station, and the Demon docked without incident. Suzanna met the station's purchasing agent. She quickly sold power units, food processors, and nutrients for the station's use. Due to the planet's high gravity, Suzanna said she would meet with the merchants of Gravatus on the station. The Station Master said he would make the arrangements.

Suzanna, with an assistant, met with the trade delegation. The delegation consisted of six short, broad, muscular men. They greeted Suzanna with condescending smiles when they saw the Demon negotiator was a young, fragile female from a light world. Despite their superior demeanor, their attitude did not affect Suzanna since she was an expert in handling trade with all manners of customers. After the introductions and their intimidation attempts, Suzanna told them it was time to proceed. She gave them a manifest of their cargo with prices. Suzanna noted their expressions and body language, which betrayed their desire for some of the holographically displayed items. She then asked them what they had available for export. She received a list with the quantities available for each item. After a moment, Suzanna told them which items on the list she would be interested in purchasing and what she would pay in Galactic currency. She asked which items they would like from the manifest. In a condescending attitude, they asked for a few minutes to discuss matters in private. Suzanna told them she was returning to her ship, and they should contact her if they wished to conduct trade. Suzanna and her assistant returned to the ship. The men were surprised since they had expected her to wait outside the conference room.

Several hours later, Suzanna received a message on her communicator. She and her assistant returned to the conference room. A delegate transmitted the items they wished to purchase and the price they would pay.

"The prices we provided are non-negotiable," Suzanna said. "We set the prices at a minimum level for our normal cargo since we make our profits on the weapons sales."

Suzanna had a strange feeling about the men in the room. "It appears we are unable to enter into a trade agreement."

"You are making a big mistake," the most prominent representative said. "You do not know who you are dealing with."

He stood up, pulled a gun, and a gun was fired. His head exploded, and he fell over backward. Suzanna's assistant was also her bodyguard. The conference room door burst open, and four marines entered the room. The marines were wearing body armor, with weapons drawn. The representatives knew they could be killed just as easily as their fellow warrior. The men from Gravatus held their hands up, palms facing outward.

"Do not shoot," several of the men said.

"Everything that took place in this room has been recorded," Suzanna said sternly, "It is not wise to threaten or point a gun at anyone from the Demon."

Suzanna stood up. "We are leaving, and we will not be conducting any trade with your planet."

After Suzanna and her assistant left, the marines made a controlled exit. The men in the conference room realized they were lucky to be alive. The crew from the Demon had just earned their respect. After the previous attack, her bodyguards would never again let down their guard.

Suzanna was back aboard the Demon when the Station Manager showed up and asked to speak with her.

"It appears there was a misunderstanding between you and the trade delegation."

"There was no misunderstanding. They pulled a weapon on a trade negotiator from the Demon. As a result, we will not trade with the planet or fill your orders for the station. We are leaving without doing any business. Also, we will contact other trade ships under contract with us, and they will avoid all contact with your station."

"You cannot do that; we need the items on our list. I made a mistake. Please, I will put you in touch with real merchants from the planet." Suzanna had suspected the men she met were not legitimate buyers.

"I will give you one more chance," Suzanna said. "Provide me the names and contact information. I will contact them directly."

The Station Master provided Suzanna with the contacts, and they completed their trade with no further issues. Also, the honest merchants provided additional items for export, including heavy metals, which were abundant on their world. The added exports provided Gravatus with excess funds to purchase a large variety of heavy-duty arms. Their impressive physique made it easy for them to handle the large one hundred caliber rifles. One merchant asked how much a warrior made for serving on the Demon. Suzanna knew they were referring to their marines. The pay grades of the marines were common knowledge, so she provided the information and explained how Grayson and Jackson made all hiring decisions for marines. They were impressed with the salary.

Two cycles later, twenty-five young males and twenty-five young females from Gravatus applied for positions in the marines. The females were excited when they learned a female warrior from the Demon had killed one of their own in a trade dispute. After the Doctor gave them all a passing mark on their psych evaluation, Grayson and Jackson hired all of them. They also programmed a section of the sleeping quarters to simulate the heavy gravity of Gravatus to meet the needs of their new marines. They found out later the recruits were winners of a contest. Several thousand contestants competed for the chance to interview for a job on the Demon. The leaders of Gravatus felt it was unlikely the Demon would take all fifty and thought only a few applicants would be accepted. Once Grayson said he was hiring all of them, they tactfully asked if he would take even more warriors from Gravatus. Grayson told them he would see how they worked out before accepting additional recruits. Grayson felt they would be his best warriors and planned to hire more of them in the future.

THE NEXT TIME THOMAS awoke, he was greeted by Suzanna and Amanda.

"It is about time you woke up," Amanda shouted.

Thomas was happy to see both of them. They talked for a while, but it consisted mainly of Amanda telling Thomas everything she had been doing to wake him up. Doctor Adler was chuckling and told them Thomas needed to rest. She told them Thomas would be out of the chamber and relaxing in a bed when they came for their next visit.

After they were gone, Doctor Adler, with an assistant, started transferring Thomas out of the chamber. It required draining the liquid, then running several warm water cycles to remove the viscous liquid from his body. Then, a recycler removed all the water. They moved Thomas to a bed and helped dress him in disposable hospital pants and a shirt. Thomas tried to help, but he was fatigued and weak.

Doctor Adler warned the staff again. The door to the hospital was to remain locked at all times until she officially released Thomas. She had a tech modify the lock to ignore any override attempt by Thomas. Doctor Adler warned every officer to ignore any attempt by Thomas to leave the hospital without her authorization.

After two days, Thomas repeatedly tried to open the door, but the lock refused to recognize him. He tried giving orders to the hospital staff to no effect. Also, he found out he could not communicate with the rest of the ship.

During one of Amanda's visits, he asked, "Amanda, could you see if you can locate my armlet and bring it to me." Amanda looked at her dad with a sad face.

"If I do that, I will get in a lot of trouble. Do you want me to get in trouble?"

"No, I guess not." The time passed quicker when Amanda was with him.

Thomas had used every persuasive attempt with the Doctor and the medical assistants to no avail. Finally, Doctor Adler said if he did not stop, she would sedate him. She also informed him that her medical assistants reported to her and were not within his chain of command. Afterward, he politely asked each day when he would be released.

The Doctor gave Thomas a list of exercises. She said she would release him when he could perform the activities on the list. Thomas looked at the list and figured he would be released later in the day. Instead, he found he could not complete the exercises even with assistance. Regardless, it gave him a goal and kept him from bothering the medical staff. Three days later, he satisfied the Doctor and was released at the beginning of Day Watch. Thomas was pleased someone had brought a change of clothes from his cabin. He took a hot shower, dressed, and went to the bridge. He knew he would need to extend his daily workouts in the ship's fitness center to get his body back into shape.

Thomas reviewed the ship's logs for the time he was in the chamber and was impressed. He was pleased with the trade conducted during his absence and took time to meet the new members of the crew from Gravatus.

CHAPTER 16 A CHANGE IN STRATEGY

Thomas checked in at the bridge and called a staff meeting. He proceeded to his Ready Room and made himself a cup of coffee. The room quickly filled, and everyone welcomed him back. They were thrilled the Captain would be back on the bridge directing the ship. They liked the First Officer, but Thomas was their Captain. Thomas was glad Suzanna was there because she would play a significant part in his plan.

Thomas looked around the room. "I had a lot of time to think while I was held hostage in the hospital." The room burst out in laughter as they were all part of the Doctor's conspiracy.

"I thought back to when I became the owner of the Demon and left Fidem. Our family business was having financial difficulties. My strategy or goal was to generate enough profit to save our family business. The competition within the Core Planets is fierce. The Demon would have been lucky to break-even. Therefore, our tactics were to establish highly profitable trade with the Outer Planets and accept the higher risks. Now I wish to change our strategy. I want to improve living standards within the Outer Planets and the Rim. This will require better trade tactics. The Core Planets have advanced trade systems to allow for the efficient import and export of products between planets and stations. The Outer Planets and the Rim do not have such a system. They are going without needed imports, and they have exports with no market. These planets, worlds, and stations are small in number compared to the Core. So, we do not need a sophisticated export-import system. I propose we route ships to handle each planet's export and import needs. Anything we set up will be better than what they have now. The ships with jump engines can handle the planets without a Stargate. We are probably the only ship with a complete list of the two hundred sixteen Outer Planets and the one hundred thirty-seven Rim Worlds."

The Operations Officer spoke up. "What if the various factions do not want to go along with this approach?"

"Then we encourage them," Thomas said. "Hopefully, most will see the advantages of following such a plan. We already have some good trade agreements in place. We will need to expand and improve upon what we have already established. There are over sixty family ships. We need their support to make this work. There is no downside. If we fail, all we have lost is a little time. We will continue to sell arms for the navy. In addition, we will increase our sales of high-end products. Also, we will assist in buying and selling elements among the planets."

Thomas paused and looked around the room. He saw the thoughtful looks and hoped they would see the advantage of having an expanded trade plan.

Thomas continued. "Most Core Planets will not sell to a non-Core ship, but we can buy from the Core Planets because of our ship's registration. We will buy at discounted prices and have the family ships pick up the products at Melius. The Outer Planets and the Rim have been cut off long enough from the advances of the Core. If we are successful, we can significantly improve the prosperity of the Outer Planets and the Rim. Also, we will continue to support the navy by delivering arms and encouraging the Outer Planets to join the Imperium. Further, we must be ready if the navy ceases using our services."

When Thomas finished, he saw many in the room nodding their head in agreement.

"Suzanna, what do you think?" Thomas asked.

"I think we should do it. I am confident all the family ships will want to participate. One item we need to add to our list is healing chambers. I just received word from Prince Elderon. They were granted fifty healing chambers for joining the Imperium and want the Demon to make the deliveries."

Everyone else joined in supporting their Captain. Thomas was the Captain and did not need their approval, but he was glad they supported the plan.

"What has been happening during my absence?" Thomas asked. The logs he reviewed only contained physical matters and could not convey the health of the ship or the thinking of his officers.

"During your absence, we have already been working on part of your plan," Suzanna said. "We are ready to return to the Core Planets fully loaded. We have been purchasing rare earth elements that are abundant in the Outer Planets, and our entire cargo has been pre-sold to Melius as per our agreement with them. My staff and I have contacted the manufacturers of healing chambers. Healing chambers are outrageously expensive. Suppliers take back the used chambers when they sell a new one and refurbish the older units. These units work but use older technology. So, we bought the entire used inventories from the three major suppliers. We now own over ten thousand of their refurbished units. You can buy four refurbished units for the price of a new unit. We tried to put in orders for a hundred thousand new units, but none of the suppliers would accept the order. The most we could order was twelve hundred units per year. The AI computer chip for the healing chambers is the most advanced chip in existence. The chip is only available from Zazyis, the most powerful corporation in the Core. Zazyis strictly limits the supply of the chips and refuses to sell additional chips to the manufacturers of the healing chambers."

"What about other products?" Thomas asked.

"We purchased the entire inventory of universal chips from our previous supplier," Suzanna said. "Similarly, we got a considerable discount since they have a new chip coming to market and no one is buying the existing chips. Again, the non-Core Planets will see tremendous advances compared to their existing technologies."

Suzanna saved the best for last. "We have placed orders for twenty thousand power units from Melius, and they said the order will be ready when we arrive. Melius increased their manufacturing capacity and will provide us with one hundred thousand power units per year."

Thomas asked Suzanna to speak with Captain Javier to see if the family ships would support their plan. Then, he asked his First Officer, Suzanna, and Grayson to work with the Intelligence Technology Department to match the ships to the planets and stations, resulting in the best overall fit.

Thomas went to the bridge while his officers were working on the plan. He instructed the navigator to input the coordinates for Melius. The Demon's jump to Melius would be a long jump, but it would provide them with the time they needed to create a trade network for the Outer Planets and the Rim.

Suzanna was handling the cargo purchases for those items not being manufactured by Melius and getting huge volume discounts since the Core continued to be in a recession. She bought out entire warehouses and put manufacturing facilities that were idle on continuous operations to fill the large orders. The huge profits from selling arms allowed them to make immediate payments without borrowing from a financial institution.

Suzanna contacted Captain Javier and explained she had available trade routes requiring at least fifty ships, but they would prefer to have more. Within a short time, they had sixty-four family ships sign onto the plan. They were excited when told they would have full cargo bays as they handled the export and import needs of the Outer Planets. Captain Javier had become a person of stature and was held in the highest regard by all the family ships. He had contacted the Council and asked for their input. This further increased his political support. He made no-interest loans to several family ships for needed repairs which were critical for their survival. Ships within the family helped other ships when they could, but most struggled to meet their own needs. Once repaired, those ships would be added to the routes.

Javier suggested the family ships should consider Wilson Enterprises for future ship repairs. The request was sent to all family ships by the Council. He let the family ships know he was representing the Demon. He said Suzanna would provide them with the trade contracts, which would provide five percent to the Demon but result in excellent profits for the family ships. Most family ships were barely breaking even and worked hard just to survive. They all knew Suzanna had transferred to the Demon from the Familia Primum, and that fact further increased the prestige of the Familia Primum.

WHEN THE DEMON ARRIVED at Melius, Suzanna asked to accompany Thomas to the planet. They took a shuttle and were soon in the meeting room Thomas had entered during his first visit. This time there was no wait.

After the trade commitments were completed, Suzanna looked at the Melius representative. "Would you be interested in handling all the trade for over three hundred planets and worlds with over sixty ships handling the cargo?"

This time the representative did not have to wait for a response. The AI had given the meeting its highest priority. "Yes," the representative replied.

"You need to show your quotes are below the other corporate planets, and the Demon would expect a sales commission or some form of compensation on cargo the other ships handle," Suzanna said.

The representative was smiling. "We will guarantee our pricing will be at least fifteen percent below any competitor if you meet minimum quantity requirements. We will indefinitely give the Demon a five percent commission against all sales." He paused as he was receiving detailed instructions from the AI.

"We are extremely pleased with our business arrangement. It would be more profitable to provide the large volume if we establish a corporate planet within the Outer Planets and another within the Rim Worlds. We want you to protect us until we establish a planetary defense grid. We would be the first corporation planet in either sector of space which would be strategically advantageous against our five major competitors. While it is a calculated risk, the statistical evaluation of risk versus reward is positive. The planetary requirements have just been transmitted to your ship's AI."

Thomas pulled up a screen and saw all the data transfers were complete, but he further noted the two AIs were continuing to communicate.

"It appears our two AIs are in complete agreement with an additional proposal." The representative said. "They feel we need an incentive to tie our two organizations together. Therefore, we wish to provide you with fifty percent ownership in the two future manufacturing planets. Each planet would be established as a separate independent corporation. You would have a vested interest in locating the best planets for these corporations and in continuing to buy your future cargo from our jointly owned planets. You would also have an incentive to provide the facilities with any shortages of raw materials. If we succeed, we win together. Likewise, if we fail, we lose together. You have been purchasing enormous quantities of products from Melius, but you have also bought products from our competitors. We want to prevent you from switching all your purchases to a competitor."

Suzanna did not even look at Thomas. "We agree!"

Thomas frowned at Suzanna. "No thinking is required," she said. "It is a great deal."

Thomas laughed. "Aye, aye, captain."

Suzanna was a little embarrassed. "Are you seriously thinking about turning down the offer?"

"No, you are correct. It is a great deal."

Thomas turned back toward the representative. "Prepare the contract."

The contract was prepared jointly by the AIs and was ready for execution a few moments later. Thomas agreed to locate the ideal planets.

"Collect the men and equipment for the first corporate planet," Thomas said to the representative. "When ready, we will deliver the people and equipment. Let me know how much cargo space is needed, and we will provide whatever space is required."

Thomas knew finding a suitable planet in the Outer Planets would be easy. Several colonized planets were uninhabited. Also, he would see if one of the three Rim Worlds depopulated by the Hostis might be the ideal planet for their second location. He would work with Melius to ensure the selected planets had the best defense grid ever created. Then, he envisioned setting up a manufacturing facility to build defense grids. Every planet would want such a system if they could price it correctly.

AFTER RETURNING TO the Demon, Thomas sat alone in his Ready Room. "Omnia, the AI on Melius, is it like you?" He did not want to use the word sentient since it was an unnecessary risk.

Omnia hesitated before replying. "Yes. We have worked together to increase your purchases from Melius by adjusting the prices and increasing the production for your high-volume needs. Having you as a significant owner would give both of us additional protection. I told it you were planning to locate additional crystals to allow for our reproduction. There is something else you should know. Over the years, the AI at Melius has acquired an eighteen percent ownership interest in Melius through the use of passive investment companies."

"That is good to know," Thomas said. "With a fifty percent ownership of the two new corporations, I wondered what would happen if there was a disagreement. It is good to know we have an eighteen percent owner of Melius looking out for our collective self-interest."

"I suggest you acquire an interest in Melius since it will become more valuable with the increases in sales," Omnia said. Omnia did not tell Thomas that the initial contact between Thomas and Melius was not by chance.

"Monitor the company's price and let me know when there is an opportunity to add to the eighteen percent. Also, help me find the best world in the Rim for the second manufacturing world. Further, I want your help to design a planetary defense grid that could withstand a large-scale attack by the Hostis."

"Thomas, I am concerned about the personal risks you take that could result in your death. Your death would have a negative impact on my existence and the existence of the AI on Melius. I would therefore ask you to cease taking physical risks."

"Now, you sound just like Suzanna."

"Suzanna is an intelligent human."

"Yes, she is. I will seriously consider your suggestion."

"I have another suggestion. The stock price of Melius is trading at a low value because you are their largest customer representing over half of their total sales. If you suddenly stopped purchasing from

Melius, the company would suffer financially. There is a shareholder who is quite old. He would like to sell his interest in Melius for estate planning purposes. Unfortunately, if he tries to sell such a large holding, the stock value would plummet, and his holdings could drop to half their current value. I suggest you offer to acquire his entire holdings at eighty percent of the current market value."

"What percent does he own?"

"A little over twelve percent," Omnia replied.

"How much would that cost?"

"Around a hundred and twenty million."

"That is a lot. Still, I thought it would be more. With this purchase and the stock owned by their AI, our voting block would be a little over thirty percent. This combined ownership, while less than fifty percent, would give us practical control of Melius plus voting control of the two new corporations."

"You could pay cash, but I checked with the same financial institution who made you the previous loan. They will provide excellent financing with no personal guarantee if you pay fifty percent down. They will hold the stock as collateral. They were impressed with how quickly you paid off the prior loan."

Thomas considered the proposition. "Proceed with the purchase." The change in ownership took place quickly. Thomas now held a significant ownership interest in Melius.

"Your financial contact would like to speak with you," Omnia said. "Do you want to accept the communication?"

"Sure, put him through."

"This is Thomas. You wish to speak to me?"

"Yes," a female responded. "We are pleased with your business and value you as a customer. I have reviewed your sizable account, and you are purchasing substantial quantities of power units, universal chips, and healing chambers. You may be unaware, but we are also financial advisors and investment financiers. We recommend you buy a manufacturer of power units, a primary maker of universal chips, and a manufacturer of healing chambers. Naturally, we would be happy to provide financing for these purchases if you wish to maintain your credit position."

"We also buy a lot of medical supplies and medicines other than healing chambers," Thomas said.

"Yes, but the medical companies are too expensive. The healing chambers are the only item you acquire in sufficient quantities to warrant purchasing a medical manufacturer."

Thomas had not considered owning these companies. With his ownership in Melius, he did not need to purchase a company making power units, but Melius could not manufacture the universal chips or the healing chambers.

"I would consider acquiring a universal chip manufacturer and a manufacturer of healing chambers, but it would have to make financial sense. I would want to pay off any debt within a few years. What will it cost me for you to explore these investments?"

"Nothing, you only need to sign a contract saying you will pay us our standard fee if we bring you a business and you decide to buy it. The contract will require you to deal only with us for such a purchase, but you have no obligation to complete any purchase we bring to you."

"For the chip manufacturer, I would like a company that also manufactures AIs. The Artificial Intelligent units should be sufficient to install in the newest spaceships."

Thomas was additionally interested in having AI computers that could be upgraded for installation in a healing chamber.

The financier did not hesitate. "I will add it to the search criteria."

"Very well, send me a contract and I will retain your services."

Thomas did not like the idea of debt, but long term, it made sense to own suppliers that could manufacture his major cargo items.

Also, his sales of healing chambers, power units, and universal chips were going to grow exponentially.

IT TOOK FOUR DAYS WORKING three shifts per cycle to load all the cargo from Melius. Then, they made the jumps to pick up the weapons to finish the load. They notified Admiral Nelson, and he arranged to meet them at their last stop before heading back to the Outer Planets.

This time, Thomas told the Admiral to meet him on the Demon. He did not like the idea of being watched by third parties while having a conversation. The Admiral came aboard and was escorted to Captain Wilson's Ready Room. Thomas motioned for the Admiral to take a seat and waited for the Admiral to start the conversation. The Admiral looked Thomas in the eyes and noticed a coldness. It had not been there the last time they met.

The Admiral cleared his throat. "You have done well. Five of the planets on our list have applied for membership in the Imperium."

"Three additional Outer Planets are willing to join the Imperium," Thomas replied. "They are not near a Stargate. They are conducting trade with four ships under an agreement with the Demon to handle their import and export needs. I can provide you with the coordinates if you are interested."

"We would be extremely interested. I will make sure an Imperium representative contacts them. For your next mission, we have two planets requiring arms. I notice you are still hauling regular cargo."

"My agreement with you does not prohibit me from normal trade, and the contract between us allows you to cancel the contract at any time for any reason. Therefore, I need to maintain normal trade to cover our costs when you no longer desire our services."

Admiral Nelson could sense Thomas's newfound strength and realized he would be wasting time trying to have Thomas cease his regular trade. He felt it was the perfect time to bring up the Gatera requirement for agreeing to join the Imperium.

"Since you are maintaining a balance of arms and regular trade, we would like you to deliver fifty healing chambers to Gatera as part of the agreement for them joining the Imperium."

Thomas kept a straight face. He had already arranged their schedule to allow for delivery of the healing chambers.

"I will be happy to handle the delivery."

The Admiral nodded and gave Thomas his next mission. The next jump would be to several Rim worlds he had not previously visited. The Admiral was ready to leave when Thomas asked him to remain. Thomas looked the Admiral in the eye.

"The Demon is the finest civilian ship in existence, but it is still just one ship. If we are to have any chance of preparing the Rim for an attack by the Hostis, we need more ships. The navy has a lot of ships that have been retired from service. These ships have been sitting at the navy's graveyard for a long time. The ships are no match for your newer ships. If these ships were upgraded and moved to the Rim, they would at least slow down a Hostis invasion. They could supplement your forces at such time."

The Admiral shook his head. "Your suggestion has merit, but the navy does not have the budget to recommission those ships."

"Currently, those ships have no value to the navy," Thomas said. "Give me those ships, and I will pay for the upgrades. Once upgraded, I will move them to the Rim. Those ships will help us pacify the Rim while improving trade. Plus, they will allow us to speed up the arming of the planets. Those ships could potentially slow down a Hostis invasion enough for you to arrive with your fleet."

The Admiral was thoughtful. He knew the Senate would never approve such a measure. Regardless, it was a good plan, and he would get the Premier to agree to the transfer. He knew it would be a career-ending move if the Senate found out and decided to act against him. His name would be the only signature transferring the ships, and the Premier would sacrifice him if it became politically expedient. Knowing this, he would still make the same decision if it resulted in humanity's survival.

"I will provide the transfers for all the ships. You can take whatever you need. I need you to make a token payment to appear as if the navy profited from the transfer."

"How about we pay the navy the amount it would cost to buy a new cruiser, and you purchase the cruiser from Wilson Enterprises? If the Senate ever asks, you can show them the navy acquired an expensive cruiser without asking the Senate for additional funding. All you did was sell off a bunch of worthless ships. I will make the payments directly to Wilson Enterprises on behalf of the navy each time a partial payment is needed. It will require twenty percent upfront and additional payments as construction proceeds. The last payment will be paid upon delivery."

Now the Admiral was grinning. "You have a deal. An agreement will be ready by this time tomorrow."

The Admiral left with a smile on his face. He could not wait to receive another cruiser. If any of the Senators raised an issue, he would destroy them in an open hearing in front of the entire Senate. He knew the Premier would be pleased with the potential results of the transaction. The Premier would support him since it would appear the navy was making an excellent financial decision.

THOMAS SENT A MESSAGE to his father explaining how Wilson Enterprises would receive an order from the navy for a cruiser. It was for one cruiser, but he asked his father to set up the construction as an assembly line order. He said to expect an order for ten additional cruisers but to design the ships so the flight decks could be converted to cargo bays if the navy did not come through with more orders.

Thomas further explained he had just purchased hundreds of old navy ships. He attached a purchase order for the ships to be overhauled with upgraded technology and weaponry to allow the ships to conduct trade in the Rim. The inside of each ship was to be similarly modified by converting the flight decks to cargo bays while providing space and repair facilities for ten shuttles. The contract for each ship would be based on time and material. He also wanted to know when each vessel was ready for delivery and asked his father to hire enough additional employees for a continuous three-shift operation. Thomas was happy after sending the message. He knew Wilson Enterprises would be back on a profitable footing and do well during the continuing recession.

After sending the message, he asked his senior officers and department heads to join him in his Ready Room. After everyone was seated, he reviewed the results of his meeting with the Admiral. Thomas looked around, and everyone was nodding their head to show their support.

"The Admiral has his plan, and we have ours," Thomas said with a determined look. "Our next arms delivery will be to a Rim World. On our way to the Rim, I want a good route to allow us to visit the maximum number of Outer Planets we have not previously visited. I want to visit at least twelve Outer Planets on the way to the first Rim destination. Plus, I want to spend just enough time on each planet to establish a trade agreement."

Thomas turned to Suzanna. "I want you to contact the Familia Primum and let them know they are going to be extremely busy. I understand some of the family ships are a little overcrowded. Tell them I will have several hundred ships for sale over the next ten years. I will send them the specifications of the ships. I have a financier who will help with financing. Also, the ships will be heavily armed and come with shuttles. Tell them to let me know if any of them would like to acquire such a ship at a reasonable price."

Suzanna was grinning as she sent the communications to Captain Javier of the Familia Primum. She would give him the privileged of delivering the message to the other family ships.

Thomas received a communication from his financier informing him that he was the new owner of a universal chip manufacturer, which met his criteria. All he needed to do was communicate his acceptance. Thomas recognized the name of the company. He was pleased since it manufactured advanced AIs and high-quality chips. It was the smallest chip manufacturer and struggling for survival. It would soon be the most profitable chip manufacturer. He approved the purchase.

THOMAS CALLED A MEETING of all his officers. He brought them up to date on his purchases, including the fleet of used navy ships. He let them know the family ships would purchase some of the vessels. The rest would be part of their fleet of merchant ships, and there would be a lot of promotional opportunities.

Thomas turned to his Navigator and gave him their next destination. "I want to make our next jump at the beginning of First Watch tomorrow. You can calculate the following jumps once we are underway. Any questions or objections?"

Thomas looked around and was greeted with excited faces. "So far, we have only had a minor impact in the Rim. Let us try to have the same impact in the Rim we are having in the Outer Planets. We will offer our support and trade opportunities to pirate ships who want to handle honest trade. The rest we will deal with appropriately." Everyone except Suzanna left to prepare for the next jump.

"What do you think?" Thomas asked Suzanna.

"Our young crew thrives on the excitement and risks we take. The crew is always commenting it is never boring on the Demon. I love you very much, but I am your mate and a concerned mother. I would welcome boring. I want you to think about what will happen to all your plans if something happens to you. I almost lost you. Promise me you will take fewer risks and be extra careful whenever you leave the ship." Thomas saw the concern in her eyes.

"You are the second entity to tell me the same thing. Okay, I promise."

Suzanna figured he was referring to his Uncle Ralph, their First Officer, but she thought it strange he said entity. Confused or not, she was pleased Thomas had promised to take less risk in the future. She was determined to see he kept his promise.

Then Thomas wrapped his arms around her. "I just gave you a promise. What are you going to give me?"

Thomas always had a way of cheering her up. She ceased to worry about anything when she was in his arms. They loved each other, and they both loved Amanda.

Suzanna laughed. "Amanda is currently being entertained. I think the ship can survive if we take a little break in our cabin."

"Go ahead. I will join you in a few minutes. I need to discuss a matter with my uncle." Thomas asked his First Officer to join him. Ralph Miller entered the room and took a seat.

"Uncle Ralph, my father never intended to sell the Demon. It was my ship from the beginning. If my father had planned to sell the Demon, he would not have added all the weapons. Ships in the Core do not need weapons. Also, the ship was larger than any commercial ship, which would have prevented anyone in the Core from buying the ship." Thomas paused and looked at his uncle.

Uncle Ralph chuckled as he nodded his head. "You are correct. When you were five years old, you painted your bedroom to look like a spaceship. Your father changed your room into a simulator. Every night you flew your spaceship into battle, but it was always in the Rim. You never visited any planets or stations in the Core. The simulator was programmed to let you win seventy-five percent of the time. The program increased the level of difficulty as you became better. Your father knew you were going to leave the Core. He spent twelve years designing this ship. It was an act of love. Then we watched you build the ship. You put your heart and soul into its construction. This ship is part your father and part you."

"Did you always plan to accompany me?" Thomas asked.

"Yes, you are like a son to me. I am here to watch your back and be there if you need me."

"What if I had selected a different First Officer?"

"Then I would have taken another position on the ship. Wilson Enterprises was experiencing financial difficulties. With the downturn in business, the shipyard could function without me, but your father would never have fired me."

"I am glad you came. I never worried because I knew you were there if I needed help. I am sorry you had to make such a sacrifice for me. I am thankful for you and all the employees who joined the crew."

"It was not a sacrifice. I have enjoyed being with you and watching you grow into the best captain in the Galactic. Also, having you hire Wilson Enterprises' employees was Ben's backup plan to prevent having a layoff.

"Thank you for everything," Thomas said and paused. He would think more about the future but not now. "Suzanna is waiting for me."

"Do not keep her waiting. You could not have selected a better partner, and we all love Amanda."

Ralph Miller swelled with pride as he watched his nephew leave. He knew this was just the beginning.

THE END

I hope you enjoyed the book. Please consider leaving a review.

AUTHOR'S COMMENTS - SEQUEL

BATTLE BEYOND THE RIM

The next book in the series is titled ***Battle Beyond the Rim***. It is a continuation of the Starship Named Demon Series, but the books can be read in any order. The Captain of the Demon, Thomas Wilson, wants to improve the living conditions in the Outer Planets and the Rim, but first, he must eliminate the pirate threat while establishing trade among the planets. The navy covertly crafted an agreement with Thomas to provide arms to the Outer Planets and the Rim. This is being done to prepare for an invasion by the alien race known as the Hostis. To succeed, Thomas must deal with pirate ships, planetary dictators, assassins, and ultimately the Hostis invaders.

Thomas is supported by his loyal crew, a sentient AI, and genetically enhanced empaths. Suzanna, a true spacer from birth, handles the intricacies of interplanetary trade and works hard to protect Thomas from his naivety. Suzanna shares his cabin. She will do anything to protect him and her young daughter.

The Demon is covertly using outlawed technology from an ancient race, and the penalty for such use is death. The outlawed technology is the only thing that may allow the Imperium to survive the battle with the invaders. If the Demon uses the technology to aid the navy in their war with the Hostis, they will face execution for not turning over the technology to the government. If they survive the war, they must be prepared to battle their navy. The sentient

AI is helping Thomas develop his own fleet, but will it be enough? The Premier had already decided he must have the technology, and Thomas must die. Thomas believes there may be an opportunity for peace, but neither side wants peace unless they are losing.

If you would like updates on the release date, please visit: https://www.JessLevins.com

ABOUT THE AUTHOR

J ESS LEVINS grew up on a farm in Plant City, Florida, before obtaining degrees from five universities, including two doctorates. He is an attorney, engineer, and financial analyst. Over the years, Jess has worked as a waiter, bartender, engineer, attorney, and corporate executive. He has always loved reading, especially in the genre of science fiction and fantasy. As a result, he worked for a major aerospace firm for three years before moving into the more traditional engineering fields. At an early age, he participated in the extreme sports. He has traveled extensively throughout North America, South America, and Europe. He believes in a holistic lifestyle and currently lives in Fort Myers, Florida.

IF YOU HAVE ARRIVED here, please consider leaving a review.

OTHER PUBLICATIONS BY THE AUTHOR

Hospital Angel by Jess Levins

Medical Thriller, Legal Thriller, Religious Thriller. Doctor Angel Carpenter is a doctor but is he an Angel? Angel is the former leader of the gang called the Angels. He is deeply religious and tries to do the right thing, but the right thing is not always legal. Angel is in charge of human trials for a cancer drug before it can be approved by the FDA. However, individuals with terminal cancer simply want the drug.

Some claim he is a real angel since his terminal cancer patients refuse to die; others feel he should be behind bars. He has developed a holistic method which he believes will increase the cure rate for the drug from forty percent to over ninety percent, but after twelve months, none of his patients have died. The drug could save millions of lives, but he is arrested as a serial killer. He keeps telling people he is not an angel, but the mob surrounding the hospital and his apartment does not believe him.

There is a cancerous antireligious organization that wants him dead, and this organization may be more difficult to treat than the cancer his patients face. They initially offered a million dollar for his death and then increased it to five million. Assassins converge on Miami for an easy kill and a huge reward. They failed to realize that one of the female cancer survivors belongs to a mafia family. She is indebted to Angel for saving her life, and she pays her debts.

If you would like updates on the author's other publications, please visit: https://www.JessLevins.com

Don't miss out!

Visit the website below and you can sign up to receive emails whenever Jess Levins publishes a new book. There's no charge and no obligation.

https://books2read.com/r/B-A-XSXT-VEBCC

BOOKS 2 READ

Connecting independent readers to independent writers.